Sherley,
    you are a joy to know.
I hope you enjoy the book.
    As ever,
        Lowell Medley
        2-25-07

Web of Deceit

Lowell Medley

Bloomington, IN Milton Keynes, UK
authorHOUSE

AuthorHouse™
1663 Liberty Drive, Suite 200
Bloomington, IN 47403
www.authorhouse.com
Phone: 1-800-839-8640

AuthorHouse™ UK Ltd.
500 Avebury Boulevard
Central Milton Keynes, MK9 2BE
www.authorhouse.co.uk
Phone: 08001974150

First published by AuthorHouse 9/12/2006

ISBN: 1-4259-1209-5 (sc)

Printed in the United States of America
Bloomington, Indiana

This book is printed on acid-free paper.

Other Works by the Author

Christmas Glory: A Christmas Play

Appointment in Galilee: An Easter Play

Poems

Dedicated to my sister Evelyn, my late wife Ona, and to all my loving grandchildren.

CHAPTER 1

Paul sat in the day coach of the train looking out the window at the landscape flashing by. He was on his way to Blakeville, Tennessee to apply for a position of assistant pastor at the Victory for Christ Church there. He had looked forward to this day that would take him away from the coal mines and the squalor of the coal camps throughout West Virginia. He hated to leave Braxton, his home and friends, but he felt there was no future for him there.

It was his first time to venture forth on an uncharted trip so he hardly knew what to expect. He was both excited and apprehensive about it: excited over the prospect the position would afford him financially and apprehensive because of the position in a much larger and prominent church. He tried to focus his attention elsewhere, rather than on the promising future the position offered if he were fortunate enough to get it. He did not want to think of the responsibility the job may entail lest he become intimidated and turn back to where he had journeyed from.

The opening for which he aspired had been brought to his attention by a fellow minister for whom he had conducted a revival. He had written a letter of application to the pastor there, the Reverend George Blakely, expressing his interest in the position and requesting an interview. Reverend Blakely had written him back and offered to meet him at the station and personally take him to the church. He had thought to bring the letter with him in case a misunderstanding should arise concerning the appointment.

Paul wondered if he would be presentable enough in looks and stature to impress Reverend Blakely. He wasn't a vain person but he had often been told how handsome he was. He was six feet one inch tall and his hair was so black it had a blue sheen to it. His eyes were bright blue, set apart by a perfectly chiseled nose. His jaw tended to be a little square but was off-set by a dimple in the chin.

As the day gave way to late evening, lights began to appear from the houses that dotted the country side and he wondered what the people did for diversion. He knew they had television: he could see the antennae jutting from their roofs. He noticed the mountains that were still visible but they didn't seem to be as majestic as they were at home. He was glad that Tennessee had mountains; it would make it much easier to adjust to the new environment. He couldn't help noticing the beautiful sunset as the last rays of the sun turned the horizon into a blaze of purple and blue and laced with pink and orange. He was filled with awe at God's handiwork.

He was scarcely beyond his beloved West Virginia hills and already he was looking back to them nostalgically. But there was something about the mountains looming ever so majestically upward that gave one the feeling of being surrounded and protected from things such as tornados and the destructive danger of nature. It reminded him of a hen as she gathered her chicks beneath her wings to protect them. Life among the hills was lived at a slower pace and people were friendly and concerned with helping one another.

He kept glancing overhead checking on his luggage to make sure someone had not taken it by mistake. Aside from the clothes he presently wore it contained the only other suit he owned. He had made a promise to himself that, should he get the job, he would buy some clothes from the first salary he received. At the moment he was anxiously looking forward to what lay ahead of him once he reached his destination. He hoped the train arrived on time so he wouldn't keep the Reverend Blakely waiting.

In any event, should the board of directors decide he wasn't the man for the job he wouldn't return home with his tail between his legs, but would seek employment elsewhere. Perhaps he may get the opportunity to fulfill a dream he had long held in his heart: to organize a church where people of every race, creed and color could come together in worship to God without prejudice, and with love for all humankind. This of itself would provide him a permanent position that would allow him to settle down in one place, get married and raise a family he so longed for.

He returned to the paperback he had been trying to read since boarding the train. Finally he had gotten engrossed in the book and was unaware of the passing of time. He happened to glance at his watch and saw it was nearing midnight. He laid his book aside and curled up on the seat to rest as well as he could. He folded his jacket to serve as a pillow and was soon asleep.

The sound of the conductor's voice calling out the next stop awakened him. He sat up, stiff from his cramped position, and looked around. Only a few of the passengers were up as yet so he went to wash his face and hands before everyone began stirring about. After having splashed water on his face and combed his hair he felt somewhat refreshed. As he stepped into the aisle to return to his seat he accidentally bumped into a vivacious looking young lady on her way to the diner for breakfast.

"Oh, I'm sorry," he said, turning to see whom he had backed into, and found himself looking into the most lovely sky blue eyes he had ever seen. The blue dress highlighted her eyes even more and a perfect blond hairdo framed her oval face while two red sensuous lips was enhanced by her flawless alabaster complexion. The fragrance of her perfume was light and delicate and smelled of honeysuckle that set his head to spinning.

"That's quite all right," she said sweetly, with the voice of an angel, and gave him a faint smile as she continued on her way.

He thought about following her, or say something to detain her for a minute—he wanted so badly to get to know her—and opened his mouth to call out to her, but suddenly his limited finances loomed up before him. He knew he couldn't afford to get involved with a lady just yet and so he stood by helplessly and watched her disappear into the next car.

Returning to his seat he took a cold, slightly mashed chicken sandwich from his jacket pocket and sat eating it dejectedly, washing it down with a cup of water. He would dismiss her from his mind, along with the dream of a home and family he always wanted, until he was more gainfully employed. He picked up his book and went back to reading it.

He looked up and saw the conductor coming down the aisle and wondered if they were getting close to his destination. When the conductor got to him he asked, "Sir, could you tell me how much longer it will be before we get to Blakeville?"

"Certainly. It's our next stop. We should be there within the next 2 or 3 hours."

Forgetting the blond vision was more easily said than done. He found he couldn't keep his mind on his book as he kept glancing up ever so often to see her when she returned to her seat. True, he couldn't afford to date just yet but there certainly wasn't any charge for looking....

Suddenly, wonder of all wonders, there she was! His spirit soared anew at the sight of her—then sank just as quickly. She was with some guy who, no doubt, was her boyfriend. From the familiarity they showed toward one another it was evident they knew each other well.

"Well, what did you expect, you idiot!" he chided himself under his breath. "After all, she is quite attractive." He watched them from the corner of his eye as they passed by his seat and for the first time in his life he was envious and jealous of the guy who appeared to be a young man of means and self-assured.

Back to his book he went seeking some sort of refuge. He would dismiss them from his mind considering the fact that it was unlikely he would ever set eyes on either one of them again. Caught up once more in his book, the few remaining hours passed by. Then, just as he finished his book, the conductor came through announcing the next stop.

"Blakeville...next stop Blakeville...all off for Blakeville. Please leave by the rear exit... Blakeville next stop...." His voice faded away as he entered the adjoining car.

Stepping down from the train he looked around for Blakely, but no one seemed to be looking for him. No one took any notice of him or his plight. Evidently, something had prevented Blakely from meeting him. Looking about he detected that Blakeville wasn't a very large town. In fact, he was to find that it was rather small, compact community where everybody knew one another. Then the thought occurred to him that maybe Blakely was waiting inside the terminal. Just as he reached the door to the terminal a small boy came rushing up to him.

"Excuse me, Sir," the boy said, "are you Reverend Paul Rangley?"

Paul smiled down at him, relieved and a little amused. "If you mean Langley, I am he. Paul Langley."

"I forgot," said the boy catching his breath. "Anyway, my Dad's here to take you to the church. I'm Carl."

"Nice to meet you, Carl," Paul offered to shake his hand but Carl rudely turned away showing an obvious dislike for him. Then a man in bib overalls came limping up to him. Paul knew at once it was Carl's father for Carl was an exact miniature likeness of him.

"No doubt you're the new preacher I'm to take to the church— Reverend Paul Langley, if I remember correctly," he said, extending his hand.

5

"That's me," Paul replied, shaking his hand vigorously. "I was beginning to think I was left to find my own way there."

"My name is Holseman. Arno Holseman. I sent my son ahead to catch you while I parked my truck. I'm the church caretaker. I wasn't aware until the last minute that I was supposed to come to pick you up. Had I known I would have been here when you arrived."

"Thank you, Mr. Holseman. I appreciate your coming. No doubt something unexpected came up to prevent pastor Blakely from coming for me as he promised to do."

Arno was ruggedly handsome and blessed with a full head of blond hair. He had been injured when a horse he was riding threw him and fell on his leg leaving him with a permanent limp. There was a slight dullness to his blue eyes due to the pressure of his job, knowing that if he made the slightest mistake preacher Blakely, with his erratic behavior, would dismiss him at once.

"Yes, as a matter-of-fact, it did," Arno said. "He asked me to tell you how disappointed he was to be unable to meet you and that he would see you this afternoon."

"It really doesn't matter," Paul replied, putting his hand on Carl's shoulder. "You have a fine looking son here. I hope we can become friends."

Carl made no reply and turned from under Paul's hand and stood looking off into the distance. He showed no interest whatsoever to Paul's attempt at being friendly. Paul knew that Arno was embarrassed by Carl's behavior and would probably explain the circumstance to him later on.

"We had best get started," Arno suggested. "Carl, take brother Langley's valise to the truck and wait for us there. It's where I always park it. We will be there shortly."

"I apologize for Carl's behavior toward you. I had hoped he would be taken with you, but I'm afraid he is still reluctant to get close to anyone as yet."

"What seems to be the trouble, if you don't mind my asking? Has he always been like this?"

"No, not at all. He used to be loving and friendly. Since I'm usually busy I don't have the time to devote to him I should have. But, I noticed the change in him came about only a few weeks ago. He refuses to tell me what happened."

They were only a short distance from the truck when Paul took hold of Arno's arm and stopped him. "Can you think of what may have happened that brought this change about?"

Arno stood rubbing his chin, thinking. "Come to think of it," he said, "I believe it happened shortly after the sudden departure of brother Allen, the assistant pastor at the time."

"Do you have any idea what brother Allen's departure may have had to do with Carl? Could Carl have possibly transferred his devotion from you to Allen during his tenure here?"

"It's possible. During the short time that Allen was here Carl did become closely attached to him. Allen was a very likeable guy and gave Carl a lot of attention—attention he wasn't getting from me at the time. In my opinion that is probably what happened."

"That sounds like a reasonable possibility to me. Now I'm beginning to understand," Paul said. "What about Carl's mother? Has she made any mention of this to you?"

"My wife passed away about a year ago." Arno replied, dropping his head at the thought of her.

"I'm sorry," Paul said, his compassion going out to both of them. "I think I know the reason for the change in Carl's personality. But, before I offer my opinion, may I ask if anything has happened recently that may have upset him emotionally?"

"Well, let me see...," He paused to give it some thought while reaching back into his memory. "Yes. Now that you mention it he used to have a friend, a black boy about the same age as Carl. His dad would drop him off here at the church every Saturday and they would spend the day playing together. Then after work his dad would pick him up on his way home from work. The preacher found out about it and had me stop the child from coming here."

"That explains it then," Paul said, and they continued on their way to the truck. "First he loses his mother, whom he must have loved very much, then he came to love Allen who, in turn, severs that bond of love by his leaving, and last, but not least, he has the love and companionship of his best friend taken away from him. As I see it, although I'm not a psychologist, he is afraid to love or get close to anyone, fearing they will be taken away from him."

"That sounds like it may well be the crux of the matter. I'm impressed. I wonder why I hadn't thought of it," Arno said.

They got into the truck with Carl sitting between them. Arno drove out of the parking lot and headed for the church. No one spoke for several minutes until Carl broke the silence by asking Paul, "Do you like kids, Reverend Langley?"

"I most certainly do! I love kids and I love you Carl."

"Preacher Blakely don't, especially boys. He says..."

"Carl!" his dad said sternly, interrupting him. "Do you want to get us thrown out on the street?" Then addressed Paul. "The preacher likes children. It's just that Carl insists on doing things the preacher forbids him to do."

"I'm sure Carl doesn't mean to be disobedient to brother Blakely or to break his rules deliberately," Paul said in defense of Carl to show him he was on his side. "Perhaps he has become stressed out and over burdened with the duties of the church causing his patience to wear thin. He probably needs some time off to "recharge his batteries". Surely he doesn't mean to be hateful and cross."

Paul took a small knife from his pocket and gave it to Carl who, with a half-smile on his face, sat rubbing it fondly. He wanted to take Paul into his heart but was simply too afraid to do so. "Thanks," was all he said, then retreated back into his shell.

"Awhile ago you asked me if I liked kids," Paul said to Carl, patting him on the head. "I'm especially fond of boys."

Arno looked over at Paul and smiled. He knew he would have no worry of Paul mistreating Carl in any way. As they drove along, Paul turned his attention to the street they were driving on and noticed it was more populated than before and figured they must be nearing the church since they were now within the city limits. He noticed how quiet Arno had become, speaking only to answer one of his questions. Carl, although still morose, had become a little more animated as they drew nearer to their destination.

"We're almost there," Carl said with very little enthusiasm. "I can see the cross on top of the steeple."

Arno made a few more turns and the church suddenly loomed up before them in all its splendor. Paul was impressed by its size and by its magnificent facade. I appeared to be well structured and, compared to his home church, it was much larger. The edifice was three stories high, the top floor was round with a domed roof and a glistening, stainless steel cross on the center of it. The second floor was recessed one foot from the edge of the first floor and in the center of the front wall there was a large oval stained glass window depicting a reproduction of the Pieta. Below this was the name of the church in eight inch high stainless steel letters. The overall building was constructed of yellow bricks that gave off a golden glow when the sun shone on it.

Arno turned to the right and drove a short distance then turned left again where he came upon two large iron gates. He pressed a button on a small device fastened to the sun visor and both gates swung open permitting them to enter. He followed the road round to the rear of the church and pulled into a four car garage.

"Come along, brother Paul and I'll show you where you will be staying," Arno said, getting out of the truck and picking up Paul's valise.

Carl leapt from the truck without a word and ran up the steps to their apartment. Paul knew it would take time to gain Carl's confidence. For the time being he would let things stand as they were. Paul didn't have a degree in psychology but he had read extensively on the subject and knew not to rush things where Carl was concerned. It would take patience as well as a lot of love and care.

Arno led Paul to the rear of the garage across a newly mown lawn to a modest brick bungalow and set down the valise. "Here you are," he said, "The door's unlocked and you'll find the keys lying on the desk in the alcove off the dining room. Miss Minna, the cleaning lady, left word that she would finish cleaning later this evening."

"If I get this job it will be nice to have someone to do the cleaning for me. I admit I'm not much of a housekeeper. Where do you live?"

"Carl and I live in the apartment over the garage," he answered. "I must go now. The preacher doesn't allow any of the help to spend too much time with idle talking."

Paul noticed that Arno was acting rather nervous as he turned to go. "I'm sorry if I have caused you any inconvenience," Paul said, "And, Mr. Holsman, I thank you for all your help. It was greatly appreciated and I hope I haven't been too much trouble."

"It was no trouble at all. I've enjoyed the time spent with you. And please call me Arno."

"As you wish," Paul concurred.

"When you get ready to go to your interview let me know and I'll show you where to go. I'll be on the other side of the apartment pruning some bushes."

"Thanks Arno," Paul said, gratefully. "I'll be glad to."

"See you later then," Arno hurried off.

Paul picked up his suitcase and carried it into the bedroom and placed it on the bed. He noticed that Arno called it a valise but he always called it a suitcase. He then took a tour of the house. He saw it was more than adequate for his needs if he should be permitted to stay. He returned to the bedroom, opened his suitcase and took out a change of underwear and his toiletries. He hung up his suit so it would be less wrinkled and was soon enjoying the stinging sensation of a good, hot shower.

When he finished dressing he checked himself in the mirror and felt a little more self-confident. He had a half hour before he was to meet with the board so he went into the kitchen to fix himself a cup of coffee if there were any coffee in there to fix—there was. By the time he drank his coffee it was time to go. He was a little nervous so he whispered a brief prayer then went to find Arno.

Arno took him to the side entrance in back of the main auditorium where they entered a hall that led them to a flight of stairs. Here they climbed the steps to the second floor then Paul was led to the foot of the stairs leading up to the third floor. Here Arno stopped.

"This is as far as I need to take you. At the top of these steps you will come to the entrance of a round room called the Skyroom. There you will find them waiting for you. Good luck."

"Arno, before you go may I ask you a question?" Arno nodded okay. "Is there an elevator in this building?"

"Yes. They have one but the help isn't permitted to use it unless it's an emergency."

"I see," replied Paul, wondering what kind of situation he was getting himself into. "Thank you, Arno. You have been very kind."

With a nod of his head Arno turned and walked away.

Paul ascended the last flight of stairs and knocked on the glass-paneled door. He could see several men grouped around an oval desk, behind which sat a distinguished looking man that had to be the Reverend George Blakely. Presently one of them came and opened the door.

"I'm Harry Stoddard," he said, extending his hand and introducing himself. "One of the members of the board of Elders."

"I'm Paul Langley." He shook his hand. "I'm here for my appointment."

"Come on in and meet the pastor and the other members," Harry prompted.

When Paul stepped into the large, round room he was captivated by opulence of it. The ceiling was indented and painted to resemble the sky. Small imbedded lights that gave the appearance of stars while a large, impressive chandelier hung above the desk. Behind the desk sat Reverend Blakely and on the other side of the desk five chairs were arranged on which were seated the remaining elders. Windows circled the top half of the room from which hung lavender drapes, thick sculpted silver-gray carpet covered the floor.

Reverend Blakely sat patiently behind the desk, smiling, while he waited to be introduced to Paul who was drawn from his astonishment of the place when he heard Harry saying, "These are my fellow board members, Bob Norris, Bill Mathews, and John Billings." Paul shook hands with each one of them as he was introduced and was greeted warmly by each of them. "And this is our distinguished pastor, the Reverend George Blakely. Pastor Blakely this is Paul Langley."

George rose from his seat and walked over to shake Paul's hand. "It's a pleasure to get to meet such a fine looking young man at last. May I offer my apology for being unable to meet you at the station as I promised. An unexpected incident came up at the last minute to detain me."

Paul was to learn that with George there would be a lot of unexpected incidents come up.

When pastor Blakely first stood up, Paul could see that he was nothing like he had mentally pictured him. He was two inches taller than Paul, making him six feet three inches tall. He looked to be in good shape and in his early fifties. His hair was thick, black and flecked with gray and fully gray at the temples. His eyes were gray-green and he sported a pencil thin mustache. Sensuous lips gave him an attractive appearance, enhanced by being impeccably dressed in a charcoal-gray suit.

Paul took his hand. "Thank you, Sir, for the compliment," Paul replied, "and thank you too for sending someone to bring me here." He regretted calling him sir, but there was something about his bearing, his tone of voice, that seemed to engender respect from his subordinates. "As we both know, a minister's life is made up of unpredictable circumstances that often arise."

"I'm glad you understand. And now if you will take a seat, the one that set over to the side, we will begin the interview."

Most of the questions asked were trivial ones and the others were directed at his personal life. Questions such as: "Are you married? Do you plan on getting married? If so, when?" The questions he anticipated strangely were never asked. Paul answered each question candidly, "No, I'm single. Yes, I plan to marry whenever I feel I can support a wife."

"How long have you been in the ministry?" asked Bob Norris.

"Approximately seven years. I have been evangelizing for the last four years after having finished my studies at the seminary."

Suddenly they were interrupted by a loud knock on the door. Before anyone could get to the door to answer it, in burst, to Paul's great and pleasant surprise, the blond girl that he had bumped into on the train. And he had thought he would never set eyes on her again.

"Excuse me, Father, for interrupting you like this, but my friends are waiting for me to accompany them to August Keep. I need some money to help the seniors buy some of the things they are in need of."

She was speaking of the nursing home where she and her friends went once a week to help bring a little cheer into the lives of some of the elderly patients who resided there. Paul sat with his mouth hanging open, staring at her in disbelief. He really never expected to ever see her again. Yet, here she was standing before his very eyes. He was certain he would wake up to find it had only been a dream.

Pastor Blakely, knowing his daughter, knew the real reason for her intrusion. It wasn't money. She had a job and money of her own. It was simply an excuse to see what the new prospective minister looked like and to meet him. He knew he was being overly permissive with her by letting her get away with this sort of thing by being a doting father, but with her being his only daughter he found it hard to be stern with her. This was the reason she hadn't hesitated to disrupt them. She knew she could get away with it. He would give her the money, mildly scold her later, introduce her to Paul in order to get her out of there so they could conclude their meeting.

He rose from his seat and with pride made the introduction. "Vivian, may I introduce the Reverend Paul Langley. Reverend Langley, my daughter, Vivian Blakely."

"How nice meeting you again," she said, extending her hand. "Had I known who you were and where you were heading, my trip could have been far less boring."

"You two have met before!" her Dad asked incredulously. "But how...where...?"

"Not really, Dad," she said, fully enjoying her father's consternation along with the attention. "But we did briefly cross one another's path."

"Perhaps I should explain before this leads to something it isn't," Paul said, defensively. "You see, while on the train on my way here, as I was returning to my seat I stepped out of the washroom into the aisle and clumsily bumped into Miss Blakely, who incidentally, was on her way to the diner."

"It was just one of those incredible chance meeting then," her dad surmised. "Here," he said, handing her the money. "Now will you please go so we can continue our meeting?"

"I'm leaving. I know when I'm not wanted." She laughed as she swept from the room.

Paul watched her disappear through the door still hardly able to believe his eyes and ears. Now she would no longer be a figment of his imagination. And he knew that their chance meeting would be a deciding factor in his being selected for the job.

They resumed their meeting although there was now a definite change in everyone's attitude. They all were more friendly and less hostile toward Paul. Then, satisfied that they had all the information they needed pastor Blakely rose to his feet and said, "Reverend Langley, would you please excuse us by stepping outside for a few minutes while we discuss your qualifications. We will send for you when we have reached our decision.

He left the room and walked down the steps then went over to a nearby window and stood looking out at the surrounding area. He had been in Blakeville only a matter of hours and already he felt a sense of belonging to it. If I'm accepted, and he felt certain that he would be, this would be an ideal place for him to settle down and start a family. Then he had second thoughts. What if they chose not to accept him—what then? He quickly discarded the thought from his mind. He would not allow doubt to cloud his mind. He had dedicated he life to God and he meant to live holy and upright before Him, following where ever He would lead him.

His thoughts then drifted to Vivian and a smile crossed his face. He scarcely knew her, yet each time he thought of her he felt a strange tug at his heart that he couldn't define. He knew her father had spoiled her, but now he knew a little more a about her too. Such as her unselfish devotion to helping others, especially the elderly at August Keep.

He was roused from his reverie by a hand being placed lightly on his shoulder. He turned to find Bob Norris standing there. He had come up so quietly he hadn't heard him.

"They asked me to come and get you. Shall we go now?"

"By all means," Paul said.

And together they climbed the stairs to Paul's future.

CHAPTER 2

As they ascended the stairs, Paul realized that the decision wasn't wholly contingent on their decision but according to God's plan and will for his life. He believed this explicitly for he was committed to God's leading regardless of what their decision might be. They entered the room and everyone seated themselves in the same chairs they were sitting in before. Paul started toward the chair he sat in previously but before he reached it Reverend Blakely came over to meet him with his hand outstretched and a big grin on his face. It was by that grin that Paul knew he had the job and emitted a sigh of relief.

"Brother Langley, it is my pleasure to extend a hand of fellowship to welcome you as my associate pastor and into the fellowship of the Victory Church." (it was always referred to by everyone as the Victory Church) I'm sure that together we shall be able to accomplish greater things, still yet, for the church." He paused for a few seconds before continuing. Now that you are one of us, it is an honor to address you as my brother in the Lord. I feel it is an endearment that draws the body of the church closer together giving the feeling of being a more closely knit family of God. And for us to have a more compatible relationship toward one another, I have decided to forego my title and you may address me as brother Blakely and I, in turn, will address you as brother Paul."

"I think that's an excellent idea. I've never been one for a lot of pomp and circumstance," agreed Paul. "Besides, it leaves little room for jealousy."

Paul was skeptical about how long this set up would last. Although he didn't know George that well he seemed to detect and air of superiority about him. He couldn't help but notice that when he spoke he had a tendency to emphasize each personal pronoun such as "I", "me" and "my", and used plenty of them.

"Another thing," brother George said, "you were unanimously accepted as my assistant. I just thought you might like to hear that."

"I certainly do appreciate hearing that and thank you for telling me. I trust that we can work together in harmony and that you will not be sorry for having chosen me."

He hadn't realized how much pressure he had been under until he had met with their approval and the assurance of a roof over his head, not to mention the salary. It gave one a secure and comforting feeling.

Then the rest of the men came to Paul to offer their congratulations and to shake his hand and welcome him into their midst. They had a concert prayer then each one went their separate way.

Paul kept trying to figure out what George meant by the term "brother" being reserved for a specific group. He reasoned with himself about this and thought, weren't all men brothers? He thought so, but the more he got to know George the more he became aware that he was a man with a lot of peculiarities. So far it had not involved anything of a serious nature, but nevertheless, he found it to be a little disconcerting. He couldn't help wondering why he said, ' "...great things for the church" ' instead of great things for Christ. Paul wasn't sure just yet but it appeared to him that, even though George was the pastor of an organization, he was adding certain rules of conduct that were of his own making. Paul had been in the ministry long enough to know there were some who, after having been the pastor of a certain church for a number of years, tended to feel the church was their own personal possession rather than a part of a governing body.

Everyone had departed the room except Harry and George and Paul. He had hesitated to leave thinking that George would want to discuss what his duties were to be or some other pertinent matter of business. But to Paul's amazement, George appeared to be more interested in discussing something with Harry rather than talking to him. From the way they were reacting toward one another it looked to him as though they were bosom buddies and involved in some sort of conspiracy together. Paul felt a little hurt by being so rudely ignored. It seemed that both of them had completely forgotten he was there. When George saw him he seemed startled that Paul was still there.

"Forgive me brother Paul for ignoring you," he said, sheepishly and offered a feeble excuse. "I've been without an assistant so long I had forgotten you were here. You're free to do whatever you like for the rest of the day. However, I would like to see you in the morning—say ten o'clock—to go over with you what your duties will consist of and to formulate a program that will permit us to work compatibly together. Then I would like to give you a tour of the church."

"I can manage that and I'll look forward to the tour. I need to get something to eat and a few letters written."

"Speaking of eating, there's a restaurant just a block down the street from the church. It's called The Beanery. It's a small place but the food is very good—you can't miss it."

"Thanks for telling me," Paul said, gratefully. "Until I can get stocked up with a few groceries, I'll probably be one of their best customers."

Before Paul could turn to leave, George laid his arm around his shoulder, implying that they were now "buddy-buddy", and said, "Once you are married, hopefully you will get a good cook. And once you <u>are</u> married there will be a substantial increase in salary to take care of added expenses."

"And what an expense!" Harry chimed in. "But they are worth it with all they do."

Paul knew that most men spoke jokingly about their wives, but when anything happened, such as a separation or divorce, and they were like a ship without a rudder tossed about aimlessly.

"I must get going; I have a lot to do." Paul said. "I'll see you in the morning at ten."

As he stepped out the door he glanced back curiously and saw them huddled together again, apparently plotting some sort of mischief. He suspected he would find out soon enough.

He stepped outside the church and had exited from the same door in which he had entered. The sun was still shining as he found his way to the gate. He was just about to pass through it when he heard someone call out his name. It was Carl out riding his bike.

"Mr. Langley, did you get the job—are you staying?" he inquired, more out of curiosity than any real concern.

"Would you like that if I did?"

"Yes. I would like for you to stay."

"Then shake hands with your new associate pastor."

Carl reached out hesitantly to take his hand. "I'll go tell Dad," was all he said.

"I'm going to the Beanery for a bite to eat. Ask your dad if you can come along. I'll wait here for you."

Carl came running back excited about going to the restaurant. "I know right where it is," he said. "I went there a few times with Mr. Allen. His last name was Barnwell."

As they walked along at a leisurely pace Paul tried to draw Carl out as much as he could by asking him, "What was Mr. Barnwell like; was he easy to get along with?"

"He was real nice. Everybody liked him and called him brother Allen."

"Then why don't you call me brother Paul? I'd like that."

"OK," he said, glancing up at Paul, wondering if it would be safe to get close to him. "I liked brother Allen a lot. Mrs. Barnwell was nice to me too."

"Do you know why he left so suddenly? Was he in some kind of trouble?" Paul asked. Some times children knew more about things than one realized.

"I don't know. I heard someone say something about an affair. But when I asked my Dad what an affair was he said, ' "never mind" '. When I asked brother Allen why he was leaving, he would only say it was for his wife's sake. She seemed all right to me."

They reached the Beanery and went in. The place was rather crowded, an indication that the food was good, and found a booth in the rear. Carl ordered a hamburger with fries and a Mountain Dew. Paul ordered the blue plate "special" of cubed steak, mashed potatoes with gravy, green beans and black coffee.

Carl enjoyed his meal and sat sipping his drink slowly so it would last longer. Paul was sure Carl didn't get to eat at restaurant very often and was glad he had brought him along; it was a way of gaining his confidence. Paul picked up on the conversation where he left off.

"Was brother Allen here very long?"

"Not too long. About nine months I think."

They finished eating and made their way back to the church. "Did you see brother Allen off and did he say anything before he left?"

"No, I didn't. I had already told him goodbye."

"By the way, you'll soon be out of school for the Christmas holidays. What will you be doing then?"

"Not much of anything. I don't have anyone to play with now. Mostly, I just try to keep out of the preacher's way."

"What happened between you and the preacher that you can't get along?" Paul asked as they reached the steps to the apartment.

"We once got along real good…but not anymore. He has hated me ever since his son Nat was drowned. But I don't want to talk about that," he said, turned and ran up the steps.

Paul stood looking after him puzzled over what that was all about. Something dreadful had evidently happened to disturb Carl so much that he couldn't bear to talk about it. He knew one thing for sure: something was badly wrong here and he meant to find out what that "something" could be. He realized that if this wasn't resolved soon that Carl could end up mentally disturbed. And that he wished to avoid by all means.

Paul went to the house, brushed his teeth, then looked for some paper on which to write a letter to his mother. He promised to let her know as soon as he got settled. Unfortunately, there wasn't a sheet of paper to be found in the house. It would have to wait until he went shopping. He did manage to find a scrap of paper to make his grocery list on. Before deciding what he needed, he went to the kitchen to check to see what there was on hand. All he could find was flour, a little corn meal, a bottle of Canola oil, and a jar half filled with instant coffee. Since he would be eating most of his meals at the Beanery, there wasn't much he would need. He didn't have a car so he would have to impose on Arno and ask him to drive him to the store. He knew Arno didn't quit work until five o'clock He would have to wait until then in order for him to go on his own time.

When they got back from the store he put away the few groceries he bought, and since he had neither a television or a radio with which to pass the time, he decided he would just go to bed early and get a good night's sleep; he was quite tired after his trip.

He slept soundly, surprised for having done so with being in a strange bed and among strange surroundings. He was up by six, had a nice, hot shower, ate breakfast, made the bed, and by the time he had done a few other things it was time for his meeting with George. He chose not to use the elevator just yet, knowing how George felt about one using it, and climbed the stairs all the way up to the top floor.

He entered the Skyroom and found George sitting at his desk busily at work on some papers. When he saw Paul approaching he quickly folded them and placed them in the middle drawer and carefully locked it. He then stood for a change, as any man would do, to greet Paul.

"Good morning, brother Paul. You're right on time—I like that. When a man is punctual it shows he is well organized," he said, shaking Paul's hand. "I trust you had a restful night's sleep."

"Thank you. I had a wonderful night's sleep," he said, letting go of his hand. "You were right about the Beanery's food. It was delicious!"

"I enjoy eating there although I don't eat there very often. Incidentally, I have a little disappointing news for you," he said, going back to his seat. "I have to rush through our discussion this morning. I've an errand that I must attend to very shortly. That's neither here nor there, but I do want to impress upon you that I take pride in filling my pulpit on Sunday morning and Sunday night. However, I do miss a Sunday evening service occasionally. You will be responsible for the Wednesday night service and the youth service that takes place once a month on Friday. Brother John Billings is the music director and brother Hiram Jones is the church clerk.

Paul took a small pad from his inside coat pocket and jotted down all the pertinent information he needed to remember. Looking at George, he said, "I can handle all that. I assume you will let me know ahead of time when you're going to be away so that I may prepare for whatever the occasion may be."

"Yes, of course. Do you have any further questions?"

"Only one. You mentioned a tour of the church. When will you get around to that?"

"I'm sorry to disappoint you, but it's hard to say. Why don't you take the tour on your own?"

"Sure. Why not?"

"Then I believe that takes care of everything. You are free to do as you wish now and I will get back with you again later." He turned to walk toward the rear exit, which Paul presumed led to the elevator.

"Just one more thing before you go. Is it possible that I could get an advance against my salary? I need to buy myself a car of some sort."

"That won't be necessary. I have an extra car—it's an old model—but is in good condition. I'll let you have it for five hundred dollars and dock your pay for whatever amount you can afford each month. Is that agreeable to you?"

"With terms like that how could I refuse?"

"That's settled then," he said, and turned toward the elevator again.

Paul wanted to ask him about Carl, but was afraid George would think he was prying. He would ask Arno later. He began his tour by going in the direction George left by and found it did lead to the elevator. Having finished his tour, and familiarizing himself with the layout of the church, he checked his watch and saw it was nearing lunch time. He would stop by to see Arno, knowing he would be home at that time. He tapped on the door and this time Arno opened it. Seeing it was Paul, a big smile lit up his face; a face that Paul didn't expect smiled very often.

"What a nice surprise! Come on in," he stepped back to let him enter. "Have a seat."

"I know you're getting ready for lunch so I won't stay long," he said, sitting down in the nearest chair. "I wondered if you would mind telling me what happened between George and Carl. He said their trouble began when George's son Nat drowned, but it must have been so traumatic that he couldn't bear to talk about it.

"You know, Carl may have just unknowingly put his finger on the problem. It was at that time this all began," said Arno, beginning to relate what took place. "I remember it well. It was during a beautiful, warm summer day. George's son Nat came by and talked Carl into slipping off and going swimming with him. As it happened, while they were swimming, Nat got cramps in his stomach and, after floundering in the water a minute or two, disappeared beneath the surface. Carl took off running to get help but by the time he got back Nat was gone. Nat was George's only son. When he found out that Nat had drowned he blamed Carl for it, accused him of persuading Nat to go swimming with him when it was actually the other way round. George was devastated and refuses to believe that it was Nat, instead of Carl, that was to blame."

"Now I understand why Carl is in the shape he is in, and how to more deal with it. Somehow George will have to be made to understand who was really at fault."

"You can't reason with him. Several have tried but when Nat's name is mentioned George goes to pieces all over again— and still does."

"Thanks for telling me this. I now know how to better understand Carl's behavior. I'll be going now so you can have your lunch."

◆ ◆ ◆

Paul could see that he was getting deeper involved in the things where George was concerned. The problem for him was: how should he go about trying to remedy the situation and, at the same time, not jeopardize his position with the church. He would just have to pray and seek God about it until he received an answer. Maybe an opportunity would be presented to him somewhere along the way. In the meantime, he would continue on as he did before.

Thanksgiving was fast approaching and he needed to get a skit put together for the youth service on Friday. He would need several of the children to participate and wondered if Carl would be willing to take a part in it. He would go by the apartment and see if he was home.

He knocked at the door and waited for Arno to answer the door. When he did he said, "I'm looking for Carl. Is he home? I'd like to talk to him about taking a part in a Thanksgiving skit I'm having for the youth."

"He isn't here right now. He left only a couple of minutes ago. I suggest you go look for him He has to be around here close by somewhere. He's out riding his bike."

"Then I'll go at once and see if I can find him. I'll see you later."

Somehow, Paul felt led to walk toward the church. He hadn't gone very far until he came upon Carl's bike laying on the grass near the side entrance to the church. He went inside, walked over to the other side of the building where steps lead down into the basement. He called out Carl's name but got no answer. He saw that several lights were on and had probably been turned on by Carl. He called out Carl's name once again and still got no reply. He stood looking about when he caught a furtive movement by someone darting behind a fold-away room divider over near the corner.

"Carl, is that you? This is brother Paul. Come on out, I know you're there."

Still he refused to show himself. Paul moved closer and could see two small feet beneath the divider. "Carl, I know you're there 'cause I can see your feet."

He crept out from his hiding place and stood facing Paul who saw he was on the verge of tears. "Hi, brother Paul," he said, timidly. I wasn't doing anything—just messing around. You won't tell the preacher on me will you?" Tears began to well in his eyes. "Please don't tell him," he pleaded.

"Don't worry, I won't breathe a word to him about this—this time," he told him, his heart going out to a hurt and bruised child. "But what if you had broken something, turned something over, anything like that. Since I'm now officially the assistant pastor I would have no alternative but to report it. Do you understand what I'm saying?"

"Yes. I'm sorry; really I am," he said and dropped his head and Paul saw a tear sliding down his cheek. "I really came to get my catcher's mitt that I had left down here," he said through tears. "There's nothing to do around here!"

Paul wanted to take him into his arms and comfort him and to show him there were people in this world who cared for him. He reached out to him to give him a hug, but Carl instinctively backed away, drying his tears on his shirt sleeve. Paul dropped his arms at his side and said,"That's okay, I believe you. It's easy to get distracted when there's nothing much to do. Isn't there anyone around here at all that you can play with?"

"Not anymore. I did have someone but, because Perry was black, the preacher made my dad stop him from coming here." Now the tears started anew.

Paul let him cry until his tears had subsided. He reached Carl his handkerchief. "Here, dry your eyes. Some people mistakenly believe that men aren't supposed to cry but that isn't true. It does one good to have a good cry every now and then," he explained.

Carl gave a faint smile, pleased that Paul understood him, and gave him his handkerchief. "The preacher don't think so. He saw me crying one time and called me a cry baby."

"He's one of those people I was talking about that doesn't believe men shouldn't cry. Forget about what he said and take my word for it. You do feel better don't you?"

"A little I guess," Carl said.

"You mustn't pay too much attention to a whole lot of what the preacher says. He obviously is under a lot of pressure and says things out of frustration he really doesn't mean," Paul explained. "I can see the preacher has hurt you. Perhaps not intentionally but unthinking. We must never harbor hate in our hearts against anyone regardless of how they may have treated us."

"I don't like him at all; he yells at me all the time."

"I came to find you to see if you would take a part in the Thanksgiving skit I'm preparing."

"Yes. I can do that."

"Now that that's taken care of, would you like to go to the Beanery for some ice cream?"

"I'd love it!" Carl exclaimed, rubbing his tummy. "Wait till I take my bike home."

As they were walking on their way to the Beanery, Paul casually asked, "What is your friend Perry's last name?"

"Warfield. He's Colby's son. I met him at school. His dad works at the Latimer Pawn Shop."

"Do you know where they live?"

"Yes. They live on the south side down by Oak Creek. It takes me about ten minutes to ride my bike there. Are you planning on visiting them?"

"Maybe, I don't know yet. I've been thinking about it. I'm going to try and get Perry back to play with you. How would you like that?" Even if he failed in the attempt he wanted to explain to them that he had nothing to do with Perry's expulsion from the church lot.

"Wow! that would be cool." Already Carl was beginning to admire Paul, but he guarded against getting too close.

They finished their ice cream and made their way back to the church. Carl asked a few questions and was excited about having Perry to play with again. "Can I go with you when you go to visit the Warfields?"

"Perhaps. We will have to wait and see."

When they reached the gate they found Arno there waiting for them. "The preacher called and asked me to find you. He wants you to come to the Skyroom. He has something important he wants to discuss with you."

"Thank you, Arno. I'll go at once and see what he wants."

He couldn't imagine what he could possibly want. He took the elevator up this time and walked to the door leading into the Skyroom but was puzzled to find it locked and no one there. Then he noticed a small note taped to the door. Seeing it was addressed to him, he took it off the door and read:

> Brother Paul,
> What I wanted to see you about can wait. An urgent matter has come up that needs my immediate attention. I'm sorry if I may have inconvenienced you. I'll see you sometime later.
> Brother George

He crumpled the note and put it in his pocket. This was getting ridiculous. There had to be some kind of ulterior motive to all of this—but what? He decided to walk back down instead of taking the elevator. He could use the exercise. When he reached the second level and started to open the door to descend to the bottom floor the door opened, as though automatically, and there stood a woman carrying a bucket and a cleaning towel. He knew she was the cleaning lady Arno had spoken to him about. She was big boned and stoutly built. Her hair was brown, which she wore in a bun on top of her head, and her eyes matched her hair.

"Excuse me, sister," he said. "If you are on your way up to the Skyroom you won't be able to get in, it's locked—unless, of course, you have a key. You look a little tired so I thought I'd save you an unnecessary climb up those steps."

"Thank you for your thoughtfulness. You must be the new assistant pastor I've heard so much about."

"I hope what you've heard had been kind. I'm Paul Langley and you are undoubtedly Miss Minna. I've heard about you too."

"I hope the report has been kind as well." She laughed. "I'm Minna Gothard, the cleaning lady, in case you didn't know."

"I would never have guessed," he said, laughing along with her. He liked her. "Aren't you working a little late?"

"Yes, a little. I'm taking the day off tomorrow so I have to get as much done as I can."

He didn't know Miss Minna very well, of course, but he judged her to be honest and straight-forward. He would chance asking her about Allen Barnwell and hoped she wouldn't think he was prying or being nosey. He didn't know how long she had been employed here but he figured she had worked for the church for sometime and would know a lot about what had been going on here prior to his coming.

"Miss Minna, may I ask a favor of you? Perhaps you can help me clear up a few things that took place prior to my arrival here. It has to do with Allen Barnwell. Do you know the reason for his leaving?"

"Before I tell you what little I know, let's sit down on those steps. I've never been one to stand when I could sit." She spread her towel and sat down on it. Paul dusted off the step with his handkerchief and sat down next to her. "I'm not sure how much of this is fact or how much is gossip, but the rumor was that he was having an affair with one of the sisters in the church. It's no excuse, but his wife had cancer and it affected their relationship. The board got hold of it and, when it was proven as fact, he was immediately dismissed and the lady was disfellowshiped. He was such a likeable person, I hated to see him go.

"Then it was nothing that involved the pastor. The way I first heard it, it had a touch of mystery to it."

"No, it was nothing more than out and out adultery. That's all."

"I've heard of the injustice the preacher done to Carl. I understand that Nat was George's only son."

"That's right," she went on, "when the preacher got word of his son's death he fell apart—lost it completely—lashing out at Carl, accusing him of taking Nat to the lake when it had been the other way around. He even accused God of taking his son unjustly."

"What a terrible injustice has been done to him and how hurtful it must have been to him. Thank you so much for telling me. I know it's getting late, and I've detained you far to long already. But before you go, can you tell me whether the preacher has made any attempt to rectify the damage he has done to Carl?"

"Not as far as I know he hasn't. Actually, he is still...I'm sorry, I have no right to say what I was about to say," she said, apologetically. "After all, my personal opinion doesn't matter."

"Only if it's relevant toward helping to solve the problem," Paul said to encourage her to continue with her story. "I assure you that what ever you tell me will be held in strictest confidence. Remember, Carl needs all the help we can give him."

Miss Minna, knowing she would lose her job if what she was about to disclose ever got back to the preacher. She turned from Paul's gaze, and while wringing her hands, weighed the consequence. She was tired of Carl being mistreated over something that wasn't his fault. Especially by a man who called himself a minister and was supposed to have love and compassion for all. Injustice from anyone made her angry, and with that anger she made her decision.

"Very well," she said determinedly, "I will tell you. As the associate you have the right to know. The preacher is being unjustly cruel toward Carl and is going to cause him to either run away from home or have a nervous breakdown. I also suspect that he is into something he is afraid of Carl stumbling onto and mistreats him to keep him at a safe distance. I have no substantial proof but in my cleaning I have come across snippets of paper with certain information written on them which has led me to believe that he is dealing in bookmaking and horse racing, and the Lord knows what else! Another thing that causes me to be suspicious is that I have a key to every room here, with the exception of the Skyroom. The only time I can get in there to clean is when he is in attendance."

Now it was time for Paul to wring his hands. With what Miss Minna had revealed to him made him realize he was in a very perilous position. It was his responsibility to confront anyone, as well as the preacher, if what they were accused of could be proven against them. Since he had no tangible evidence with which to prove any of this, he would just have to wait, bide his time and see what, if anything, turned up.

"It looks like I have a time bomb on my hands just ready to explode!" Paul stated gravely. "If what you suspect turns out to be true I certainly intend to see the guilty parties brought to justice. I would appreciate what has been discussed here remain confidential between the two of us."

"I understand your position. Of course not one word of this will ever pass these lips of mine. I promise you that."

"Nor mine. Now I must be on my way. It looks like I'm going to be rather busy for awhile," Paul said, taking his leave. "Goodnight, Miss Minna."

"Goodnight, brother Paul."

Once on the outside he paused to take several deep breaths of fresh air to ease the tension he felt. He walked toward his house, his mind in turmoil. He had just arrived here and it appeared he had walked right into the middle of a lion's den. He had no one with whom he could confide in or to ask for advice—except God, of course. Whatever direction he took it would be of His making. He kept hearing the words ' "…will stumble onto," ' and wondered what all they might entail. All he could do at the moment was remain quiet and keep his eyes open. If anything dishonest was going on, he was sure there was, it would come out sooner or later. Did not God's word declare in no uncertain terms: "…Be sure your sin will find you out."

It was dark out now. He had spent more time talking with Miss Minna than he thought. He reached his front door and was surprised to see it standing wide open. Could he have forgotten to lock the door? he wondered. He stepped inside thinking that Miss Minna, who probably had a key, must have left intending to return in a few minutes. Here, he thought, was probably where Carl had wondered in. He then walked into the kitchen and there found the back door wide open too. Carl must have walked through the house and, seeing no one was there, left by the back door, thoughtlessly leaving both doors open since that was the way he found them. He closed the door and locked it, securing the house for the night. Then the thought: why am I blaming Carl for this; could someone have broken into the house instead. He began checking to see what, if anything, was missing.

Stepping into his bedroom he stopped abruptly, staring unbelievably at what met his eyes. His suitcase, which he had left laying on the bed, had most of its contents scattered over the bed. It was obvious someone had been searching for something. But what, he wondered, could they have been searching for; who could it have been? He gathered up his things and put them away in the drawers then put his suitcase on the top shelf in the closet. If anything was missing he didn't know what it could be. Then suddenly it came to him. It was the small five inch jade figurine of St. Francis of Assisi that he had stored in the side compartment of his suitcase. He rechecked the compartment again and, sure enough, it was missing. A close friend at the Seminary had given it to him and he cherished it for sentimental reasons as well as its value.

For the time being he would dismiss the jade from his mind as he felt there was nothing he could do about it.

The next time he had met Miss Minna, he told her what had happened and gently scolded her for going off and leaving the door open.

"I'm so sorry about that, brother Paul," she had apologized. "I had intended to be gone only for a minute and got busy doing something else and completely forgot about leaving the door open. I promise it won't happen again. Please forgive me."

"All is forgiven and forgotten," he assured her and they parted amicably. He went to his desk, took out a sheet of paper he had remembered to buy, and began the letter he had promised his mother he would write. He had so much he wanted to tell her and his dad he hardly knew where to begin. He didn't want to write it all in a letter for fear that the preacher, or one of his cohorts, would get hold of it.

Dear Mother and Dad,

I'm sorry to have taken so long in writing you as I promised but I am kept pretty busy. I arrived safely here in Blakeville, Tennessee and I've finally gotten settled in. Another reason I hadn't written because I didn't have any paper to write on and had to wait until I went to the store to buy some and to get some stamps.

This is a lovely church and much larger than the one at home there. But it looks as if I have stepped into the middle of a very complex situation. It's much too involved to explain it all to you now, so I will explain it in more detail when I can get around to calling you on a pay phone.

I hope you are getting some rest and that Dad is doing a lot better. Write me a long letter and let me know how you both are doing. Remember me in your prayers and much love to you both.

Your loving son,
Paul

He sealed the letter, put a stamp on it and set it aside. He would mail it first thing in the morning. It had been a long day so he got up and went straight to bed. He stretched out on the bed luxuriating in its clean freshness. He fell fast asleep and dreamed he was back home where he was free of all worry and care. His mother had prepared him one of the most delicious meals he had ever eaten. He awoke at six o'clock and lay there for a few minutes dreading to get up and face the day. But one thing he was pleased about, his Thanksgiving skit had went over nicely and the children performed almost to perfection.

The next thing he had to do was prepare for Christmas. The children loved to perform in a play so he would write his own and present that to the church for the holiday. So far he only had to fill in for George one time. He was sure the number would grow until he would practically be carrying the whole load.

As he lay thinking about what lay ahead of him he felt like he was both Daniel and Moses combined. It appeared that he had been placed in a lion's den, from which he hoped to be delivered, and it was up to him to lead these people out of a troubled church.

CHAPTER 3

Paul got out of bed and dressed to the sound of clattering garbage cans. It was, no doubt, garbage pick-up day and he didn't have his garbage ready yet. But he had plenty of time for they didn't pick-up until ten o'clock. That was one thing the preacher, (he had started thinking of him as "the preacher" as all the others did) had neglected to tell him. If he did he didn't remember him doing so. It didn't matter for he didn't have much garbage today anyway. He shaved, washed his face and combed his hair, then went to prepare his breakfast of cereal, toast and jelly, along with a cup of hot black coffee. The responsibility that lay ahead of him was monumental. He hadn't the slightest idea how to go about solving it and so he simply was trusting God to lead, guide, inspire and direct him. May His will be done. One thing he did know and was certain of and that was he would have to tread cautiously. He was fully aware that he did not possess sufficient knowledge or wisdom to solve this on his own. He could do nothing within himself. Therefore, he would be totally dependant on the Lord for strength and guidance. He felt the Spirit drawing him to his secret closet of prayer. He was fully relying on the Lord to lead him and desired to always be in the center of His will.

He began to pray softly and in earnest: "My heavenly Father, I come before you with praise and thanksgiving for all your many blessings. I thank you for thy great love and for the privilege to love and serve you. I believe I have been placed here for a specific purpose, Lord, but I can do nothing of myself. I ask you to please guide and keep me in the center of thy will. Grant that I may boldly proclaim thy word, holding high the blood stained banner of Christ, in whose lovely name I pray. Amen.

After he had finished praying he felt uplifted and much encouraged in the Lord. He had been thinking about taking a more extensive tour of the church and decided that today would be the day to do it. He was sure there was some things he had missed. Who would be the most qualified to give him a complete tour of the church, he wondered. He then thought of Miss Minna; she would be the ideal one. And since she was the one that cleaned the church she had to know every nook and cranny of it. He went in search of her and found her on her hands and knees scrubbing the vestibule.

"Good morning, Miss Minna. How are you this morning?"

She stopped scrubbing, straightened up and looked up at him. "I'm fine, thank you. And, how are you feeling this day?"

"As well as can be expected, I suppose. I wondered if you would do me the honor of giving me an extensive tour of the church—that is, if you can find the time."

"Me, give you a tour of the church! And what might the preacher think of that?"

"Never mind what he thinks. Will you do it?"

"Sure, if you think it's okay."

"I don't know anyone who would be more qualified than you."

"When do you want to begin this tour—right away?"

"The sooner the better."

"Then give me a minute to put away my bucket and we'll get started."

"We may as well begin here," she said, taking him into the sanctuary. As they walked through the double doors Paul was taken anew with the beauty of the place. The pews were finished in cherry and covered with wear resistant material of lilac and blue and were positioned in a semicircle of four sections. Each section had twelve pews that tapered down slightly as they neared the front. The carpet, of wear resistant material also, was a purple. Five aisles gave easy access to each row of pews. The pulpit was a perfect match to the pews, as were the ones for a hundred voice choir. There were a number of inverted lights in the ceiling over the choir and three chandeliers hung just to the front of the pulpit. On the wall behind the pulpit was an elaborate oil painting of the Christ, with arms outstretched, depicting his ascension into heaven. The lighting was beautiful throughout and lighting enhanced a large painting of the Lord's Last Supper displayed on the back wall. Spotlights were conveniently placed to highlight the person speaking and for the performance of plays that were presented during the holidays. Closets for storage space were plentiful and a conference room completed the first floor. She then took him by elevator to the second floor where they stepped through the doors into a large hallway. Along each side were six Sunday School rooms and at the end of the hall was his and the secretary's office. Here, too, was the front wall that featured the Pieta in stained glass.

"There's no need to go up to the Skyroom. I've already been through that <u>and</u> the basement."

"That completes the tour then. I hope it was informative."

"Very much so. You did a good job and I don't think we missed a thing. Thank you so much," Paul enthused. "I hope I haven't caused you to get too far behind with your work."

"Not at all," she said. "I really must get back to work though or I <u>will</u> get behind."

After having reviewed the church and its architecture Paul was impressed by what the preacher had accomplished. He had to have built this building at a great sacrifice to himself and the membership. It was indeed a tribute to what he once had been. He must have possessed a tremendous personality at the time. It was dangerous when one gained success and prosperity and became self-sufficient. They became deceived into believing they did it on their own and no longer needed to rely on God.

It showed the promise of another beautiful day. So far, Paul noticed that the weather here wasn't too much unlike the weather back home. July and August never seemed to be as warm as they really were due to the cool breeze that blew from off the lake.

He looked forward to the young peoples' services. He enjoyed every minute he spent working with them. He decided to go by Arno's again and have another talk with him about Perry Warfield. He wouldn't mention the suitcase incident just yet until he had a chance to talk to Carl about it. Even though Carl seemed to be the most likely suspect it didn't necessarily mean that he was the guilty one. He didn't know if Arno would be home at this time but he would go by and see.

He knocked on the door and could just barely hear Arno call out for him to come in. He assumed that Carl wasn't home and he wasn't. He stepped into a dimly lit room and made his way to the bedroom where he found Arno lying in bed.

"What are you doing in bed at this hour of the day—is something wrong?" he inquired, stepping up closer to the bed.

"I've been feeling pretty bad since yesterday and running a fever. I cut my leg while cutting down a dead tree a day or so ago. I didn't think much about it at the time, thinking it wasn't too bad and would heal on its own with a little home remedy thrown in. But early this morning the pain became so bad I sent Carl to get some Epsom Salts to mix in some hot water in which to soak my leg in."

"Do you mind if I raise the shade and turn on the light so I can take a look at that leg?"

"Go right ahead," Arno said. "I was going to straighten up a bit around here this morning but when I started to get up I couldn't stand any weight on my leg."

Paul removed the bandage wrapped round the leg and stood staring gravely at the inflamed laceration. "I hate to tell you this, and it is only my opinion, but unless something more than first aid is done it's possible that blood poisoning would soon be claiming that leg." Paul could see red streaks running above and below the wound down to the ankle as he replaced the bandage. "Soaking it in hot water with Epsom Salts may help alleviate the pain but it won't clear up the infection. I really think you should have a doctor take a look at it."

"Do you really think it's that bad?"

"Yes. I really believe it is," Paul replied, "And if I were you I'd hold off on the hot water treatment until the doctor has checked it. Whom should I call?"

"If you think it's that serious then call ole "Doc" McPharson. He's from the old school of medicine. He's a drunk but he's a good doctor."

"Paul called the number Arno gave him and a deep, gravely voice said, "Doc McPharson here. What can I do for you?"

Paul explained to him the reason for the call.

"I see," said the Doc. "Tell him I said not to soak his leg in hot water but to pack it in ice instead. I'll get there as soon as I can."

Paul hung up the phone and said, "It's a good thing I called him. He said not to soak your leg in hot water but to apply an ice pack to it until he gets here."

Arno's esteem for Paul went up another notch. Just then Carl came back with the salts. For some reason he wasn't paying much attention to Paul and avoided looking him in the face. This caused Paul to think he was guilty of taking the jade figurine more than ever.

"Set those salts aside. I'm sorry, you'll have to go back again and get me a bag of ice. The doctor said I needed to put ice on my leg instead." Carl hurried off to get the ice.

"Now that that's taken care of what did you want to see me about?"

"I came to talk with you about Perry Warfield. Do you have any idea why the preacher stopped him from coming here to play with Carl?"

"I have a good idea, although I'm not at liberty to say," he said, defensively. "I did only what I was ordered to do."

Paul got a chair and placed it near the bed and sat down. "I realize that. But didn't he give you any reason for dismissing him?"

"None whatsoever. He called me on the phone and told me what he wanted me to do. He isn't one to talk to you face to face about any-thing unpleasant. He gave me no reason and I asked for none. I can't say anymore than that. I could lose my job."

"As I understand it, even though this is your home, you aren't per-mitted to have whomever you want in for a visit?"

Arno squirmed uncomfortably, choosing his words carefully. "Not exactly; it hasn't gone that far yet. Since my wife's passing, my friends have been few and far between. No objection has ever been made before. Therefore, I suspect it's nothing more than prejudice because Perry is black."

"The preacher must have had a valid reason, other than that, for doing what he did. And I believe that reason was the aftermath caused by the death of his son; he's held a vendetta against Carl ever since," Paul concluded.

"How did you find out about that—who told you?"

"Why, you did. Don't you remember?"

"Yes. Come to think of it, I do remember. I'm getting so forgetful anymore."

"That happens to all of us."

"I hated it real bad that Nat drowned but the preacher should know that what happened wasn't Carl's fault. It could as easily have been Carl instead of Nat, or, for that matter, both of them."

"Thank God, at least one of them survived! Say, have you had anything to eat?"

"Yes. I had a bowl of cereal before I sent Carl to the store. I wasn't very hungry anyway." Arno, becoming a little impatient while waiting for the doctor to arrive said, "Where could that doctor be? He should have been here by now!"

"I thought so too. I've got to be going soon. I'll wait a little longer. Maybe he will show up shortly. But, before I leave, tell me when would be the best time to pay a visit with the Warfields?"

"That depends. They both work and don't get home till around six in the evening. She gets off work at five, drives by to pick up Colby, who doesn't get off until five thirty," he said, rubbing around the wound on his leg, his face reflecting the pain there. "You know, of course, that if the preacher finds out you have gone there he will dismiss you immediately."

"That's a chance I'll have to take. Anyway, as things presently stand, I don't believe he would make an issue out of it," Paul said, without explaining. "As it is, I can't go anytime soon. I have a few things I have to do before I visit them."

At last there was a knock at the door. "That's probably the doctor now. I'll go let him in. I'll check with you later this evening to see what he had to say about your leg."

Paul opened the door and the person standing there said, "I'm Doc McPharson. This is the Holseman residence isn't it?"

"Yes. Come in. I'm Paul Langley, the associate pastor here," Paul said, introducing himself and shaking his hand. "You'll find the patient in the back bedroom. I was just leaving. Nice to meet you Dr. McPharson."

The ice pack eased the pain somewhat but it still ached pretty bad. The doctor removed the ice pack and treated the wound against further infection. "Stay off your leg for two or three days and I think you'll do fine. Here's some pain pills to be taken as needed for pain and if you have anymore trouble with it you can give me a call."

"How much do I owe you, Doc?"

"Thirty dollars ought to take care of it," he said, looking forward to the bottle of booze it would afford him.

Arno's leg healed without any further complications and he was grateful to get back to work. The preacher was considerate enough not to dock his pay and for that he was thankful."

Paul had now been assistant pastor for eight or nine weeks now and he found himself thinking of Vivian more frequently lately. He had been trying to come up with a good excuse to call her. Then he got an idea. This being the end of the year he would ask her to celebrate New Year's Eve with him. Presuming that she still lived at home he called her there.

"Hello," said a slightly slurred voice. "Mrs. Blakely speaking."

"I'm sorry to disturb you. This is Paul Langley, the assistant pastor. May I speak with Vivian please."

"I know who you are! Why haven't you come to see me?" the whiskey giving a rudeness to her voice. "I'm not well and I don't get to come to church very often," she whined, wallowing in self pity.

"I apologize for being remiss but I have been rather busy. I'll try to drop by soon and call on you. Now, may I speak with Vivian.?"

"I'll be expecting you," she answered flippantly, then got to her daughter. "As for Vivian, she doesn't live her anymore. She has her own apartment now," Adra said. "She's probably at work at The Botique. It's a dress shop." She gave him the number.

"Thank you so much. Bye now."

He called the number Adra had given him and got an answer right away. "Hello. This is The Botique. Vivian speaking," she said cheerfully.

"Vivian, this is Paul. How are you?"

"Oh, Paul, how nice to hear from you," she said, pleased that he had gotten round to call her. "I'm doing great, how about you?"

"I'm hanging in there. The reason for my call," he explained, "is to ask you to go out with me New Year's Eve to celebrate. It's only a few more days away you know—that is if you don't already have a date."

"No, I don't have a date at this point in time. My boyfriend and I have called it splitsville. I'd love to go out and celebrate with you." Paul was pleased to hear that. "Call me at the office when you get home. If I'm not there call me at home," he said, giving her the both numbers although she probably already had the church number. "I need directions how to get to your apartment."

"Will do," she said.

Paul wasn't aware of it but at the moment he reached the Skyroom, George was on his way to the church and would soon be heading for the garage.

He rang off from talking to Vivian and went to the Shyroom in hopes of finding the preacher there. He wanted to be shown what the controls on his desk was for and how they worked. When he got there he was disappointed to find there was no one there. He wondered where the preacher went to stay gone so much. He was to find out later, much to his chagrin. He didn't expect to be able to get in but tried the door anyway. To his surprise it was unlocked. This was very unusual to say the least. Then he became suspicious, thinking that it had been left unlocked on purpose to try and catch him poking into things. In spite of that, he opened the door and went in. He went to the desk to try and figure out how to work the controls himself. There was a panel of buttons on the left side inset into the flat surface of the desk itself. He noticed that above each button was written what each button was for with the exception of one or two that had noting at all written on them. He noticed, too, the center drawers had no handles to open them with so they undoubtedly were controlled by the buttons that had no names. He was simply using common sense and figuring it out as he went along. He got an idea. He slid his fingers under the edge of the desk top and, sure enough, there they were more buttons. He pressed one at random and the left drawer slid open. It came up empty. Instinctively, he pressed the same button again and the drawer closed. He pressed another button and it opened the drawer on the right. He started to press the button to reclose it when his eye caught sight of what appeared to be a ledger. He picked it up, curious to know what it contained. Ordinarily, he wouldn't have thought of looking inside to see what was written there but, with the cloak of suspicion hanging over the church, as well as the suspicion of the unlocked door, he didn't hesitate to look inside. On the front page was written: The International Bank of Switzerland, followed by a column of numbers with specific amounts of money, with the dates of deposit. He couldn't take the chance of reading any further so he closed the ledger, replaced it in the drawer and closed it. Just as he turned away from the desk and stood looking around in walked the preacher. He seemed to think nothing of Paul standing there, thinking that the things in his desk were safe. He didn't think Paul would have the slightest idea how to open the drawers. He began to explain where he had been.

"I was here earlier, which you probably figured out by the door being unlocked, but had to go and get the portfolio I forgot. I didn't want you to be locked out if you should get here before I got back. I wanted to show you the papers that shows the value of the church and the property. Also, the insurance papers and the date the payments are due, so that you would be able to take care of it in case I might be gone or incapacitated for some reason.

Paul was somewhat confused. The only thing he could figure out was that it appears George had planned a meeting with him, thinking he had told him, when in actual fact he forgot to do so. Since he was here he would just go along with it and pretend that was his reason he came up there. It covered up the real purpose for his being there.

He waited for Paul to finish looking over the documents and gave them back to him. He replaced them in his folder. "I want to commend you for the way you have handled your responsibilities here. You are an assistant any man would be proud to work with. Now, let's get a little more light in here," he said, pressing a button and the drapes parted.

Paul wondered where all this praise was leading to. He found it hard to believe that George could be anything other than compassionate and honest. He simply had an aura about him that gave one that impression.

"Thank you for those kind words and for your faith in me. I hope I can prove to be worthy of them. What else do you have on the agenda?"

"Nothing more, unless I've forgotten something. If I have we will take it up later. But, since you are so young and energetic, I hope you can come up with some exciting and innovative ideas that will keep our people interested and enthusiastic," he challenged.

"I'll do my best. I do have some ideas that I hope aren't too far out. I think they will go over great with the young people for the monthly service."

"May this old and experienced preacher give a young and upcoming one some timely advice?"

"You certainly may; I'm always open to constructive criticism."

"Yes, well…uh…," he stammered. "What I was going to say is: don't get too overly ambitious. It has been the downfall of many a good man. Remember, Rome wasn't built in a day."

"I thank you for your sage advice and council," Paul said, thinking, how could he possibly give me such advice when he has failed to heed it himself. He must be trying to intimidate me, to keep me at a distance from finding out about his questionable activities. "Come to think of it, what was it you wanted with me when you had to leave so suddenly a few days ago?"

"Oh, it wasn't all that important. Actually, I wanted to remind you about the garbage and the day they pick it up since I had forgotten to mention it to you earlier. Also, I wanted to personally introduce you to our secretary Nora Letty."

Later, Paul would come to realize why George had been so reluctant to introduce them. "That's all right. I met her during my tour of the church. As for the garbage and pick-up day, Carl told me about it," he said, without thinking what Carl's name might evoke from him. However, he didn't say anything, but Paul saw his eyes suddenly go dark with contempt at the mention of his name.

Satisfied that he had covered everything he wanted to talk with Paul about, George suggested they step out on the terrace. They stood looking over the landscape and he pointed out to Paul several of the city's landmarks. He then walked back into the Skyroom.

"You did say that you had already toured the church, did you not?"

"Yes. I was very impressed." Paul wondered where his mind was. It didn't seem to be on the business at hand. "However, I was never shown how to operate any of the electrical wizardry connected with it."

"I'll show you how it works here in the Skyroom," George graciously offered. "There's nothing complicated about it really. Nevertheless, I must ask you not to open any of the drawers as they contain very important and personal papers, and <u>things,</u> of mine.

Paul kept a straight face, careful not to smile or give himself away. "I'll remember that," was all he said.

George gave him a quick demonstration then said, "I seem to always be dashing off but I have an important meeting with someone (it was with Harry Stoddard), so I have to be going. Until later then...." he turned and walked away.

Paul thought George was acting very peculiar; he wondered about his mental faculty. He went to the church office to talk with Nora, to see if anything new had come in that needed his attention. He tapped lightly on the door before entering as she called out, "Come in!"

"Busy as usual, I see. How are you?"

She quit typing and turned to face him. "I'm doing fine. Yes, there's plenty to do around here. How are things going with you? Have you got settled in yet?"

"I'm doing okay, I guess, and catching up on things. And, yes, I've finally got settled in. Say, if I can ever be of any help to you please don't hesitate to let me know."

"You're very kind. And if the occasion ever arises where I need help I'll let you know."

He liked Nora right away. He liked the sound of her voice; it was soft and not too high pitched. She was small in stature and stood about five feet tall and was rather attractive. Long eyelashes accentuated her dark blue eyes and honey colored hair framed her face, cut short and styled in a fashion very becoming to her.

"I thought I'd check to see if anything had come in that needed attending to right away— not that I don't have anything to do."

"A call did come in this morning from someone needing monetary assistance, but, George ...er I mean brother George, took care of it."

Paul caught the slip in addressing George and wondered about the familiarity, then dismissed it from his mind. "Well, I'll be in my office, if you need me for anything give me a call."

"Sure thing," she said. "Nice talking with you."

Paul straightened up his desk and then began jotting down some ideas for the youth to participate in. Having finished with this he got ready to go to lunch when he noticed George was back. He seemed to always be popping in and out. He appeared to be headed for Nora's office but seeing that Paul was in his office too, and to throw off suspicion, he stopped by Paul's office instead. Seeing that it was nearing lunch time, and using that as an excuse, he asked Paul, "Have you had lunch yet?"

"Not yet. I was just getting ready to go and eat."

"I'm taking Adra out to lunch to stop her from harping about my never taking her out anymore. Would you like to come along; you two can get acquainted."

"I'd love to meet her. I talked with her a few minutes the other day or so on the phone."

"Incidentally, how is the car doing?"

"It's a great car. I really like it."

"I'm glad you're satisfied with it."

"I'm still waiting for the extra key."

"I'll get it for you when I go to pick up Adra."

He searched high and low for the key. Try as he may, he couldn't find it anywhere. "Adra, where is the extra key to my old car?"

"I don't have any idea where it could be. Let's go and I'll look for it when we get back."

George took them to one of his favorite Italian restaurants called Lueggi's. Things went along nicely and Adra comported herself with dignity, taking care not to make a scene. She knew if she embarrassed her husband in front of Paul, he wouldn't take her out anymore. He hardly ever took her out as it was.

George drove back to the house where he dropped Adra off then took Paul back to the church. He waited for Paul to get out of the car then drove away without saying another word. Another one of his peculiarities, he thought.

Paul went to his office and sat down at his desk to compose a sermon to use in an emergency should the need arise unexpectedly. He was just about finished with it when the phone rang. interrupting him. "Paul Langley. May I help you?"

"Brother Paul, it's Nora. A call has just come in for brother George. He doesn't seem to be around anywhere. It's Bill Matthews calling. Do you want to take the call?"

"Yes. Put him on."

"Brother Paul, this is Bill Matthews, one of the board members as you know. I can't get hold of the preacher and I need someone to go to the city jail and talk with my son Tilden. He's been arrested but claims he's innocent of what he's being charged with. Do you know how to get to the jail? It's…" and he proceeded to give him directions how to get there. "Have you got that?"

"Yes, I've got it. I'll get there as soon as I possibly can and see what can be done."

He hurried over to the parsonage to get the extra key to the car from sister Adra. He knocked at the door and waited. Presently, she came to the door. She looked disheveled and un-kempt and a little unsteady on her feet. Obviously, she had fortified herself after getting home from the restaurant.

"Sister Adra, did you find the extra key to the Plymouth brother George sold me? If so, would you get it for me please. I need it badly."

"No, I haven't found it yet. Come in and I'll look for it again if you don't mind waiting."

"Not at all," he said, and she went in search for it again. He felt sorry for her. She must be a very sick person.

She returned with a key chain holding three different keys. "These may be the ones you want. They are the only ones I can find."

He took the keys, thanked her, and hurried to the garage. To his relief one of the keys fit the ignition. He would return the other two keys to her later when he had more time. He backed the car out of the garage and headed for the jail. He had no trouble finding it, got out of his car and went inside. A man was sitting with his feet propped up on the desk eating an apple.

"Good afternoon. I'm Paul Langley, assistant pastor to George Blakely at the Victory church. I understand you're holding a young man by the name of Tilden Matthews. I'd like to speak with him for a few minutes if I may."

"I'm sheriff Jake Dudley," he said, swinging his feet to the floor. "So you're the new preacher at Blakely's church. I'm pleasd to meet you," he said, offering his hand. "Preacher Blakely is one fine man!"

He shook Jake's hand. "That's right I am. It's nice meeting you too, Sheriff Dudley." Paul wondered why he referred to the church as being Blakely's church. He said nothing though and let it pass.

Jake got the key and opened the steel door leading into the corridor where the cells were located. He opened the steel door, they stepped into the corridor, he locked it behind them and led Paul down to the middle cell where Tilden was incarcerated. "When you're ready to leave call out my name and I'll come and get you."

Paul always got the feeling he was being incarcerated himself whenever he had occasion to visit a jail. He stood before the cell door and there sitting on a cot, to his great surprise, was the same young man he had seen on the train with Vivian. He sat holding his head between his hands, the perfect picture of dejection.

"Tilden, you don't know me, of course, but I'm Paul Langley, assistant pastor to George Blakely," Paul said, introducing himself. Not until the mention of George's name did he raise his head and look at Paul. He stepped over to the cell door and waited for Paul to continue. "I don't know what, if anything, I can do to get you out of here but I'll do what I can. Would you mind telling me why you are here?"

Tilden stood quietly studying Paul, no doubt wondering how he could possibly be helped by a young preacher who had only arrived in town a few short weeks ago. "Please don't misunderstand me, Preacher," he began. "I appreciate your coming but how come Blakely didn't show? I <u>know</u> he could get me out of here."

Paul was curious to know why he was so certain that George could get him out and he couldn't. He was so confident that George had the power to bring about his release. "I realize I don't have the clout that Reverend George has but, like I said, I'll do what I can."

Paul kept prodding Tilden trying to find out why he was in jail but he kept evading the question. He seemed to think a lawyer had to be present when crucial information was given. "I can't do very much for you if I don't know what I'm fighting against."

"I'll say this much. It had to do with marijuana, commonly called "pot". That's all I'll say until I've spoken with a lawyer."

"Well, that's a start. I'll be on my way then. Maybe George can be located and do whatever it is that he does and get you out of here."

He called out Jake's name and was soon standing outside of the jail breathing freely of the outside air.

CHAPTER 4

Paul returned to Arno's late in the evening as he promised to do. He found him much improved and on his way to a full recovery. Doc McPharson had cleaned and sutured the wound, prescribed a regimen if antibiotics and some pills for pain. Paul was glad to see he was doing so well and would soon be up and about again.

As for Tilden, Paul didn't have much hope of getting him out of jail but he wouldn't tell Tilden that. He intended to go back and talk with him again, perhaps find out what had taken place that caused him to land in jail. He had to go wash his car and from there he would go to the jail.

He walked into the jail with a little more confidence than he had before. Jake was sitting at his desk reading a newspaper. There was some clamor going on back in the cells so more prisoners must have come in.

"Good day, Sheriff. I'm here to talk with Tilden again."

Jake took him back to the cell as he did before. "Matthews, preacher Langley is here to have another talk with you." To Paul he said, "Stay as long as you need to and call me when you're ready to go."

When Tilden heard Paul's name he jumped to his feet and came over to the cell door. "I'm glad to see you again, Preacher. Am I any closer to getting out of here?"

"Not just yet, but I'm working on it. I need you to give me more information. Why you are in here and what brought it about." Paul said.

"I'm in here because I was at the wrong place at the wrong time. I admit I was at this friend's house where some dudes were smoking "pot". But, believe me, I wasn't one of them," he said, turning and pacing his cell. Then he came back, grasped hold of the bars and pleaded with

Paul. "You have to find Blakely. I appreciate you trying to help me, but Blakely is the only one who could possibly get me out of here!"

"Now calm down. Since we can't find Blakely you'll have to contend with me until we do. Maybe I won't be able to get you out of here but I can try. It would help to know the name of this place and what you were doing there where they were using illegal drugs. Tell me the truth, what were you doing there?"

"Nothing! Absolutely nothing! It was a private party at a friend's house. I just happened to go by there and went in to see him for a few minutes. I know it sounds like a feeble excuse. It had been a while since I last saw him and I...oh, what's the use. No one is going to believe me anyway. It all sounds like a cock and bull story," he finished hopelessly. He went back and sat on his bunk.

"You must give me the name of your friend, where he lives, and where he can be reached. I've got to have a talk with him."

"You sound as though you don't believe me," he spoke from his cot.

"You said yourself, it sounds like a cock and bull story."

Tilden got up from his cot and came back to his cell door. "His name is Joe Talley; he lives at 123 on Woodman Drive."

Paul thought about asking him if his dad had been by to visit him, but, not knowing what kind of relationship existed between them, decided not to. Now that he had a name and address he had something to work with.

"I'll check this out and get back with you. Hang in there and I'll see you later," Paul said. He walked to the steel door and called out Jake's name. He came at once and opened the door and when they got to the front of the jail Jake said, "Do you think the boy is guilty? He doesn't seem to be the type to get involved with something like this."

"It's hard to say. Personally, no, I don't believe he is. Tell me sheriff, is this his first time being in jail?"

"I believe it is, if I remember correctly," he said, hanging up the keys.

"Thanks. That lets me know he hasn't been a trouble maker," Paul said, explaining his reason for asking. "I'll see you later, sheriff."

"Just call me Jake, ok?"

"Then you call me Paul. So long for now, Jake." He left and went to his car.

He decided to drive around awhile and better acquaint himself with the streets and the business district. He noticed the further he drove south the more run-down the area seemed to be. He then drove eastward for a short distance then turned down the next street he came to and was surprised to find he had come upon Latimer's Pawn Shop. He made a mental note of its location, drove on by, made a right turn and found himself back where he started from. He checked the time, saw it was nearing one o'clock and drove to a fast food place and had a burger and a Coke.

He pulled into the garage and parked in the same place the car had been before. He returned to his office to see if anything new had come up while he was out. Seeing there was nothing of importance, he went over to talk to Nora a few minutes and found she wasn't there. He figured she had gone to lunch and hadn't returned yet. Since it was still early evening he would drive around and see if he could find the Talley residence. He found it, parked his car, went to the door and knocked. When Joe answered the door Paul saw standing before him a clean-cut young man that looked nothing like he had expected.

"Yes sir, what can I do for you?" he asked politely with a smile.

"I'm looking for Joe Talley. I was informed he lived at this address."

"He does and you have found him. I'm Joe Talley."

"I'm Paul Langley, the assistant to George Blakely at the Victory Church," Paul remarked. "I'm here on behalf of Tilden Matthews, who, at the present time, is in jail. You two know each other?"

"Yes, he's a casual friend of mine. We went to school together. Would you like to come in where we can discuss this more comfortably."

When they were seated, Paul continued by saying, "I have a few questions I'd like to ask you, if you don't mind."

"I don't mind at all. And you say he is still in jail?"

"As a matter-of-fact, he is. Which is why I'm here. I understand there was some pot smoking that went on here. Can you tell me if he smoked any pot while he was here?"

"I know for a fact, he did not. Neither did I. I had a party going on here in full swing when he happened to drop by. I don't know who brought the pot, but, in the interim, someone called the cops and they rushed in and grabbed everybody in sight. Actually, he was only here about five minutes. I never touched the stuff and neither did Tildan."

"How did you manage to get released from jail and Tilden made to stay; shouldn't he have been released the same time as you were?"

"He should have been—I thought he was. Somehow, there must have been some kind of mixup."

"No doubt, there were. May I ask who posted bail for you and got you out?"

"I really don't know. I was told I was free to go and I asked no questions. They told me I would be informed when the trial would be."

"That's all I wanted to know. I thank you for your time and cooperation. I hope everything turns out well for you."

Paul drove straight back to the jail. Jake was on the phone when he arrived. Without a word, he laid the phone down, unlocked the door and returned to the phone to resume his conversation.

When Tilden saw that Paul had returned he rushed to his cell door to hear what he had to say. "What did you find out; am I getting out of here now?"

"Sorry, not yet. I went to see Talley and wanted to let you know what he had to say."

"What did he have to say?"

"He verified what you told me and assured me that neither you or him had smoked any pot. He was released from jail and thought you had been too. He doesn't know who sprung him —at least that's what he told me—but I intend to try and find out. I hope to have you out of here no later than sometime tomorrow."

"The sooner the better if you ask me. I thank you for what you're doing on my behalf. I thought you might like to know, my Dad came by for a short visit right after you left."

"If Talley was bailed out why doesn't your dad bail you out?"

"He doesn't believe that I didn't smoke any pot. He thinks this should teach me a lesson."

"Well, I've got to get moving if I'm going to get you out of here." Turning to leave he said, "I'll keep you posted." He called for Jake to let him out and as they walked to the front he said, "Matthews hasn't given me any trouble since he's been here. I hope you're successful in getting him out."

"We'll see," he said. "We should know by tomorrow whether I've succeeded or not. Thanks for putting up with me."

"Just part of he job, Preach...er, Paul—just part of the job."

When Paul got back to the office he saw that Nora still had not returned. If she had only gone to lunch surely she would have been back by now. Evidently, he thought, she must have gone home. If she had, he wondered why she hadn't mentioned it to him. He noticed she had had been taking a lot of time off here lately and, of course, he had no idea why. He then thought of Vivian and gave her a call. He hadn't had a chance to talk with her since their New Year's Eve date. One of the other sales ladies answered the phone and he asked to speak to Vivian.

"Hello, this is Vivian."

"Vivian, this is Paul. I hope my calling you at work doesn't jeopardize your job."

"No, they don't mind as long as we're not busy."

"I just wanted to call and say hello. I didn't want you to forget me. I would call more often but I'm kept so busy," he explained. "As soon as I get a few things straightened out we will get together and take in a concert."

"That would be wonderful! I wondered why I seldom heard from you."

"I hope that can be remedied before too much longer. I'll call you as soon as I find out when the concert will be."

"That's fine. I'll be waiting on your call. Until then, " Bye."

As soon as he hung up he headed for the library. He wanted to look up some information on a Hawaiian Luau. He planned to have one for his next monthly youth service. Then it was back to his office once more to begin preparing for the Luau. School was out for the summer and it was hard to believe that the Christmas holidays had come and gone and summer was here again already. The annual church picnic was on the last Sunday in June and Paul looked forward to it. True to the promise he made to himself he bought those clothes he so badly needed. Now he had some decent clothes to wear whenever he had to go anywhere.

While sitting in his office it occurred to him that most of the calls that came in to the church were mostly for him. It was as though he was the pastor rather than George. Paul knew that George was aware of his growing popularity but what his feelings were about the matter would never be known. He still couldn't understand how George had manage to procure Tilden's release from jail so quickly. He had failed to do it after devoting so much time and effort to it only to be met with failure at every turn. It was obvious that he didn't have near the clout that George had. Once he had returned from his trip he had resolved the whole affair in a matter of minutes.

As it turned out, the trial that took place was hardly mentioned in the papers or otherwise. There had been a few minor charges, some fines were paid, and the matter quietly dismissed. The news that Harry Stoddard's son David had been involved was leaked to the press. Then it was bantered about that Tilden had been told about the party and the pot, but there was no truth to any of it. So much for gossip. The truth is that he just happened to be passing by there and dropped in to see Joe for a minute and had been innocent of the whole affair.

As Paul sat summarizing about different ones his mind came back to Nora again. He was coming to realize that something odd was going on where she was concerned. He knew she had been absent a lot lately and wondered why she didn't get someone to fill in for her if she were ill. So much depended on her being at her desk, especially when George was gone so much. The phone rang causing him to jump, startling him out of his reverie. It was Miss Minna and she seemed very distraught over something. He was unable to get much info from her that made much sense, except that she was at Arno's and something about Carl being missing. He quickly threw on his jacket and hurried over there to see what had actually happened.

He found Arno in front of the garage calmly washing George's white, Fleetwood Cadillac. "How long has Carl been gone? Are you sure he isn't somewhere about the grounds?" he asked.

Arno turned off the water hose before answering him. "I have no idea how long he has been gone, nor why. He has never done anything like this before." Paul could see that he was quite upset. "I have to finish washing the preacher's car before I can go look for him."

"Do you know if he has had a run in with anyone recently?" Paul inquired.

Miss Minna, having seen him talking with Arno, came hurrying down the steps and rushed over to where they were.

"Not that I know of. But I don't always know about...." Arno's words trailed off.

"As you may know, I've always said this would happen. He has had a few spats with the preacher, which is what I think has caused this."

Paul knew what she meant. Carl had told him about a few of his encounters with the preacher. He had, no doubt, wandered into off limit territory and had been severely reprimanded by him.

"Is his bike still here? Then again, I guess not. It would be rather difficult for him to run away without his bike. I have a pretty good idea where he may have gone to."

"I'll go see if I can find his bike anywhere just in case," said Miss Minna, hurrying off to search for it.

"Let me know whether you find him or not," Arno said as he resumed washing the car. "If he isn't where you suspect him to be I'll go looking for him after the preacher leaves."

Here Miss Minna came hurrying back. "His bike is nowhere to be found!" she exclaimed.

"I hope that proves my hunch is right," Paul said, heading for his car.

Paul was sure Carl had fled to the Warfields; there was nowhere else for him to go. By going there to look for Carl, he would avoid having to chance visiting them on his own. He had been unable to persuade the preacher to let Perry return to play with Carl. He was going to do nothing to favor Carl in any way. Paul fully intended to talk to Perry's parents and try to explain to them his position on the matter. He hoped he could make them understand. But, before going to the Warfield's house, he decided to go by Latimer's Pawn Shop and talk with Colby.

He entered the shop and the jingling of the bells on the door brought out from the back room a well dressed gentleman who came up to him smiling and said, "May I help you?"

"I'm Paul Langley, the associate at the Victory Church," he said, extending his hand.

"Oh, yes," he said, still smiling. "I've heard of you." He shook his hand. "I'm Jesse Latimer, the proprietor. What is it you're looking for?"

"I understand that Colby Warfield is employed here. I would like to speak with him if I may."

"Yes, he works here. He's in the back room. I'll get him for you."

Colby came walking toward Paul and he could see the self confidence in his walk. He was clean and neatly dressed in jeans and a chambray shirt. He was well built, which was proof of a good workout, was five feet eleven inches tall, and had a pleasant personality.

"You wish to see me," he asked with perfect diction.

"Yes. I'm Paul Langley, the…"

"…Assistant pastor of the Victory Church," Colby laughed, finishing the sentence. "I'm glad to meet you. Forgive me for interrupting you, but I've heard so much about you from Carl that I feel I already know you." He offered his hand, "I'm Colby Warfield. I hope my son hasn't caused you any trouble."

"No, not at all," Paul shook his hand. "Believe me, I'm truly sorry for what happened to Perry. When I have more time I'll try and explain it to you. That's partly why I am here. Carl has run away and I'm sure he's at your house since he has no where else to go. Do you suppose you could get off for a half hour or so and drive out to your place?"

"I'll ask Mr. Latimer and see. It takes about fifteen minutes to drive there from here."

Colby walked back to where Latimer was. "Mr. Latimer," Colby began, "may I be excused for about an hour? Reverend Langley wants me to drive out with him to my house."

"Sure, go right along," Jesse told him. "Business is slow for the time being. Just be sure to be back in plenty of time to sweep and lock up the shop."

They drove along chatting amiably. No mention was made about prejudice and Paul felt they were to become good friends. He didn't want to discuss anything about Perry until he had the time to discuss it with his mom and dad together.

"Have you seen Carl lately?" asked Paul. "I know he's very fond of your son Perry and it seemed to me to be the most logical place for him to run to."

Colby evaded answering his question by saying, "They get along very well together. Perry was very badly hurt by what happened. He's just too young to understand this sort of thing. How does one expalin prejudice to a seven your old child?"

"The damage had been done. That I can't deny. But I mean to rectify it somewhere along the way," Paul assured him. "I'm working toward that end now. But you haven't answered my question of whether you have seen Carl lately or not."

He delayed disclosing to Paul whether Carl was with him or not. He wanted to be sure not to give away his whereabouts too soon. "He really <u>has</u> run away then hasn't he?"

"Yes, I'm afraid so. I suspect he will ask Perry for his help; he really has no one else to whom he can turn to."

"Turn right onto that dirt road just ahead there," Colby directed, "and follow it along the river's edge. I live on the other side of those trees there up ahead."

Paul stopped the car in front of a crudely constructed three room house that could hardly be called little more than an oversized shack. Just as he got out of the car he saw the boys dart behind a clump of bushes and stayed hidden there. He knew his hunch had been right; he had found Carl's place of refuge.

They went into the house and Paul could see that everything was spotlessly clean. The walls looked freshly painted and the curtains were starched and ironed to perfection.

"Won't you sit down brother Paul?" asked Colby. "My wife isn't here, she's still working."

"No, I don't have the time. I've got to find Carl and get him back to his dad. He's worried to death over him. Aren't you going to admit that he's here?"

"All right, I'll admit it. But if Carl finds out I told you he will be awfully hurt and not trust me anymore. You'll have to pretend to find him on your own. Those two boys are very good friends. Carl is a frightened and insecure little boy and we will do what we can to help him."

"What you say is true. I'm trying to do all I can to help him too. Now I'm going out back and call out to him and see if I can't get him to come out from where he's hiding."

Paul walked out into the back yard and loudly called out Carl's name. "Carl, come out from behind those bushes. I know you're there 'cause I saw you and Perry run behind them when I was getting out of the car."

Paul waited for him to come out but he didn't show. "All right, Carl," Paul said, "you have never seen me angry and I'm getting very angry at you. I know you're there and you better come out to five. One…two… three…four…."

Carl came out then, his head hanging down, very scared, on the verge of tears and not wanting to face Paul. "I'm sorry, brother Paul. Please don't be angry at me. I had to run away! I just couldn't take any more of the preacher's yelling at me!" Here the dam of tears broke and overflowed.

Paul didn't scold him but leaned down and hugged him real tight. "Your Dad is very worried over you by your running away. Are you ready to go home now?"

"No. Nothing can ever make me go back there!"

"Can you tell me why? Your Dad needs you more than you know and he does truly love you," Paul cajoled him. "Whatever happened to cause you to leave will be taken care of in time. I promise you."

He finally persuaded Carl to return home. "Once you're home, stay there. Don't go anywhere near the church until we get this matter straightened out. Now, let's put your bike in the trunk of the car and we'll drive Mr. Warfield back to his job." When they got back Paul pulled up in front of the shop and stopped to let Colby out. "Thank you brother Colby for your help. I'll be talking with you again later. I have a lot I want to discuss with you and your wife."

To Paul's great surprise, Carl got out of the back seat and got up front with him. He believed he was gaining ground with him. He was confident he would eventually win his trust. He saw that Carl was quiet and somewhat withdrawn. He guessed it was because he was dreading the confrontation with his dad. Paul casually mentioned how boys often ran away, hoping to draw Carl out of his apathetic state, so he would tell him the reason why he ran away.

"Want to tell me what happened that caused you to run away? I promise not to repeat it to a single soul," Paul said. He put his arm around Carl's shoulders and pulled him over closer to him. His love and tenderness, warmth and affection toward him soon won Carl's trust and confidense and he slowly began to open up to him.

"Well…it all began…," he started out haltingly, "when I accidentally got into an off limits place that I…well, I didn't even know it was off limits. Honestly, I didn't know I wasn't allowed to be there. Anyway, I bumped smack-dab into old preacher Blakely. I don't know what he got so all fired angry about but he started acting real crazy like and told me that if he ever—and I mean <u>ever</u> he said—caught me snooping around again my dad would be looking for another job." Here he burst into tears again. Paul gave him his handkerchief. "You have every reason to cry. It makes me want to cry right along with you."

Paul could feel the anger rising in him—real anger! Anger he hadn't had or felt in a very long time. "When we get back I want you to be extra, extra careful and stay out of the preachers way as much as you possibly can. Will you do that for me?"

"I'll try."

"In the meantime, I'll be looking into this to see if there is anything that can be done about it. OK?"

"OK," he said, drying his tears with the handkerchief. "I didn't mean to go in there, it just happened." He gave Paul his handkerchief.

"Where is this room you're talking about?"

"The storage room. It's next to the furnace room in the basement. I had Supermouse with me and I was just messing around in the basement. Supermouse got away from me and ran under the door into the room. I opened the door, it was unlocked, and I went inside looking for him. The preacher happened to be in there and that's when he bawled me out. I wasn't snooping, really I wasn't!"

"I believe you," Paul said, messing his hair. "Let's forget all about it shall we? Promise me that you'll keep Supermouse at home from now on, or at least don't take him into the church. You promise?"

"I promise," he said, as Paul drove into the garage.

Paul went with Carl to the bottom of the steps where Arno waited at the top for Carl to come up to him. As he waited for Carl to reach him he said to Paul, "Thank God, you found him!" He enfolded Carl in his arms saying, "Don't you ever scare me like that again!"

While Arno was rejoicing in the return of his son, Paul returned to the garage and took Carl's bike out of the trunk and left it at the foot of the steps. Arno came down to where he was. He reached out his hand to Paul. "Thanks," was all he said, and Paul knew how much meaning went into that one word.

Paul then went to his home and went inside. It had been a long and trying day. He was more determined than ever to find out what was going on with George and why he got so upset with Carl for going into the storage room. He hadn't known about that particular room and it hadn't been pointed out to him. Paul knew George had to be up to no good for him to threaten a little boy so severely. What could he have possibly been doing in that storage room, Paul wondered.

CHAPTER 5

As soon as Paul closed and locked the door he went to his room and knelt down by the bed to pray. He was emotionally drained and needed a spiritual uplifting. Not only that, but he felt guilty for getting so angry with the preacher. It was at times like this that made him realize his need to seek fellowship with his heavenly Father and prayer was the only way that could be obtained. He prayed earnestly to be completely led by the Spirit, and that God's will be accomplished in his life. When he finished praying he felt a definite renewal of his own spirit and had a strange sense that he would soon have the answers to many of the things that had been going on since his arrival here. On thing he was certain of: whatever was done to uncover what was going on uncover the preacher's activities would have to be carried on from within the confines of this house. It was the only place that whatever he may discover would go undetected. He went into the kitchen for a light snack before going to bed.

He fell into bed almost too tired to sleep. When sleep did overtake him he slept fitfully and dreamt he was being chased by a large black bear. He was glad when the time came to get up. After he had eaten breakfast he went to the office and was surprised to see Nora hard at work trying to catch up on the days she missed. He went into her office to talk with her, hoping to find out why she was missing so much work

"Good morning," he greeted her, "how are you doing?"

"Very well, thank you. There's several messages that may be of interest to you. I'll group them together and bring them over to you."

"A good idea. And I thank you." He thought she would mention the reason for being away from work so much, but she didn't offer a single excuse. He returned to his desk. She brought the messages over, gave them to him, then turned without a word and went back to her office. He sat looking after her and thought he had detected a slight bulge to her stomach. Could she be pregnant? he wondered. No, it couldn't be, he told himself, she's isn't even married. I must be getting paranoid.

None of the messages were of an urgent nature that required his immediate attention so he laid them aside. He went back to talk with Nora about her work. "Sister Nora, do you have any idea how much more you're going to have to be off? I was thinking if you did perhaps we could get someone to come in and fill in for you. That way, you wouldn't get so far behind with your work and wouldn't have such a hard time trying to catch up."

"No, I have no idea. It's due to circumstances beyond my control." She wouldn't comment beyond that.

"Maybe I could talk to brother Blakely about the problem and he could work something out for you. He does seem to have an eye for you."

She looked up at him with a hurt look in her eyes. "Sarcasm doesn't become you," she said. "I would not have believed that of you."

"I'm sorry. Please forgive me. I was way out of line. I have no right to take my frustration out on you. Whatever your problem is I trust it will be resolved soon."

"Now, that sounds more like you. I forgive you. Anyway, a little compassion never hurt anyone. The day will come when you will know and understand more than you care to," she said, unaware of how prophetic she was being. "I'm truly sorry to have missed so much work, especially when I need the work so badly."

Paul looked at her more closely and noticed, for the first time, the light circles forming around her eyes and how pale she looked. Evidently, she has been more ill than he thought. To change the subject he asked her, "Would you happen to know where brother George has gone to. I haven't seen him for a day or two."

"You mean he left without telling you where he would be or when he would be back," she asked evasively. "Perhaps he left a message for you on the dictaphone. I'll go and see."

She hurried away and was back in about five minutes or so. Suddenly it dawned on Paul that she had a key to the Skyroom. Strange, he thought, why would the preacher give her a key to the Skyroom and not give one to Miss Minna, the cleaning lady. It didn't make any sense. He had told her, no doubt, to guard the secret well. She had just slipped up and given herself away.

"Just as I suspected," she began, unaware of her goof, "he left word on the dictaphone for you. He had to go out of town on business and expects to be back by late this afternoon. I'm sorry. I should have remembered to check that."

Paul wondered when the preacher had begun neglecting his church. It probably would give him a clue as to when all this trouble started. "Thank you Sister Nora," Paul said, and returned to his office.

Certainly the preacher's behavior was getting more outlandish as time went on. Now Paul understood why brother Allen had left when he did. He must have discovered a few of the things the preacher was into and got out before getting caught in the middle. He was afraid his wife was not strong enough to withstand the aftermath of it. Apparently, he hadn't had an affair after all, that it all had only been a rumor. Paul came to the conclusion that the preacher had given him the position as assistant because of his inexperience and age. The preacher knew he was "green" at a lot of things and that would be to his advantage. He also must have thought he wasn't any too smart and wouldn't be able to detect a lot of what was going on. He thought it odd the preacher kept the Skyroom locked whenever he was away. It had to be because of his covert activities, he reasoned, although he had no solid proof of his guilt or innocence. He wasn't aware of it at the time but it wouldn't be long before an incident was to take place that would bring the preacher's covert activities tumbling down around him.

Although Paul had met Adra for a short while when he went out with them to eat, he never had the opportunity until now to pay her that visit he had promised her. He knocked on the door and stood waiting for her to answer it. When she came to the door she looked real nice for a change. She was dressed as if she expected to be going out.

"Why, brother Paul, how nice that you could find the time to come by. Please come in." She stepped back for him to enter.

"It appears you're getting ready to go out. Maybe I should come back at a later time."

"No. Sit down, we have plenty of time. Vivian and I are going shopping for a little while and she won't be here for another hour or so yet."

As they sat talking, Paul learned a lot about the state of their marriage and such. From what she told him, he deduced that their marriage wasn't on the best of terms. She also disclosed a few of his faults, undoubtedly, to justify her reason for drinking.

He noticed the time was getting away from him so made ready to leave. "Sister Blakely, it has been a joy talking with you, but I must be getting along. Perhaps I can find the time to come by again sometime."

"That would be nice. Thank you for coming. I'm glad we could have this little talk together. Since I'm not well I don't get out very often. It gets lonely sitting here all alone. Please do come back again, won't you? If you call to let me know you're coming we can have some coffee and cake."

Paul's heart went out to her. He knew she was trying to ease her emotional pain with alcohol which, he knew, brought more harm than good. After he left he went to check out the storage room. It was the one room he had never been in.

He stepped inside the room and could see it contained a lot of history of the church. There were several trophies setting on a shelf, as well as a few plaques, a testament to the preacher's past accomplishments. There was even a couch that converted to a day bed which puzzled him. He wondered where this had been used and why it had been stored here. He continued looking over the things in the room and came upon an old filing cabinet. He pulled on one of the drawers, expecting it to be locked but, to his surprise, it wasn't. How strange, he thought, for the preacher to leave this filing cabinet unlocked. This has got to be an oversight on his part. Curious, he took out a file and looked at it. It was a file showing the original building plans for the church. He replaced the folder and pulled out another one. Soon he was so engrossed in the cabinet's contents he didn't realize how much time had slipped away from him. He put the folder back and was going to close the drawer when saw an envelope that wasn't in a folder at all. He picked it up and pulled out its contents. He couldn't believe his luck, for in his hand he held an old bank statement showing personal cash deposits made at one of the local banks. He put it in his inside coat pocket to check out later. He made sure all the drawers were closed and left the cabinet just as he found it. Since he had lost track of the time he knew the preacher could show up at any time. He took a quick glance over the rest of the room and spotted a pair of small gloves that he was sure belonged to Nora, but thought nothing more about it. He would later find out how they got there. He left the storage room, then was off to the Beanery for something to eat.

When he got home he could see that Miss Minna had been in and done some cleaning. That meant he would have a clean bed to sleep in tonight. He went over to his desk and addressed a card to his dad who was celebrating his fiftieth birthday. With that taken care of he began to write that long letter he to his mother that he had promised to write her. He covered every thing he thought she would be interested in. Then he added a P.S. I can't wait for you to meet my girlfriend. Her name is Vivian Blakely, the pastor's daughter here, and she's gorgeous.

The day seemed to have passed by so quickly for some reason. Knowing a clean bed was waiting on him, he took a shower and went to bed. He slept soundly throughout the night and wakened later than usual. By the time he got dressed, grabbed a bite to eat, it was nearing eight o'clock by the time he got to the office. When he got there he saw Nora was already at her desk. She was early, very seldom did she get there before nine. He went over to speak to her.

"Good morning. Aren't you the early bird this morning. The first morning I'm late and you get here before me."

"And a good morning to you. I know you're curious as to why I'm earlier than usual this morning. Well, I've turned over a new leaf. I've resolved to be on the job as early as I can each day, no more missing work, and to get my work caught up and back in order."

"Then I'll not detain you, since you are in such high spirits, and leave you to your work."

He didn't know it then, of course, but there was an incident about to unfold that would bring to light a trail of hypocrisy and deceit the preacher had perpetrated over the past year or so that would bring shock and disbelief to all who knew him and a reproach to the church.

Paul had only been back in his office a few minutes and gotten seated at his desk when he heard a crash like something had fallen. He jumped to his feet and rushed over to Nora's office to see what had fallen. It was Nora. He found her lying in a heap on the floor. It appeared she had fainted knocking over her chair. He didn't know what to do other than to call the only doctor he knew, Doc McPharson. While he waited for him to arrive he folded her sweater he found laying on the floor and put it beneath her head. He then covered her with his own jacket and sat down to wait for Doc to arrive. After what seemed like an eternity Doc arrived just as Nora began to stir. She opened her eyes, looked about to see where she was, then sat up.

"You must lie still young lady until I can check you to see if there is anything seriously wrong with you. I'm Doc McPharson. You have just fainted and you need to be examined to see if we can find out the cause of it."

"I'm all right; I don't need a doctor." She stood to her feet swaying slightly. "Who called you?" she asked, and promptly passed out again.

"Preacher, would you please step outside until after I have examined her?"

Paul left and returned to his office.

The Doc worked at reviving her so she would know what he did while he examined her. She was embarrassed and too weak to resist any further. When he finished his brief exam he said. "Fainting is a sign that your body needs attention and that something could be seriously wrong. However, in your case, you have nothing to worry about. It isn't life threatening. From what I can determine, without doing a more thorough exam and some testing, is that you are pregnant."

"Oh, doctor, are you sure? I just can't be!" she said, and promptly burst into tears. "As I said, I can't be positive without a complete exam, but that's my honest opinion as it presently stands," he said, helping her to her feet. "Can this be kept quiet until I decide what to do?" she inquired.

"To a certain extent but not altogether. I do have to report it on my records. It won't go any further than that as far as I'm concerned."

"I appreciate that. Please send me the bill and I'll take care of it later."

He wrote down her address, left her standing in her office and went over to talk with Paul. As soon as he entered the office Paul said to him, "I hope nothing is really seriously wrong." He was totally unprepared for the answer he got.

"No, nothing that a few more months can't take care of," he replied. "I would have to do a thorough examination to be certain but, in my opinion, the young lady is pregnant."

Paul had just risen from his chair but after a bombshell like that he had to sit down again. "Then you don't think there's any margin for error?" he asked incredulously.

"I'm about as positive as one can be at this point. But, like I said, only further tests would bear me out."

"Why, she isn't...she...." he stammered, realizing that he came close to disclosing to the doctor Nora's lack of a husband. Regaining his composure, he rose to his feet and asked, "How did she accept your diagnosis?"

He changed his hat to his left hand and scratched his head. "That's what puzzles me. Most mothers to be are usually overjoyed at hearing they are going to have a baby. But not her! The first thing she did was put her face in her hands and burst into tears. Well, I've got to get back," he said, and turned to go.

Paul walked to the door with him. "Since I was responsible for calling you, I would appreciate it if you would send the bill to me. Here's a card with my home address on it." Paul stood where the doctor had left him, wondering what he was expected to do in a situation such as this. Should he pretend the doctor hadn't mentioned her pregnancy or should he let her know that he knew and offer her advice. He bowed his head and prayed silently, asking God for wisdom and knowledge. He went over to his chair and sat down. Just then Nora came out of her office with her coat on and carrying her purse.

"Are you feeling any better?"

"Yes. Thanks. But I'm too upset to try and do anything more today. I'm going home." She turned and walked briskly down the hall.

He stood and watched her until she was out of sight, his mind in a whirl. Of course he had no idea who the father of Nora's baby was. Then came an alarming thought. Since he was not yet married, and since he and Nora had adjoining offices, it was likely that he would be accused of being the father. He knew, of course, he wasn't, that time would prove him innocent, if it came to that, but what was he to do in the meantime? With all worry and concern he presently had, now this! He could always think better while sitting so he went to his chair sat down.

And then the phone rang. "What now?" he asked aloud.

"This is Paul. How may I help you?"

"Paul, this is Vivian." He noticed it was the first time she had addressed him by his first name. "I hate to bother you with this but would you go over to the house and check on Mother? She doesn't answer the phone and I can't go by there until I get off work. She never goes out —well hardly ever—so I don't know if she is there or has fallen and can't get to the phone."

"I would be more than glad to do that for you. But, say, while I have you on the phone, how about you and me getting together this evening after you get off work and have a sandwich and something to drink."

"I'd love to. Do you know where the Coffee Shop is on Smithville Road? I'll meet you there."

When he hung up the phone, he heard the phone in Nora's office ringing. He went over to get his jacket and answered it while he was there. "Hello," he said. He got nothing but silence. Evidently, whomever was calling wasn't expecting a male voice to answer, so he said, "Hello," again.

"Uh…is this brother Paul?" came the voice on the other end.

It was the preacher whom he recognized at once. "Yes, this is he," Suddenly, for some unknown reason, the thought came to him that George was the father of Nora's baby. With that thought he couldn't bring himself to address him as brother.

"Where's Nora…er, I mean sister Letty?" he quickly corrected himself. "Why isn't she at her desk, or do you know?"

"She was taken ill and had to go home," he answered as calmly as he could, careful to keep his voice under control and being sure not to mention that she had fainted.

"I see," he said, and Paul thought he probably did. "I'm sorry I had to run out on you. Did you get the message I left for Nor…er, sister Letty to give to you?"

"It was a little late getting to me, but, yes, I got it."

"Well, the reason for my call was to tell her that I'm not going to make it back tonight after all. That leaves you to have to fill in for me." He took a deep breath and continued. "Would you please call the Mrs. for me and tell her that I'll be in sometime tomorrow. I would appreciate it very much."

Paul hung up and looked at his watch. He rang Adra and would give her both messages at the same time. He let the phone ring for a long time but, like Vivian, got no answer either. He hung the phone up and walked over to the parsonage to personally check on Adra. Something was not right. Getting no answer at the front door he went round to the back and knocked again. Still no answer. He tried the door, found it was unlocked and stepped inside and was met with deadly silence. He called out her name but got no response. He went in search of her.

He expected she had had an accident or had passed out somewhere. He went through the whole house but she was nowhere to be found. He couldn't imagine where she could have gone, for Vivian had said that she seldom ever left the house on her own. Well, for some reason she has left it now, he thought. Later, he would be shocked to find out what that reason was.

He didn't return to the church, but left the parsonage and went to his house, there to freshen up before going to meet Vivian. He would give her George's message and also tell her that her mother wasn't home, how he had went over and searched for her.

The Coffee Shop was crowded and bursting with activity when he arrived. It was obviously a popular place for the younger crowd. He made his way through the crowd to the rear of the shop where he found Vivian waiting for him. He was slightly disappointed in the place for it wasn't very conducive to what he had in mind; he wanted a quiet place with a more romantic atmosphere for what he had in mind. They had a wonderful time talking and found they had a lot in common. She was a Big Band fan, so was he; she loved to curl up with a book on a rainy night before a blazing fire, so did he; she loved swimming and walking for exercise, so did he. They spent the better part of an hour in the shop together then he walked her to her car. Because of the noise in the place he waited until now to give her both messages.

"I called her but never got an answer. So I went over there to see if anything had happened to her and to give her your dad's message. But she wasn't anywhere to be found. Your dad wanted to let her know he wouldn't be home till tomorrow."

He could see she was embarrassed and he knew the reason why. She knew the house wasn't always in the best of shape and not always as clean as it should be. "I'll have to go by there and see if she has gotten home yet and find out where she has been. I suppose I ought to be getting over there. It's getting close to church time, and since you will be speaking, I'll see you there."

She drove away and he headed for home to get ready for the service. He showered and dressed in his black suit he mostly reserved for funerals. Why he had chosen to wear black tonight he didn't know. As it turned out, it was an omen to what would happen shortly after the close of the service.

He stepped behind the sacred desk and faced the congregation. "Your pastor has been detained once again. So the mantle has been passed to me to deliver the sermon tonight." He had prepared the message that God had laid on his heart, to which he gave the name of "Trust and Unity". He was nearing the end of his sermon when he saw Vivian slip in quietly and sit in the back near the door. As soon as he had dismissed the service he hurried to her to find out about her mother. He saw the worried look on her face as he whispered to her, "Wait until the people are gone so we can talk."

When the last person had congratulated him on his sermon and left he hurried over to where Vivian stood waiting for him. "I can see by the look on your face that something's wrong. Isn't she home yet?"

"I don't know if anything is wrong or not but she still hadn't come home when I left for church. I'm hoping she will be there by this time. This is so unlike her to do something like this and to be gone so long."

"Somehow I can't feel it's anything to be alarmed about just yet. She has probably gone to get some "nerve medicine". Vivian knew what he was referring to. "I'll go home and change clothes and if she isn't back by then, give me a call and we'll go drive around and look for her."

"Thank you, I will," she said, gratefully, and hurried to her mother's house.

Paul hung up his robe and was just exiting the sanctuary when Carl came running up all excited and out of breath. "Brother Paul," he said loudly, "there's been a murder! Dad sent me to tell you in case you hadn't already heard…"

"Shhhh, not so loud," he interrupted him, "and calm down! Are you sure someone has been murdered?"

Carl took a deep breath then calmly began again. "Dad hear it on the radio. Mr. Latimer got shot and they think Perry's dad did it. He didn't…, I know he didn't do it! He wouldn't do a thing like that." He was then overcome with tears.

Paul pulled him close to him to comfort him with the words that it would be all right, that the police would find the guilty one. "You could be right about Colby being innocent. Just because he has been accused doesn't make him guilty. Now, let's get rid of those tears and be brave for him—and Perry. Go tell your dad I said thanks for sending me word—and don't worry. I'm with you. I don't believe Colby did it either."

Carl smiled bravely up at Paul, confident that Colby would be proven innocent. He knew Colby could not afford a lawyer, that the court would appoint him one, but he wanted him to have a private one and thought of the young lawyer that had bumped into his car. After inspecting his car and seeing there was no discernable damage done, he never filed any charges nor accepted any compensation. The young lawyer was impressed with Paul and having just started his practice, gave him his card and had told him that if he ever needed anyone to represent him in a defense case to give him a call. His name was Charles Haverman.

Paul didn't think there would be any use in trying to talk to Colby before morning so he went home instead. Besides, he had yet to hear from Vivian concerning her mother. As soon as he reached the house he called her to see if Adra had returned home yet.

He detected the sound of relief in her voice when she said, "Yes, she's home now. She wouldn't tell me where she had been, or what she had gone out for, only that she was on an errand. I helped her to bed, she was so exhausted. She's already asleep."

Knowing she was still upset over her mother, he declined to mention anything about the Latimer incident. It would only upset her the more. He was sure she would hear about it first thing in the morning. "Is there any chance for me to see you this Saturday—say at eight o'clock?"

"That can be arranged. Eight will be fine."

"Eight it is then. Goodnight,"

He was pleased that his relationship with her was going as well as it was. If he ever got married he was sure she would be an excellent wife. He was already deeply in love with her.

He knelt beside his bed and thanked God for His guidance and blessings. He had been so busy he didn't realize how tired he was until he stretched out in bed. He didn't have to lie there very long, in spite of other's misfortune's, until he was sound asleep.

Chapter 6

A persistent pounding at the door awakened Paul. He put on a robe and slippers then went to see whom his early caller could be. There stood Jake, the sheriff, a look of fatigue on his face. "I'm sorry to disturb you so early in the morning but there's been a possible homicide I have to check out. I say "possible" because the victim is still alive but remains in very critical condition. I have a few questions I need to ask you."

"By all means. Come on in. I'll be glad to help in any way that I can."

Jake took a small pad from his shirt pocket and sat down. "We have a suspect in custody from the shooting. He's the black guy that works at the pawn shop. I understand you went to visit him a few days ago."

"That's correct, I did. I went to see him about going with me to his house to search for a boy that had run away from home. That's where I suspected the boy was hiding. Why is Colby a suspect, if I may ask?"

Jake debated whether to disclose this bit of information or not. "I see no harm in telling you. Jesse was unable to identify the person who shot him, but he did see that it was a black person before losing consciousness."

"That doesn't sound too good. But then, there's other blacks around here besides Colby.

"Which brings me to my next question. Does he and his wife get along very well—and what about his little boy?"

"As far as I know they're getting along fine, as is their son. They are some of the nicest people I've ever had the privilege of knowing."

"That's all I need to know. I'll be going. Thanks for your cooperation."

"Do you think I could have a talk with him right after I've spoken to a lawyer on his behalf?"

"Sure. I see no reason why you can't. But take my advice, make it brief and get out of there as soon as you can. There's trouble brewing over this and you could get caught in the middle of it." He put his pad in his pocket and stood up to go. "Remember my advice," were his parting words, "this could turn real ugly."

Paul dressed and sat down to eat a bowl of cereal and drink a cup of coffee. As soon as he finished eating he left for Haverman's office. He was admitted by a lovely statuesque, blue-eyed blond. He was definitely attracted to blonds. Haverman's office was moderately furnished and it was obvious he was still struggling with his career, looking for the "big break" to come his way. This place is definitely below the status of his impressive looking receptionist, he thought to himself.

"Welcome to the rising and thriving firm of me, myself, and Haverman," he laughed, extending his hand, "—Charles to you. I'm delighted to meet you again."

"You may not be after I tell you why I'm here. But, before I do, may I say your receptionist is a knockout. How do you manage to hold on to her?"

"Yes, isn't she. I'm fortunate to have her. She could easily get a more lucrative position than this one, but insists she likes it here—and her boss. And, well…here she stays."

"Do you suppose being a promising defense attorney who has hair the color of ripened wheat, eyes that reflect the blue of the sky, and Robert Redford looks could have anything to do with it?" Paul asked, teasingly.

"Saying all those nice things about me," Charles said, laughing heartily, "must mean you have a "nobody else wants case" you want me to take."

"You're very perceptive…and it could be jut that," Paul said. "Seriously though, the reason I'm here is to take advantage of your offer, which I assume would be at a very special rate. Actually, it isn't me, but a friend of mine, that needs your service."

Charles swung his feet to the floor, sat up in his chair before giving Paul his answer. "As you can see, things aren't going as well as I hoped," He motioned for Paul to have a seat, "but I'll still do it for you at a reduced rate. Who is it then that is certain to be my downfall, if I may ask?"

"A man named Colby Warfield. I'm sure he's innocent in spite of the incriminating accusation of his employer Jesse Latimer. After all, he never saw the person well enough to actually recognize who shot him. He only saw that the person was black before passing out."

"Then your friend is black. Right? It's one of those catch cases: if you win you can do no wrong; if you lose you lose everything."

"That's about the sum of it. I realize that should you take the case you would most certainly be jeopardizing your career. I believe that after you have met and talked with him you will be as convinced as I am of his innocence. You are his only salvation."

"I like the way you put that—salvation, rather than the more commonly used term chance or hope." He drummed his pencil on the desk as he wrestled with his decision of what to do. He got up, still not saying anything, and went over to the window and stood looking out.

Paul kept quiet, saying nothing either, as he waited for him to make his decision.

Finally, he turned from the window and faced Paul. "It's a big gamble. There is no doubt about that. But if I should win I would have it made. No more struggling to climb the corporate ladder. I'm getting nowhere as it is, so I've got more to gain than I have to lose." He came back over to Paul and reached out to shake his hand. "Your friend has got himself a lawyer."

"You won't regret your decision and neither will you be sorry," Paul predicted. "Justice will triumph!" He took his hand, giving him a firm handshake.

"I'll begin scouting around to come up with as many clues, witnesses and the like—you know, the usual procedure. I'll depend on you to help in doing the same. We've got to have as fool proof case as we can possibly construct. We can't afford to expect anything less that the best we can do."

As Paul prepared to leave he said, "Thank you for your help and your courage to try this case. We shall win! Of that I have no doubt. Incidentally, I'm on my way to see your client. Will it be all right to tell him I have procured a lawyer to represent him?"

"You go right ahead and do just that. Also, tell him that I'll be by sometime this afternoon to see him myself."

While driving to the jail Paul recalled what Jake had said about trouble brewing and he hoped the people didn't try and take the law into their own hands. What kind of trouble was Jake referring to he wondered. Could it be a lynching? If so, he would try to get out of the jail as soon as he possibly could. When he arrived he noticed a few men loitering around outside the jail. As he was entering the jail he saw one of the men pull his hat down to hide his face and turn aside to keep Paul from recognizing him.

"You missed a little excitement," Jake said, "and I'm not sure it's over with yet. There were about six men that was threatening to take my prisoner a little while ago. I managed to calm them down and they left. I see a few of them are back with renewed determination and looking for some action. Bottled courage is at work out there."

"If that's what they have in mind, what can you do to protect your prisoner; how safe is he in here; can they get to him if they storm the jail?"

84

"Well, you know how it is with a mob crazed with liquor and incited by some power hungry leader. No jail is completely safe from a gang of men determined to take the law into their own hands. If forced to, I would have no alternative but to use my shot gun."

He got the key and took Paul back of the jail where Colby was incarcerated. It was much darker here and the cell much smaller. He unlocked the cell and let Paul inside with Colby. Colby was sitting on his cot, his back against the wall, his legs drawn up to his chest and his head between his knees. He never looked up until Jake spoke and told him Paul was there.

"You have a visitor, Warfield. Take as long as you like, Preacher," he said, and left.

Being in the cell with Colby gave Paul the same feeling of being locked up as he had before. He pitied anyone who had to stay locked up in a place like this and he knew Colby didn't deserve to be there. Paul sat down beside Colby, yet he didn't move. He was totally depressed and without hope.

"I know this is hard on you, but you must not give up hope. Now move over here beside me. I've some good news for you."

He scooted over next to Paul. "I could use some good news. I've heard nothing but bad news for the past few days. What am I going to do, Preacher? I swear it wasn't me that shot Mr. Latimer! Why would I shoot a man who has gone out of his way to help me? It makes no sense— no sense at all!"

"That's how I see it too. You're right, it doesn't make any sense whatsoever. I don't believe you shot Mr. Latimer either. I want you to know that. However, you've got to believe in yourself and keep your spirit up. Are you doing any studying while you're in here?" He looked over the cell but there were no books to be seen. "Why aren't there any books here?"

"Because they wouldn't allow me to bring any of my books with me when they transferred me to this cell. They barged into the other cell, grabbed me and practically threw me into this one."

"I'll check into this and see why they have taken your books. If they say it's okay for you to have your other books I'll get them back to you. Besides that, I'll bring you some on my next visit."

"Thank you brother Paul. You have been so good and kind to me; you have been a true friend. I hope you know how much I appreciate it. I won't forget it!"

"You're more than welcome. Your books will help pass the time in here and keep your mind off things. Now, how about shaking off that cloak of despair and defeat and tell me what happened to cause you to end up in here. "There really isn't much I can tell you. I don't know what actually happened either. Anyway, we closed the shop just like always and went our separate ways. I was at home alone when all this took place. Unfortunately, I can't prove it for there was no one there who could vouch for my being there. Armeda had taken Perry and gone to a friend's birthday party. Oh, it wasn't much of a party but it sure knocked me out of the only alibi I would have had." He paused for about thirty seconds. "I don't see any way that I can possibly prove my innocence."

"Just keep the faith. You don't have to, your lawyer will do it. If you truly are innocent, and I believe with all my heart you are, we (when I say "we", I mean Charles, your lawyer, and me) will find a way to prove it. By the way, I've engaged a lawyer to represent you. That's the good news I was going to tell you when I first came in. "

"Honest! But…but…who would do that for me?" he asked unbelievingly. "There ain't no way I can pay…"

"I think you can. He's doing it at a reduced rate, which I so graciously asked for," Paul said, interrupting him. "Your lawyer's name is

Charles Haverman and he said to tell you that he would be by to see you sometime this afternoon. Is there anything you can think of that you might want to mention before I go?"

"No…wait a minute. There is something I want to mention, something I'm curious about. What did Mr. Latimer return to the shop for?"

"I don't have any idea. It seems likely that he probably forgot something, walked in on the intruder, surprising him, and was shot…" Paul broke off speaking and stood listening. Although he barely could hear it he thought he heard the clamor of voices. Then Jake came rushing back to where they were.

"Quick, Preacher, you've tot to help me talk some sense into those men outside before they get completely out of control."

Paul wasn't sure he could say or do anything that would deter them from their unlawful mission but he could try. Jake and Paul stepped outside together and stood on the top step before this angry group of men. They raised their hands to get them to quiet down so they could reason with them. But with a gang of men hellbent on an act of unlawfulness and bolstered with courage from a bottle, it appeared they were losing more ground than they were gaining. Then Paul suddenly caught a glimpse of a face in the crowd that filled him with shock and disbelief. The ring leader of this vociferous, ill-begotten crowd was none other than John Billings, the church's music director, an upstanding family man and a respected member of the church.

"You, brother Billings, both perturb and surprise me. How is it you, a prominent member of the church, can stoop to the level you have here today. You are supposed to be an example to these men by showing love and compassion as well as equality and justice."

"I still have all those attributes, but it's time someone had the guts to step forward and put a stop to an injustice such as this one. We have a man in the hospital right now hovering between life and death, all because of an ingrate who repays the man's kindness by trying to murder him!" He turned and faced the men around him. "Isn't that right men?"

A loud roar of approval went up from the crowd.

It appeared they were not going to listen to reason and began to surge forward toward the steps leading into the jail intending to take Colby by force. It was precisely at that moment that the Great Orator, George Blakely, suddenly and miraculously appeared. He stood where all the men could see him and raised both hands for them to quiet down. He then began to speak.

"Brothers and friends, I know how you must feel. And, to a certain extent I don't blame you." He sympathized with them putting himself on their side. "Even if your motives are justified, your intentions are wrong—very wrong! Think about this for a minute: suppose you carried this out and avenged our good friend Jesse and your deed was deemed justifiable. You would have no reason whatsoever to feel guilty. Now, let's look at another view point. Suppose after the deed has been done and new evidence has been uncovered and the man is exonerated; he wasn't the guilty one after all. You would certainly feel guilty then for you snuffed out the life of an innocent man. Think about it! How would you feel then? How could you face your families? I beg you, please consider what I have told you and what the result would mean to you later."

Paul knew that George was adept at painting a vivid word picture and could be very persuasive. Never had he been more eloquent than at this most crucial time. He saw the men, though fortified with Satan's brew, drop their heads in shame as the impact of his words penetrated their sodden minds and they departed in mass. His parting words spoken to their backs were: "I suggest we all go home and let the judicial system take care of this. If the man is guilty he will be justly dealt with and will suffer the consequences."

With the mob dispersed and peace restored George turned to Paul, wiped his brow, and said, "Whew! That was close! I heard the news on the radio as I was driving on my way back and rushed to get here as soon as I could. Do you have any idea who was behind all of this?"

"I couldn't say." Paul answered evasively. He wasn't about to finger John Billings and make an enemy for life. He mentioned something about some men's weaknesses and let it go at that.

"I've got to get home and report in," George said, smiling. "Do you want to ride back with me?"

"Thanks, I have my car here. I'll see you back at church."

Paul went back in to talk with Colby then stopped to talk with Jake on his way out. "Is there a rule restricting Colby from having books in his cell? If not, I'd like to bring him a few."

"No. Not that I know of. When he was moved to the other cell they wouldn't let him take his books out of spite because he is black. I'll see that he gets them back. I want to compliment you and the preacher on the way that mob was handled. You both did a terrific job!"

"All the credit goes to George. If he had not got here when he did, I shudder to think what could have happened. Thank God, nothing did!"

While driving back to the church Paul reflected on what must have taken place at Latimer's Pawn Shop the evening he was shot and who could have shot him. He hadn't the slightest clue as to whom it could be. He was gratified to know Jesse would survive.

He had not, as yet, let the preacher know that he knew about Nora being pregnant; or that he suspected him of being the baby's father; or that things at home weren't going as smoothly as he would have everyone believe. It occurred to him that the reason for part of the preacher's absences were possibly connected to Nora. No doubt, he was busy arranging a place where he could hide her away until the baby was born, in order to keep it hidden from the public and the church.

Still yet, another scenario popped into his head: that it was possible that Adra could have been the one who took his jade figurine to pawn it. It was a far-fetched idea, but she could have shot Jesse. She was absent from home for a long period of time, especially when she seldom ever went out before, and wouldn't tell Vivian where she had been. The idea didn't seem as far-fetched as he first thought. It could provide him with a lead and a clue toward solving the case. He would discuss this with Charles and see what he thought. It certainly would bear looking into.

However, there was a catch to this theory. By suggesting Adra as a suspect could put his relationship with Vivian in jeopardy. Yet, the more he thought of it the more plausible it became. He knew there were times when alcoholics became desperate for a drink and needed money for alcohol to satisfy their craving.

He pulled into the garage then went to his house. He had to talk with Adra without Vivian or George finding out about it. At least, not until he was certain of her guilt or innocence. But what could he use for an excuse. Then he had an idea. He would take her a small cake with one candle on it for her birthday.

Also, he wanted to find out Vivian's sentiments concerning Colby's misfortune. He hoped she felt the same as he did. He would find this out later and, since she now had her own apartment, it would enable him to talk privately with Adra.

He picked up the cake and, not to appear too conspicuous, went to Adra's back door and knocked. He waited, giving her time to get to the door. When the door opened he was astonished to see Vivian standing there. He decided to be honest with her and tell her the truth.

"What are you doing here?" he blurted out. "Er…what I mean is, I didn't expect to find you here. I thought you would be at your home."

"So I see by the look on your face," she said, stepping back to let him in. "Mother called to ask me to come and help her with the payment of some bills. Otherwise, I would have been. Come in."

"I happened to remember your mother had a birthday coming up and I wanted to give her this little cake I thought she would like for her birthday."

"Of course she would. Who wouldn't want a small cake for their birthday? Now, tell me the real reason for your covert action."

"You're getting to know me pretty well. But, I'll be honest with you, I wanted to talk to her about that period of time when she was gone so long. Could I, do you think?"

"I thought you had a devious intent on your mind. You figured she would be alone and you could talk with her privately—am I right?" she laughed softly at her cleverness. "That's why you were so surprised to see me here."

"Could be," he grinned at her. "Before you get your mother, may I ask you what were your thoughts when you heard that Jesse had been shot and Colby was accused of it?"

"It's a shame he was shot, but somehow I just don't believe Colby is the one that did it. That's like biting the hand that feeds you. Besides that, I feel sorry for him. I just wish there was something I could do for him."

"I'm glad to hear that. Those are my sentiments exactly. That's really why I'm here—to get a lead on this thing. I got to thinking about your mother being gone for so long and wondered if she may possibly have gone to the pawn shop to pawn something (he had not, as yet, told her about the missing jade piece) and, by chance, saw the person that shot

Jesse. Oh, I know it's grabbing at straws, but if we can get a lead on this, however insignificant it may be, it could save an innocent man's life."

"I'll get her, but she may not want to talk about that."

Adra, dressed in a robe and wearing house slippers, came in and sat in the chair across from Paul. He thought she looked pale and thin. Vivian sat down on the sofa next to Paul.

"What is it you wanted to talk to me about?" she asked Paul. "I thought it might be important."

"You were right about it being important—it is!" Paul began. "Sister Blakely, I know it's none of my business where you went alone a few days ago, but if you don't mind telling me it could help in saving a man's life."

"I understand. Go on."

"Did you, by any stretch of the imagination, happen to go by Latimer's Pawn Shop? And, if you did, did you happen to see who it was that shot Jesse Latimer? Anything you may have seen that could lead us to a possible suspect."

She sat looking at Paul for a moment through bloodshot eyes, blinking back tears that were welling up in them. His heart went out to her, he was a very compassionate man. "Do you think anything this old lady may have seen would be taken seriously by anyone?" Those tears had welled to overflowing and ran down her cheeks. She wiped them away with her hankie. "Look at me and tell me! Do you?"

"I would," he said, humbly. "And, if what you say leads to any conclusive evidence, a whole lot of people will have to believe it too."

"Wait a minute," Adra said, getting up from her chair, "I want to show you something." She left the room, then came back with a small object wrapped in flannel. "I believe this belongs to you." She handed it to him.

It was his St. Francis of Asisi figurine.

"So it was you who took it," he said, though not unkindly, glad to get it back. "I would never have suspected you as the one who took it. But why?"

"I'm ashamed to tell you why but I might as well. Most everyone knows about me anyway. I'm an alcoholic—as if you didn't know. That's one reason George stays gone so much. He's ashamed of me and well he should be. I'm pretty well disgusted with myself as well. But getting back to the figurine. Well…I needed some money and when I couldn't find any here at the house, I sneaked over your house to see if I could find a dollar or two laying around over there, for, you see. I was beginning to get the shakes pretty bad. Had I found any money I fully intended to pay it back. However, I didn't find anything except the jade figurine. Because it was jade I took it, thinking I could pawn it at Jesse's shop. When I got there the front door was locked so I went round to the back door, thinking he may be in the back of the shop and let me in. You must understand, I was desperate for a drink! It was then I realized the shop was closed for the day." Although Adra didn't know it, Jesse was in the shop. He had returned to get something he forgot that he had wanted to take home with him. "Then I heard someone coming and I ran and hid behind the garbage bin. I was so scared I was almost too afraid to look—but I did. Someone stood up close to the building smearing something black all over their face, neck, and ears. Afraid of being seen I crouched a little lower too scared to chance taking another look. It really didn't matter because I couldn't see well enough by then to make out who it was anyway. After a few minutes I dared to take another peek and saw whoever it was enter the shop. It was then I got out of there as quickly as I could, not looking back once. That's all I can tell you. Please forgive me for doing what I did. I'm truly sorry!"

"Of course we forgive you, don't we Vivian?"

"We certainly do. But, Mother, how did you get to the pawn shop with no money?"

"How else, my dear. I hitched a ride all the way there and back."

"Oh, Mother, how terrible! You must promise me never to do anything like that again. That could be very dangerous and you could have gotten hurt!"

"Now if you both will excuse me, I'd like to lie down again. I'm very tired." She got up and went to her room.

Paul got to his feet, overjoyed at what he had just been told. Without thinking, he grabbed Vivian and kissed her on the lips. When he realized what he had done it rather embarrassed him. Vivian, on the other hand, gave no indication that she thought his impulsiveness was anything out of the ordinary. It was their first kiss.

"I don't believe your mother realizes how important what she told us is. Nevertheless, since it is so late, I'll have to get to that pawn shop first thing in the morning to look for that tin the make-up was in, in case it was thrown in the garbage bin or on the ground at the back of the shop. Our only hope is that they haven't picked up the garbage yet.

Since he had already kissed her, he kissed her again, bade her goodnight and went home to get a few things done before going to bed.

CHAPTER 7

Paul was up at the break of dawn, ready to go within the hour to search the garbage bin and the grounds around the back of the pawn shop for any incriminating evidence he could find. His main concern was finding the make-up tin in hopes of getting a clear fingerprint. He hoped to get there and get his searching done before Mrs. Latimer (her first name was Sophia, but everybody called her Sophie) came in to open the shop. Jesse was home now and doing well, but had to have a nurse with him around the clock, while Sophie ran the shop.

The first thing Paul searched was the garbage bin, hoping they hadn't picked up the garbage yet. He raised the lid and drew a sigh of relief. They hadn't done so. He rummaged through the things laying on top as best he could but didn't find the tin. However, he did find a blue chambray shirt over in the far corner and noticed the black smudges around the collar and the cuffs. He could hardly believe his luck! This had to ge the shirt worn by the intruder. He began looking for the makeup tin at the rear of building, as that was where Adra saw him applying the makeup. Just as he suspected, he found it by the steps next to the entrance. He picked it up with his handkerchef, being extra careful not to smudge any fingerprints that may be on it. The name brand was on the lid and all they had to do now was check the stores in the area that sold this particular brand and hopefully get a description of the person who purchased it.

He hurriedly left the place and headed for Charles' office to give him the "treasures" he had found. Charles would have them bagged and numbered for evidence. He was sure they were closing in on the person that had shot Jesse. Colby's incarceration would soon be over.

Amidst all this, Paul's mind turned to the upcoming church picnic due in one week and the youth service taking place this evening. He then went to his office to work on a program that he hoped would hold their interest. He would write a short biographical sketch on four of the apostles and see if they could guess who they were. After the service several of the young people came by to tell him how much they enjoyed the service. He could see they weren't hard to please. He went home, sat down and wrote his mother a long letter telling her all the details of his sojourn to date. He would post it first thing in the morning. He made sure to tell her about Vivian. One day soon he hoped to make her his wife and he was anxious for them to meet. He knew she would love her almost as much as he did.

He wakened early, as he usually did, and after having breakfast, began preparing for the picnic. He had already reminded the ladies to make sure there would be plenty of food. He had to devise the games for the old and young alike so no one would feel left out. He was look-ing forward to his date with Vivian, but he had yet to decide where he wanted to take her. With that all taken care of, he backed his car out of the garage to wash it. While he was doing so, Carl rode up on his bike and got off to help him. Paul could see a great improvement in him lately and felt he was going to be all right now, especially since Miss Minna and Arno were now dating. She devoted a lot of love and care to him, but made no attempt to take his mother's place in his heart.

"Things are a lot different at your house now that Miss Minna is dating your dad, isn't it?"

"Not too much different."

"What do you think about them getting married? I believe she will make you a good mom."

"She will never be as good as my mother was, but she's okay," he said. "She's been real good to me. I like her a lot."

"Are you coming to the picnic that's coming up next week?"

"I'd like to come, but I don't know if we're coming or not. I heard them talking about going somewhere else."

"It's going to be a lot of fun...."

"I like you almost as much as I did brother Allen. You don't act like a preacher."

"Thanks. I'm very glad to hear that," Paul laughed pleased. "I hope you won't dislike me less if I do get to acting like one." He stepped back and looked at the car, "That looks like a good job to me. Thanks for your help."

Miss Minna came out on the porch and called down to Carl to come and eat. Carl wiped his hands on his pants. "Gotta go. I'll see you later."

He watched Carl as he rode his bike to the house and thought, There's definitely a change in him.

The day was finally over and the time for his date with Vivian had come. He had decided where he wanted to take her and had it all planned. He wanted it to be a date as romantic as any date could be. He had tickets to a classical concert for them, and a reservation at a nice, quiet restaurant where one could dine to the music of a live pianist.

"Are you enjoying yourself? I know you have a lot of other things on your mind." Paul asked her.

"Oh, yes, this is so romantic! I love it," she assured him. "But, Paul, isn't this rather expensive?"

"A little, but I wanted it to be special—just for you."

While they were talking the pianist was playing and singing "Stardust".

"Isn't that a lovely song the pianist is singing? It's so beautiful."

"It is, and I christen it "Our Song"."

They were so at ease and comfortable with each other. Before they knew it, time had slipped away and it was getting very late. Neither one of them wanted it to end but it did. She had to work in the morning and he had a busy day ahead of him. Paul took her to her apartment an walked her to the door.

"It was a lovely evening and I enjoyed it. I had a wonderful time. Goodnight."

"I'm glad you did," he said and kissed her. "Goodnight, my love."

She let herself in and Paul returned to his car and drove home. He lay in bed thinking what a swell time they had. He had to have more money so they could do that more often. He made a decision to ask the preacher for a raise in pay the first thing in the morning. With that decision made, he turned onto his side and went peacefully asleep.

He rose early as he usually did, had a light breakfast and left to go by and see Charles. He was anxious to know if he had found out whom the person was that had purchased the black makeup and at what particular store. He went to his office, rather than call, as he wanted to make sure no one got wind of what evidence they had come up with. He entered the office and his receptionest told him to go right in. He didn't yet know her name.

"Say, you're almost as good as I am at collecting evidence," Charles remarked. "We have gathered an impressive amount of evidence between us. Did I tell you that I uncovered some new fingerprints that look very promising. It seems our "criminal" was a little careless about where he or she left them. I discovered them on the mirror in the rest room at the pawn shop. They are running a check on them now."

"That's great! Did you find out where the makeup was bought and who bought it?"

"I've found out where it was bought but not to whom. We're getting close though."

"Incidentally, what is the name of your receptionist?"

"Her name is Davina. Her friends call her "Vina".

"Davina, huh? Very fitting."

"Not to change the subject, but it won't be long before we will be going to court. Keep your fingers crossed.

"I will. Well, I've got to be going. I've got a lot more work to do. Give me a call if anything new comes up, okay?"

The day for the picnic finally arrived. The weather was just short of being perfect. Although there was a slight chill in the air due to fall arriving a little early, changing the leaves in to their Autumn splendor, particularly the Maples which were arrayed in yellow and gold. The large Oak tree in the back yard would be the last to give up the green of its leaves and the last to shed them. By ten o'clock the church grounds were swarming with people. It's strange, Paul thought, some people could always find time for food and entertainment, but very little time to come to church. He supposed, as in any church, there were always a few people who came to church solely for the fellowship and social aspects of it. There were even a few that came out for picnics, for the Easter and Christmas play, then never seen again until the same time next year.

The picnic committee saw that tables were in place, that the food would be ready to be served by twelve thirty. Paul had never seen so much food. Suffice it to say, everything anyone could want to eat could be found on one of the tables. The people of Blakeville appeared to be a generous group. Games for the children and the adults were carefully orchestrated to keep the youth from getting bored or feeling left out. Paul was having as much fun as the children were. He pitched horse shoes, something he hadn't done for a long while, then joined the sack race, in which he became entangled in a pile-up of sacks with others. In the middle of this tangle came the ringing of the bell calling everyone to eat.

He filled his plate with so much food he was almost ashamed for anyone to see it—and well he should. On his plate he had a piece of succulent, baked ham, baked beans, potato salad, some olives and pickles, two rolls, a piece of apple pie and a cup of steaming, black coffee. As he sat eating, he kept looking around searching the grounds for Arno, Minna, and Carl. He was at a loss for a reason why they weren't there. George wasn't even there. But, then, he wasn't too concerned about the preacher. He knew he would show up in time to make his grand entrance. Still, he was really disappointed that Carl wasn't there. He finished eating his food and was about to take a bite of pie, when he saw the preacher coming toward him with some friend in tow.

The friend was of medium height and rather rotund. His hair was gray at the temples and his mustache was black, with a little gray mixed in. He was nattily dressed in a gray, pin striped suit, and a charcoal-gray fedora hat, which he graciously tipped to all the ladies, made up the rest of his appearance. Paul knew he must be someone of importance or the preacher wouldn't be associating with him. He got up from the table and stood, waiting to be introduced.

"Brother Paul, may I introduce you to our esteemed mayor, Josh Adams. Josh, this is my associate, Paul Langley."

Paul's mouth dropped open in spite of himself. He was taken aback that they knew each other so well they were on first name basis. That, in itself, didn't impress him as much as it intrigued him. His first thought was: what could they possibly have in common? He quickly recovered his composure.

"I'm pleased to meet you, Mayor Adams," he said, and shook his hand.

"My pleasure, I'm sure. George is a close friend of mine, I had to meet the man he chose to work with him. I knew it had to be someone special." He took out his handkerchief and wiped his brow. "As you can see, I'm used to an air conditioned office. Even though it has turned a little cooler, it's still much too warm for me."

Paul was tempted to say it wasn't the weather but the girth, he didn't of course. Then he heard the preacher putting words to his thought.

"It's not the weather Josh," he said, patting him on the stomach, "it's the pounds and the girth."

They must be really close, Paul thought, for George to say something that intimate to him. The mayor placed his hands on his stomach and commented, "That's the price one has to pay for being the mayor. Every achievement has to be toasted, you know, and every lady kissed." They both laughed at his repartee. "By the way, Reverend Lnagley," the mayor continued, "why haven't you ever been by the club?"

"The club," Paul echoed, "what club?"

"Uh…he…that is…" George stammered, "I don't believe I've ever mentioned it. Have I?"

"If you did, I don't recall it," was Paul's reply. "But, it doesn't matter. I've not had the time for it anyway. I haven't even played a game of golf since arriving here."

The mayor saw at once that he had goofed; he had unwittingly let the cat out of the bag by disclosing one of George's guarded secrets. "Sorry if I stumbled into uncharted territory. My mistake. Now, if you'll excuse me, I hate to run, leaving all this delicious food that I don't need, but I've got to get back to my wife and kiddies. I promised to take them out for a drive this afternoon." He shook Paul's hand. "It was nice meeting you."

"Nice meeting you too."

Paul was surprised that George left with the mayor and didn't stay for the rest of the picnic. He expected that George would berate the mayor for having spoken out of turn. He got another cup of coffee and finished eating his pie. He got up to mix and mingle with the people and to fellowship with them. It was then he caught sight of Vivian and her mother. He was so proud of her for not being ashamed to be seen out in public with her mother. Also, for persuading her to go to the picnic with her. Paul and Vivian both had been trying to coax Adra to enter a sanitarium for treatment, but so far without success.

Vivian had shampooed Adra's hair, giving it luster and body, then styled it in a way that was very becoming to her. She had put on makeup to hide her paleness, giving her face a little color. She dressed her in a pretty cotton dress of pink and yellow, added a pair of sunglasses for concealment and she looked like a different person. Adra sat sipping a cup of black coffee, striving to keep the tremor of her hand from showing. Paul knew she would be leaving before too long and go to the house for a temporary "cure" for those tremors. Vivian was wearing an apple green dress, her hair tied back with a matching scarf.

"This has to be two of the loveliest ladies at the picnic today," Paul complimented them. "And I'm so pleased, sister Adra, that you could come." He didn't know why, it just seemed the right time to call her by her first name.

Adra set her cup down on the napkin she had laying on her knee. "You might say that's due to the persuasiveness of my beautiful daughter and a certain young minister the church board were wise enough to engage for his services."

"I think I have a bit of credit coming for having a hand in it too," Vivian said in mock jealousy. "I do think she looks real pretty, don't you Paul?"

"I most certainly do." he replied. "I'm so proud of her for having the courage to come regardless of what others may think. Not to change the subject, but have you ever seen a more beautiful day for a picnic than this?"

"It is near perfect isn't it," Vivian said. "How I wish that Colby were here to enjoy it with us instead of having to sit all alone in that cell."

"Look at it this way: after next week he will be free to enjoy whatever he wants. He isn't as despondent as he once was. He has his books now that he enjoys."

"Then his trial is coming up next week, isn't that right?" asked Vivian.

"Yes it is. It's scheduled to begin in September, right after Labor Day."

Adra set her cup down on the table and rose to go. "If you don't mind, I believe I'll go and lie down for awhile. I'm getting tired."

"Here, take my arm," Paul said, "and I'll walk you home—that is if you don't mind."

"I don't mind at all. In fact, I would be both flattered and honored," she said. taking hold of his arm.

"Mind if I tag along," queried Vivian.

"Not at all. We would be glad to have you."

When they were far enough away from the crowd where they couldn't hear what was being said, Paul said to Adra, "Sister Adra, wouldn't it be wonderful to be well again? I know you want to regain your husband's respect and your strength. Won't you let Vivian and me find a nice quiet and peaceful place where you can be treated privately?"

"Dad can well afford it, Mother. You could be so happy once again!" Vivian said encouragingly, holding back the tears. "You do want to get well again don't you?"

"Oh yes, more than anything in the world! But I don't believe it would do any good."

"We won't know unless we try. I'm sure it would help immensely," Paul added. "It's a sickness, just like any other illness. The thing is, you have to make up your mind you want to get better, you want to want to get cured. There are any number of places one can go to be cared for. What do you say…help us by letting us help you."

They reached the parsonage and stopped in front of it. "I'll think about it," Adra said. "I promise to give it some serious thought." Before going inside she said, "Thank you for walking me home. You're very sweet. Vivian, you go back with Paul and enjoy the rest of the picnic. I'll be fine now."

On their way back, Vivian said, "I believe in time she will consent to go if we keep after her. I think she realizes it's her only alternative."

"Then we will keep after her if that's what it takes," Paul agreed. "Will you be able to attend any of Colby's trial?"

"Only the last day of it. I'll have to trade off with one of the girls to do that."

They reached the picnic grounds and noticed the crowd had thinned out considerably. By early evening most everyone had left, with the exception of a few volunteers to help clean up. Within an hour everything was clean and things stored away. There wasn't much left for Arno to do.

There was never any service on Sunday night due to the picnic, so Paul went to visit Colby. He drove up to the gate and about to get out and open it (he still had not been given an automatic control for it) when Arno drove up. He waited for Arno to open the gate and pull in beside him with Miss Minna and Carl.

"What happened to keep you guys from coming to the picnic, if I may ask?" said Paul.

"We had a picnic of our own," Arno explained. "Minna has a bad cold and thought it best not to come." Paul noticed he had dropped the Miss from her name.

"I'm sorry you have a cold. But you missed a good one. It was one of the best we have ever had."

"We hated to miss it for Carl's sake. Still yet, we had a good time," Minna said, leaning across Arno. "Didn't we Carl."

He didn't reply but only shook his head yes. Paul knew by that he had been disappointed. Arno noticed the grounds were restored to some semblance of order.

"I see you've cleaned up most of the mess which is a lot of improvement over last year. I know I have you to thank for that."

"You're welcome. I thought a little help wouldn't hurt. I'm sorry you missed it. I'm glad you had a good time though. Now I'm off to visit Colby," he said, and slowly pulled away.

He reached Colby's cell and found him busily studying his books, which was good. He could tell he was getting tense as the days drew nearer to the trial. When Colby saw Paul come up to his cell, he laid aside his book and went over to talk with him while standing and holding to the bars. Paul placed his hand over Colby's.

"It won't be long before you're out of here, a free man and able to be with your family once more. I'm looking forward to that, as well as you are."

"You're a good man, Preacher, to help me like you have. I hope you're right. I've missed being with my family a great deal. They were by for a short visit earlier today." Paul saw the tears that filled his eyes.

"That's great! I'm glad you could see them for a few minutes." Then he asked him something that had long been on his mind. "Colby, are you a praying man?"

Colby dropped his head. "No, Preacher, I'm sorry to say, I ain't."

"It would help a great deal if you were."

"For awhile back, I had the distinct feeling that I was going to have to learn mighty quick when that mob was after me. I thought I was a goner for sure."

"Now is a good time to remedy that. Won't you surrender your heart to the Lord right now? You would feel much better by doing so and you'd be happy that you did."

"You know, Preacher, you have certainly shown Christian love toward me. I'd like nothing more than to be saved right now."

With heads bowed, Colby prayed the sinner's prayer along with Paul and knew the moment his sins were forgiven. "You were right, Preacher. I feel much better all ready. So clean and happy in spite of these bars that surround me. May I call you my brother now?"

"You certainly may, brother Colby," Paul said, giving him a hand of fellowship. "As soon as your trial is over, the first thing we will do is baptize you, along with some others who have been waiting to be baptized as well, if that's agreeable with you."

"I will be looking forward to it."

"I'm happy that you have given your heart to God. And now I must go. I want to go by and visit Jesse and speak with him for a few minutes."

"While you're there tell him that I definitely wasn't the one who shot him."

Paul meant to visit him earlier but the doctor asked that no one visit him until he had regained his strength. He had no trouble finding the house and tapped lightly on the door. The nurse came to let him in, then said to Jesse, "The Reverend Paul Langley is here to see you," then sat down to continue her crocheting. Jesse lay in bed watching television.

"Now, that's what I call a man of leisure. How about me trading places with you for a day or two?" He reached to shake Jesse's hand.

"Appearances can be deceiving," Jesse replied, switching off the television, not realizing the irony of the words he just uttered. "I would be only too happy to trade places with you. I never thought I'd ever want to get away from a bed as bad as I do this one."

"I'm glad you're on the mend. Is there anything I can do for you?"

"No, but thanks. Sophie is doing a wonderful job of taking care of things."

"I wonder if you would mind if I asked you something. It concerns Colby, who, by the way, asked me to tell you he definitely wasn't the one who shot you."

"I would rather not…"

Ignoring his objection, Paul charged ahead with the question. "He tells me you and he left the shop together, after closing it. Would you care to tell me why you had cause to return?"

"I see no harm in answering that. Yes, we did leave together. In fact, I got all the way home before discovering I had left my wallet on the counter where I had laid it. I returned to get it when I heard this noise in the back and thought Colby had come back too."

"And that's when you came upon the intruder, right?"

"Right. But I don't want to say anything more until after the trial."

"The trial starts in about a week, as I'm sure you know. Are you positive he's the one who shot you?"

"Not beyond a doubt. I'm sure he's the one who did it."

Two visitors walked into the room and Paul excused himself. "I see you've got visitors so I'll get out of the way." He went to the door, turned and said, "I'll see you there," and left him to his company.

He would get back in plenty of time for the evening service. While driving along he turned the radio on and got to thinking of the ledger he had seen in the drawer in the Skyroom. Now that the preacher had given him a set of keys to the church, including one to the Skyroom, he would check to see if it was still there. He had also finally given him an automatic opener to the gate, which was a great convenience not having to get in and out of his car. When he drove into the garage he noticed the preacher's Cadillac wasn't there. So he knew he wasn't in. He decided not to go to the Skyroom just yet, but to his office instead. The first thing that caught his eye when he stepped into his office was the sheet of paper sticking in his typewriter. He pulled it from the typewriter and read:

> Dear brother Langley,
>
> This letter will explain, in part, the reason for my absence, not being able to work very much lately anyway.
>
> I have talked with brother Blakely and he has agreed with me that it would be best, for the time being, for me to take an unspecified period of time off until I get to feeling better. I will return to work as soon as I am physically able.
>
> I am going to visit with my aunt, in hopes that a drier climate will help with my recovery more quickly....
>
> Nora

Paul concluded there was a lot of subterfuge concealed in this note. He knew the truth behind the real concocted reason for Nora's absence, although neither she nor the preacher were aware that he knew. He threw the note into the wastebasket. Then he got to thinking how odd it was that she had managed to come in, type the note, then leave it in the typewriter without being seen. She was sick, no doubt about that, for she would almost certainly have morning sickness. He was of the opinion that the preacher would keep her hidden away somewhere until after the baby was born. He retrieved the note and studied it more closely.

If Nora was going to type a note to leave in his typewriter, she would reasonably use her own typewriter. Thinking this out he got an idea. He went to her desk and inserted the note into her typewriter and typed a few words on it to compare the type. He then returned to his typewriter and did the same. He did detect a similarity in them but noticed a slight difference in the letters "Y" and "F". This led him to believe that Nora hadn't written the note at all, that the preacher had probably typed it himself and stuck it in his typewriter. He hurried to the Skyroom to compare the preacher's typewriter to his and Nora's, remembering to bring along a flashlight with which to do his sleuthing. He knew if the preacher saw a light on in the Skyroom he knew it would attract his attention.

He tried the door and found it locked as usual. He found the key and entered the room. In the meantime, unknown to Paul, George was just pulling into the garage. However, Paul went to the typewriter, removed the cover, nervously inserted the note and, as expected, the letters were a perfect match. He quickly replace the cover, then opened the drawers to get the ledger. To his dismay, the ledger was gone. He searched no further for he knew, now that he had a key, anything with any significant value would long have been removed and cleverly concealed elsewhere. He closed the drawers, went over and sat in the preacher's chair, and just sat there relaxing. It was then he glanced over at the door and there in the open doorway stood the preacher. He had forgotten to close the door and had no idea how long he had been standing there watching him.

George walked over to the center panel of the desk and flicked a switch, turning on the overhead lights. Paul was in an awkward predicament, to say the least, sitting there in the preacher's chair with a flashlight in his hand. He made a quick decision, if he should ask he would tell him the truth but would not volunteer anything.

"You startled me, brother Blakely," (he was back to calling him brother again) he said lamely, getting up from his chair. "I didn't hear you come up."

George walked over to Paul and stood face to face. "Why the flashlight, Paul; wouldn't the overhead light better enable you to find what you were searching for?"

Paul caught the omission at once of leaving off brother from his name, which he always held to religiously. Could this mean dismissal for him, Paul thought, and knows that I am closing in on him? As they stood facing one another, Paul noticed a strange look in his eyes as if they were made of glass.

"What could I be searching for? I've just always been fascinated with the technology incorporated into this desk and was seeing how it works." he answered, his voice sounding high in his ears. He knew to remain calm and try not to agitate him further. "I thought by leaving off the ceiling light it would save you a trip up here unnecessarily. I knew if you saw the light you would rush up here, thus my reason for using the flashlight."

"How considerate of you," he said, sounding and looking more like himself. "There was something here I wanted to show...." He fell forward and Paul grabbed him to keep him from falling, helping him to his chair. Whatever the attack was it passed as quickly as it came. He sat rubing his temples trying to ease his headache.

"Have you seen a doctor yet about these attacks."

"I'll be all right now. It's these excruciating headaches I've been having for the longest time. They make me awfully dizzy."

"You really need to have a checkup."

"You're right, I should. I just keep putting it off. I'll call the doctor and make an appointment first thing in the morning," he said, the glazed look now gone from his eyes. "I thank you for your concern."

He seem to have forgotten what they had previously been discussing. So Paul asked him, "Did sister Letty say anything to you about going away to visit one of her aunts? I found a note from her stuck in my typewriter."

"I knew she was going. She mentioned that she wasn't feeling very well. Actually, it was I who suggested to her that she take some time off until she felt more like working." He took a letter from his inside coat pocket and handed it to Paul. "This is what I meant to tell you about awhile ago. I've already got a replacement for her."

It was an acceptance letter from Ethel Anders, a widow who was well thought of by the church people. Paul was sure she was given the job for obvious reasons. He finished reading the letter and gave it back to him.

"You've made a wise choice," he said, moving toward the door. "I'm going to the house to get ready for tonight's service. I'll see you there."

He stepped through the door, not waiting for an answer. Then he thought of his messages. He had completely forgotten them.

CHAPTER 8

September came bringing warm days of sunshine, not unlike August, except there was less humidity and the air was noticeably cooler. The yellow and gold of the Maples had deepened, along with the hues of russet, orange, and red of the other trees. The lawns were showing splotches of brown due to the lack of rain.

Labor Day came, then passed uneventfully, bringing the day for Colby's trial to begin. Paul tried to help gather evidence as best he could and hoped that, together with what Charles had collected, would prove to be sufficient. Paul asked Charles not to mention that he had helped gather evidence, for if it was discovered, he was sure to be accused of taking sides which would only succeed in making enemies for him.

Paul rose early, as was his custom, in order to make it to the trial on time. He intended to attend as much of the trial as he could. He arrived in plenty of time, taking a seat in back of the courtroom. He looked round and saw that the place was packed. He knew Adra was to testify and would be sequestered in another room off to herself until called to testify.

To the left, in front of the spectator's gallery, sat the defense, and to the defenses' right sat the prosecution. The Jury was to the left of the defense along the wall. The Judge's bench was elevated on a raised platform, giving him the advantage of looking down on his constituents. To the left of the Judge's bench was a table with the collected, or otherwise, evidence on display.

Paul was pleased to see Colby sitting next to his attorney. He sat with his head bowed, dressed in a navy blue suit with a matching tie. It would help to impress the jury and show he wasn't destitute enough to have to rob anyone to subsist. The main door to the courtroom was now closed, allowing no one else to enter, and the trial bagan.

The voice of the bailiff rang out loud and clear announcing the Judge's entrance into the court: "His Honor, Judge Daniel Snow." Everyone rose to their feet until the judge was seated, they then were reseated. He rapped his gavel three times and declared, "This court is now in session!"

To Paul, the judge appeared to be a man of wisdom and. hopefully, compassion. He was an elderly man, experienced, and judged a man by his character rather than his color or nationality. His hair was perfectly white and suited to his name. He was a man who kept himself in shape and stood five feet eleven inches tall. A handsome man in his mid-sixties.

"This court will now come to order. No sudden outbursts, shouting, or whistling will be tolerated, and anyone becoming unruly or boisterous will be immediately ejected from this courtroom. Mr. Prosecutor, are you ready to begin the trial?"

"Yes, your Honor." the prosecutor, Mr. Weatherall, promptly complied. When he had fisished laying out the events leading up to the trial, he turned to the judge and said, "Your Honor, I call to the stand my first witness, Mr. Jesse Latimer."

When Jesse entered from a side room, his left arm cradled in a sling, it brought a stir of excitement from the crowd as he made his way to the witness stand and sat down. The bailiff stepped to his side and said, "Please stand, place your left hand on the bible, raise your right hand. Do you swear to tell the truth, the whole truth, so help you God?"

"I do."

"You may be seated."

Mr. Weatherall stepped before Jesse and began his questioning. "Mr. Latimer, would you please state your name and occupation."

"Jesse Latimer, owner of Latimer's Pawn Shop."

"Now Mr. Latimer, would you relate to the court what you were doing at the time of the robbery and what led to your being shot?"

"My helper, Colby Warfield, and I closed the shop and left for our respective homes. Shortly after I reached my home I discovered my wallet was missing and realized that I had left it laying on the counter in the shop and returned to get it. While I was checking my wallet to see if anything was missing, I heard this noise in back of the shop and went to see what it could be. It was then I came upon this black person who had broken into the shop. In my attempt to disarm him, we fell to the floor and, in doing do, I was shot in the left shoulder. By this time it was more dark than light, and as I had turned only one light on, I was unable to see this person well enough to recognize him. All I could see was that he was black. He then forced me to give him what money I had in the register and he then quickly fled the shop."

"Were you threatened in any way?"

"No. I can't remember him threatening me."

"Did the accused say anything to you that you can recall?"

"Only, ' "Give me all your money." '

"Do you see anyone in this courtroom that resembles your assailant?"

"In all honesty, I cannot say that I do. As I have said, and I repeat, I did not recognize the person who shot and robbed me, only that he was black. I have a black man working for me and he is the one I thought it might be. It was my assumption that it was he who did it."

"Is that person within the confines of this courtroom?"

"Yes, he is."

"Would you point him out to the court?"

Here Jesse was a little hesitant of outright accusing Colby of being his attacker. After looking down at the floor, he raised his head and reluctantly pointed to Colby.

"Thank you, Mr. Latimer," said Mr. Weatherall. "That's all the questions I have for this witness at this time."

"Do you wish to cross examine the witness, Mr Haverman?" asked the judge.

"Yes I do, your Honor," Charles said, walking over to stand next to Jesse. "Mr. Latimer, do I understand you to say that you recognized your assailant to be Mr. Warfield as the man who shot and robbed you?"

"No. I did not say I recognized him as the man who robbed and shot me. Only that he resembled him, since the person shot me was black."

"By black, do you mean black as we ordinarily know black, or do you mean a lighter or darker shade of black?"

"Well, there wasn't that much light to enable me to determine the difference in shades. I suppose it could be more described as just ordinary black."

"Would you look at my client now, Mr. Latimer, and describe his coloring for me?"

Everyone became very still as Jesse looked over at Colby. "As well as I can see from here he looks like…uh…looks dark brown rather than black. But…"

"Then your answer is that he isn't ordinary black. Is that correct?"

"That's correct, he isn't."

"Thank you, Mr. Latimer," said Charles. "No further questions, your Honor."

"You are excused, Mr. Latimer," said the judge. Then to the prosecuting attorney he said, "Mr. Weatherall, your next witness, please."

"I call to the stand, Mr. Hyram Jones."

After being sworn in, the prosecutor began his questioning, taking Mr. Jones through the repetitious part of his testimony, and that he lived directly behind the pawn shop, then bringing him up to the main part of his testimony. "...and so you were looking out your back, kitchen window. Tell us what you saw there."

"Well, I saw several people running around the back of the pawn shop. One of them ran over and hid behind the dumpster, I couldn't make out what gender they were, and as one came cutting across, another one came running out of the shop and knocked the person down. He stopped, came back to help the person to their feet, then took off running again. Those two appeared to be two males. It was too dark to make out whether they were black or white."

"Did the one hiding behind the dumpster ever come out in the open again?"

"No, I don't recall seeing that one again. After that, I lost interest and went on about my business."

"Thank you, Mr. Jones. Your witness, Mr. Haverman."

"Mr. Jones," asked Mr. Haverman, "do you recall whether the person that knocked the other one down was wearing gloves or not?"

"No, I could not distinguish that from the distance of my window."

"Thank you, Mr. Jones. No further questions."

And so it went until the prosecution had exhausted their entire list of witnesses. It was now nearing twelve o'clock noon and Judge Snow called for a lunch break. The jury was cauioned not to listen to the radio, watch television, read the newspaper, or discuss any aspect of the trial with anyone other than among themselves. They were dismissed and instructed to return to the jury box at precisely two P. M.

***

When the court reconvened, it was the defense's turn to present their case, so Colby's attorney, Mr. Charles Haverman, carefully lined up his cast of witnesses, taking care not to make any grave mistakes.

When everybody had settled down, and Judge Snow had called the court to order again, Charles stepped forward and announced, "I call to the stand my first witness, Mr. Colby Warfield. There was a buzz of excitement, for it had been banded about that Colby would not be testifying on his own behalf, which proved, of course, to be nothing but a rumor. Colby walked to the witness stand with his head erect, looking neither to the left or to the right. and seated himself, then he was dutifully sworn in.

There actually wasn't much that Colby could testify to since he had no proof that he was at home at the time the robbery occurred, neither had he seen what had taken place. Charles knew he was risking Colby's chances, but he felt he must show the people what type of person he really was. He pointed out his studies; his ambition to make something of himself; of his attendance record on the job, and that he had no need to rob <u>anyone</u>. After carefully pointing out these characteristics he began his questioning.

"Mr. Warfield, would you state your name and occupation for the record."

"Colby Warfield, clerk and handy man at Latimer's Pawn Shop."

"What do you mean by handy man?"

"I clean and sweep the store, things like that."

"I see. And how long have you been employed at Latimer's Pawn Shop?"

"I have been there approximately six years"

"Have you ever had an occasion to be away from work due to illness or any unforeseen mishaps?"

"I have missed only two day work in all that time due to illness."

"Mr. Warfield, did you shoot Mr. Latimer and rob him of an unspecified sum of money?"

"No sir, absolutely not!"

"No further questions, your Honor."

"Does the prosecution wish to cross examine the witness?" asked Judge Snow.

"Yes, your Honor," said Mr. Weatherall, who then turned to face the witness."

"Mr. Warfield, do you categorically deny that you robbed and shot your employer, Mr. Latimer?"

"Absolutely!"

"Can you prove where you were during the time of this altercation?"

"I was at my home, but I cannot prove it. My wife and son were gone to a birthday party during that time. Therefore, I was home alone."

"Thank you. Mr. Warfield. No mor questions, your Honor."

"Mr. Haverman, your next witness please," said the judge.

"I call to the stand, Mr. James Barris."

Everybody turned to look at this unknown witness few had ever heard of. He was a mousey little guy who would hardly be noticed in a crowd. Charles suspected he was only looking to be noticed. After being sworn in, Charles began his questioning.

"Mr. Burris, would you relate to the court what you told me previously?"

"You mean about my running into the suspect—or him running into me?"

"That's right, about your encounter with the suspect."

"Well," he began, "I was on my way home from visiting one of the local pubs and was walking behind the pawn shop on my way home. I live about a block behind the shop. As I was walking past the rear of the shop this fellow came rushing past me and knocked me down. He paused, came back to help me up, then took off running again. As he was helping me up I could see that his face was black but his hands were white. Evidently, he had been wearing a pair of gloves."

Mr. Weatherall jumped to his feet. "I object! Obviously, this man was drunk and could not have known half of what he professes to have seen. I ask that Mr. Burrises' testimony be stricken from the record as null and void."

"Overruled," said Judge Snow. "There's no way we can determine, at this late date, whether this man was drunk or sober during the incident."

"No more questions, your Honor."

Mr. Burris sat smiling, pleased with the attention he was getting. From here he would return to obscurity just as he was before. He seemed to be content, as well as satisfied, with his fifteen minutes of fame.

"I now call to the stand, Mr. Tilden Matthews," said Mr. Haverman.

As soon as Mr. Matthews had been dutifully sworn in, Mr. Haverman began by saying, "Mr. Matthews, would you please relate to the court the event that took place between you and David Stoddard prior to the robbery?"

"As you know, once before I got mixed up in something I wasn't guilty of by listening to my friend David. This time, when he approached me about a scheme he had in mind, I refused to go along with it."

"What scheme was that?"

"He told me he was taking me into his confidence and asked me to help him; that he had a plan for getting some quick money to have a big time on. He said no one would ever know who did it. I listened to what he had to say, and when he had finished speaking, I told him I wasn't having anything to do with it. He left and I never saw him again until several days later, at which time he told me that he had carried out his plan."

"What did he mean by plan?"

"He said he was going to don a pair of denim jeans and a chambray shirt, blacken his face, neck and ears, put on a pair of gloves, and old man Latimer would think it was the black man that worked for him."

Mr. Haverman walked over to the table and picked up a piece of evidence, returned to the the witness and held up a 22 caliber pistol for Mr. Matthews to see. "Have you ever seen this gun before?"

"No. I have not."

"Your cross, Mr. Weatherall."

"Then you don't know if Mr. Stoddard intended to use a gun or not. Is that right, Mr. Matthews?"

"I don't recall him mentioning anything about a gun."

"Thank you, Mr. Matthews. No more questions, your Honor."

"Your Honor," Mr. Haverman said, I call to the stand Mrs. Adra Blakely."

Adra was escorted to the witness stand and her nervousness was evident. She held her head up determined not to be intimidated. Everyone could see she was frail and sickly as she took her seat. After she was dutifully sworn in, Charles walked over next to her and very gently began his questioning.

"You are Mrs. Adra Blakely, is that correct?"

"That is correct."

"Mrs. Blakely, please relate to the court how you came to be in back of Latimer's Pawn Shop on the evening this incident we are trying here today took place."

She began relating what had taken place, making no mention of her alcoholism, which was a mistake on her part. She was sure to be humiliated later when it would be brought out later by the prosecution on cross examination. When she finished speaking, Charles picked up the shirt and held it up in front of her.

"Have you ever seen this shirt before?"

"I don't know if I have seen that particular shirt before or not; they all look alike to me."

Charles knew she was being evasive.

"Does it look like the one the person was wearing when that person broke into the pawn shop?"

"Yes, it does."

"Did you notice what kind of pants the intruder was wearing?"

"As well as I could see, they looked like a pair of jeans."

"Please take this shirt and tell me what you see on the collar and cuffs."

"It has black smudges on it."

"Now, look inside at the collar and tell me what you see there."

Adra held the shirt with trembling fingers and, after putting on her glasses, peered at the shirt collar. "There are the numerals 0447."

"Now, look above the left pocket and tell me what you see there."

"The initials "HS".

"And now, would you mind telling the court what you were doing at the pawn shop at that hour in the evening?"

"I had gone there to pawn a jade figurine. When I got to the shop it appeared to be closed so I went round back to see if there were anyone in the rear of the shop that would consider letting me in. I had just got behind the shop when I heard someone coming. I became afraid and ran and hid behind the dumpster."

"Thank you, Mrs. Blakely. I have no further questions."

Mr. Weatherall rose to his feet, approached the witness very gruffly to cross examine her, making Adra more nervous than she already was. "For the record, Mrs. Blakely, I would appreciate it if you would please repeat a portion of your testimony. What was your purpose for coming to the pawn shop?"

"As I said, ' "I had a small jade figurine...I wanted to see...," Adra stammered nervously.

"Come, come, Mrs. Blakely, let us not falter and mumble. Please speak up so the court can hear you."

"I had a jade figurine I wanted to pawn."

"I see. Are you lacking in funds, Mrs. Blakely, that you have to patronize a pawn shop to supplement your income?"

"Objection!" boomed Mr. Haverman. "The prosecution is deliberately debasing and badgering the witness. She has every right to patronize any business establishment she chooses."

"Objection sustained," said the judge.

"Very well, your Honor. I thought it might be of interest to the court to find out what the wife of a prominent minister, the Reverend George Blakely, should have the need of the service of a pawn shop. If I may continue, I would like to bring out a topic that I'm sure will prove very interesting and have a great deal of bearing on the case."

"Then you may continue. But it must bring credence to the case at hand."

"Thank you, Your Honor," said Mr. Weatherall, turning back to face Adra.

"Mrs. Blakely, does your husband give you money for household expenses, things like that?"

"Yes, he does."

"Does he give you sufficient funds to cover everything or, on occasion, do you find that you have come up short?"

"Yes. Occasionally I do run short of funds."

"Does the money allotted to you include the purchase of alcoholic beverages?"

Again, from Mr. Haverman. "I object! It's a personal matter how she spends the money allotted to her."

"Sustained," intoned the judge.

"Rephrasing my question: do you have occasion to purchase alcoholic beverages?"

"I don't think that…"

"Please answer my question, yes or no, Mrs. Blakely."

"No, of course not!" she answered, knowing that she was perjuring herself. She couldn't bear to face the truth.

"Then you deny that you purchase a quantity of liquor for personal consumption from the money allotted to you?"

"Yes…er no…oh, I don't know!" she said, getting perturbed and confused.

"Isn't it a fact that you consume a substantial portion of alcohol every day?"

"I don't…I don't…," she stammered, breaking down and beginning to cry. "How could you be so cruel and unfeeling!"

"One more question, Mrs. Blakely. Are you and alcoholic?"

Exasperated and ashamed she cried out in her frustration, "Yes! Yes, I admit to that. Is that what you want to hear!" she spat the words at him, buried her face in her hands and continued to sob piteously.

Charles had heard enough and jumped to his feet. "I object. Prosecution is badgering the witness!"

"Objection sustained," concurred the judge.

"I have no more questions Your Honor," said Mr. Weatherall and returned to his seat.

"The witness is excused," said the judge.

Adra, too ashamed to raise her head, now faced the stark reality of her condition and was forced to see herself as she now was.

"Would the attorneys please approach the bench?" requested the judge. When they stood before him he continued. "Gentlemen, I would admonish you to conduct yourself in a more humane manner. We're not in the business of destroying anyone's character. Are you ready for the summarization?"

Both answered in unison. "Yes, your Honor."

Then you may proceed, Mr. Weatherall."

"Thank you, your Honor."

He turned to address the jury. "I hope I haven't appeared to be merciless and heartless in your eyes, but I felt it was imperative that you know the state into which Mrs. Blakely has succumbed. With her admission that she is an alcoholic—and I suspected she was all along—we are made aware of the inaccuracies that often occur in their judgment of what they have actually seen. With that in mind, can we accept their testimony as the truth knowing their mind is often impaired from an over indulgence of alcohol? Can an honest decision be based on that? I do not attempt to sway you in your judgment, for that decision is entirely yours, but I urge you to honestly follow the dictates of your conscience. Thank you."

"And now, Mr. Haverman, if you please."

"Your Honor, ladies and gentlemen of the jury, I just want to say what you have seen and heard presented to you today are the facts, as far as we know them. I'm sure that from what you have heard you have got to be convinced that my client, Mr. Colby Warfield, is completely innocent of this crime for which he has been charged. If you follow the dictates of your heart you can come to only one conclusion: not guilty. That's all I have to say. Thank you."

The judge speaking to the jury said: "Before you are dismissed to begin your deliberation I must admonish you not to watch television or listen to the radio. You are not to discuss any part of the trial with anyone other than between yourselves. You will be sequestered in a room which no one will permitted to leave until you have reached a unanimous decision. You must consider all the facts and make your decision as to whether the defendant is guilty or not guilty beyond a reasonable doubt. Again I must warn you not to discuss the case with anyone other than amongst yourselves. When you have reached a verdict you may pass it to the bailiff who will, in turn, bring it to me. You are hereby dismissed to begin your deliberation."

Time dragged slowly by while everyone waited for the jury's decision. Actually they had deliberated for only two hours before reaching a verdict but it had seemed far longer. When the judge received word that a verdict had been reached he had the jury return to the courtroom and called the court back to order.

When judge Snow received the verdict he looked it over and addressed the jury. "Is this your final decision, so say you all?"

"Yes, Your Honor, it is," replied the jury foreman.

"Will the defendant, Mr. Warfield, please stand?"

Colby stood to his feet and Charles rose to stand beside him to give him moral support. If one could have seen Colby's eyes they would have seen the look of fear in them. He was certain that he would be found guilty simply because of the color of his skin.

Judge Snow paused dramatically for a few seconds before reading the verdict. Then in a clear voice he intoned, "We, the jury, find the defendant, Colby Warfield—not guilty!"

The court erupted into a loud burst of applause, whistling and yelling and hugging one another. When order had once again been restored to the court, Judge Snow announced, "This court is now adjourned." He then rose from his seat and entered his chambers.

Armeda rushed to her husband and threw her arms around his neck, kissing and hugging him, while laughing and crying at the same time. "Oh how wonderful!" she exclaimed. "Thank God, you're free!" She then turned to face Charles. "We can never thank you enough, Mr. Haverman, for what you have done for us!"

"It has been a pleasure to have had the opportunity to serve you. If there is anything further that I can do for you don't hesitate to call."

Paul sat with Vivian the last day of the trial and when the verdict was announced he grabbed and hugged her. He was overjoyed that Colby had been proven innocent. He went over to speak with Charles and to introduce him to Vivian.

"I, too, thank you Charles for all that you have done. Now, may I introduce my dearest friend, Vivian Blakely. Vivian, my friend and very successful attorney, Mr. Charles Haverman."

Vivian extended her hand. Charles took it and said, "How nice to meet you. You have a prize in this man. You would be wise to hold on to him."

"Nice meeting you, too, Mr Haverman. I'm of the same opinion and I intend to do just that."

"Now that you've won this case, I predict more business will come your way than you will be able to handle," Paul said.

"I hope that's one prediction that comes true," Charles said, laughing and turned to gather his papers together.

Paul took Vivian over to congratulate Colby and to introduce her to Armeda. "I'm so very happy for you Colby," Paul said. "If justice ever triumphed this is one time it did!" He then introduced Vivian to Armeda. "Armeda, I'd like you to meet a very dear friend of mine, Vivian Blakely. Vivian, this is Colby's wife Armeda."

"How glad I am to meet you," Vivian said, giving her a big hug. "I hope we can become real good friends."

"It's nice meeting you too. I'm sure we will and I would like nothing better."

Vivian turned to Paul and said, "I must go and look for Mother and see that she gets home all right. I'll see all of you later. Bye."

"Bye hon. I'll call you later." Then to Colby he asked, "Do you have a way home? Is there anywhere I can drop you off?"

"No, thank you brother Paul; you have done enough already. Armeda has our old jalopy here so I'll be driving back to our place with her."

"May I add my thanks again to you, Reverend Langley, for all you have done for us." Armeda said, extending her hand to him. "Without your help I suspect we would have come up the losers."

"Your both are more than welcome. I was only happy to do what little I could and to help in some small way," he said, letting go of her hand. "Please feel free to call me anytime I can be of help to you in any way. I mean that sincerely."

"Brother Paul, bring Vivian and come visit with us anytime. You will always be more than welcome in our home," Colby said.

"Thank you, I'll do that," Paul replied, taking his leave of them and going to his car. He would go back to the office and see what, if anything, had come up while he was away. As for George, he didn't expect he would attend the trial but felt he should have been there in support of his wife. After having given it a little more thought he came to the conclusion that his absence was due to Adra having to testify. He was a very proud man.

He intended to talk with Vivian about her mother to see if they could persuade her to enter a treatment center before she recovered from her humiliation at the hands of Weatherall. He was sure she would consent to go after what she had just endured . He had just about reached his office when he heard voices coming from what was now Ethel's office. He recognized the voices as being that of George and Harry Stoddard. The door was slightly ajar so he stood next to it to see if he could hear what they were talking about. He hadn't meant to eavesdrop but as their voices became louder he became more curious to know what they were bickering over. He was sure George wasn't aware that the door wasn't fully closed.

"But you can't be serious!" he heard George say.

"I was never more serious in my life," came Harry's reply. "Effective at the end of this week I'm resigning from the board."

"What happened? Just a short while ago you were gung-ho about becoming sheriff of this county. We have things worked out to where it's almost a shoo-in for you." Their voices became lower but Paul could still make out what they were saying. "You know the election will soon be coming up," George said.

"I'm sorry, George," came Harry's reply, "but David means more to me than anything you have to offer. I have already failed him badly enough and I don't intend to repeat my mistake. If he gets out of this mess he's gotten himself into I mean to stand by him and be the father I should have been all along."

Harry's addressing George by his first name must mean there was a very serious rift between them. Then their voices got lower yet again and Paul was drawn like a magnet closer to the door to better hear what was being said. "What has being elected sheriff got to do with being a father to your son?" George asked. "It might be the best thing you could do for him. When he gets old enough he may want to become a policeman himself."

"You're wasting your time, Preacher. I've already told you, I'm not interested anymore. You almost had me sold on the idea but I've come to my senses. After all, you only wanted me to have the job so you could have more of the law on your side."

"Now, Harry, my brother, is that any way to talk to me after all the good times we have had together?" George got up from his chair, went over to Harry and put his arm around his shoulder. "I admit it wouldn't be bad having the Chief of Police on my side."

Harry turned from under George's arm and started for the door, afraid to trust himself to George's persuasiveness and be talked into changing his mind.

"Again, I'm sorry, but my mind is made up. I'm grateful to have been one of the "Chosen Few", even one of the "Insiders", as it were. It was exciting and a lot of fun. I'm getting out before it's too late. Don't you understand—David almost killed a man! I can't chance that ever happening again."

The telephone rang but George ignored it as he continued trying to persuade Harry to change his mind. "You know, of course, to leave our circle you put your life, and David's, in grave danger. After all, you have been privy to some things that would be very damaging to the rest of us it should ever get out; things that many in the church don't know exist."

"Are you threatening me?" Harry asked angrily and incredulously. "You can't be serious! If you are it won't work with me. I don't scare that easily."

"That's up to you. But if I were you I would give it some serious thought. You may decide to change your mind."

"I have already thought about it. I had to make a choice between David and you—I chose David. Wouldn't you have made the same choice had it been Nat and he were still alive?"

George turned as if stricken and stumbled to a chair and sat down. "Why did you have to bring Nat into this? Oh, Nat...Nat!" he moaned. "Why did you slip off and go swimming with that awful Holseman boy?" He seemed to have forgotten Harry was there. "I still miss you so much." With that he buried his face in his arms and continued to sob heartbrokenly.

Paul had heard enough and slipped away and went to his office. He had barely gotten seated when he heard Harry leaving. He still wondered why George had used Ethel's office instead of the security of his own. Harry closed the door and left. He had never seen George in the state he was in before. He recalled his threatening words and simply concluded that he must be heading for a nervous breakdown.

CHAPTER 9

The moment Tilden Matthew finished testifying about his encounter with David Stoddard, the police were dispatched to arrest him for the "Pawn Shop Caper" as it was now being called. They found him at a local pool hall, arrested him and took him to jail. The irony of it was he was incarcerated in the same cell Colby had been confined in.

The local radio station broadcast the news of David's arrest by stating that it had been reported that David Stoddard was considered a suspect in the Pawn Shop Caper. He had been indicted on charges of robbery and attempted murder of the shop's owner, Mr. Jesse Latimer.

They rushed his case through the required channels as fast as they could and scheduled his hearing one week later. Finally there was David standing before Judge Snow to plead one way or the other. "There's no need to drag this out so I will come right to the point," said judge Snow looking down at the young boy standing before him. "Young man, you stand before this court today accused of robbery and the maiming of one, Mr. Jesse Latimer. How do you plead?"

David was so scared. He mumbled, "Not guilty", but the judge didn't hear him.

"You must speak up young man. I can't hear you."

"He pleads not guilty, Your Honor," his court appointed lawyer, Josh Billings. said.

"Your trial will be before a jury and will take place on the fifteenth of September. In the meantime, I suggest you work in compliance with your lawyer, Mr. Billings, and we will see you in court. You will now be remanded to your cell to await your trial."

Now that Harry had severed his ties with George and resigned from the board, there wasn't much he could do about getting David released from jail. He would just have to toughen it out until his trial date came up. It was at times like this that Harry could see the advantage of belonging to George's inside circle of friends. But that was the price he would have to pay. All he could do now was wait for the trial to begin and hope for the best.

In the meantime, Judge Snow would familiarize himself with the evidence against David which would enable him to make a just decision toward David's sentence. He heard a replay of Tilden Matthews and Rick Morrison's testimonies and was shown the shirt recovered from the dumpster with the initials "HS" and the number 0447 on it. It was believed that the initials stood for Harry Stoddard, the father of the accused, and the numbers were the laundry mark. Paul didn't attend David's hearing; therefore, he didn't know when his sentence was to be. He would find out and be there for moral support for both the father and son. Meanwhile, he was to meet Vivian at her mother's house where they would try to persuade Adra to enter a recovery center while she was still smarting from the trial. He rang the doorbell and Vivian went to answer it. Seeing that it was Paul, she said, "Come on in" and he followed her into the kitchen where she and her mother were eating.

"Won't you have some soup with us?" she asked.

"No, thank you. But I would like a cup of coffee, black. no sugar, please." He took a seat next to Adra, who looked at him and smiled weakly, still slightly embarrassed over her having to disclose her alcoholism.

Vivian served him the coffee then seated herself close to Adra on the other side. "I think you're will be pleased with what Mother has to tell you. Tell brother Paul what you told me just a few minutes ago."

Adra wiped her mouth and looked him in the eye for the first time. "I told you I would give some serious thought about going in for a cure. Well, I have decided to go as soon as a place can be found for me."

"That's wonderful news and I am pleased. You won't regret your decision. You will feel like a new person once you are cured. I will start looking for a suitable place first thing in the morning."

"After that experience on the witness stand it can't be soon enough for me, I assure you," Adra said.

Vivian got up and put their cups in the sink. "I'll discuss this with Dad this evening. I'll let you know what he has to say."

Paul finished his coffee and rose to go. "I'm terribly sorry for what happened to you during the trial," Paul said to Adra. "I believe it did help you realize you needed help. I believe it was your testimony that helped to sway the jury to clear Colby of all the charges against him, regardless of what the prosecutor said." He patted her on the shoulder and she lay her hand on his.

"It was dreadful, I won't deny that, but what will happen to that boy? He's just a kid." she wanted to know. "He's not more than fifteen; he's so young to be sent to prison."

Paul found it heartening to hear her speak with concern for someone else. It was something she hadn't done for a long time. "This is his first offense. Perhaps they will be lenient with him. It certainly was a drastic thing that he did to get his dad's attention."

Vivian walked him to the door. "Do you know when his trial is to be?"

"I don't have a clue or of what the outcome is going to be for him. But, I'll find out."

"When you do let me know, okay?"

"Sure thing. I intend to keep in touch with them and give them both as much support as I can. I know they both can use a friend just now. I've got to go. I've some things I've yet to do before I can call it a day." Then he whispered to Vivian, "Step outside with me for a minute."

They stood in the yard where Adra couldn't hear them. "I don't want her to find out how rough the treatment might be, She probably wouldn't go."

"When you go to look for a place for her try to find one that's not too far out," Vivian said. "I'd like to visit her as often as I can to give her moral support."

"She will need all the support we can give her. I understand the first week is pretty rough and that no visitors are allowed. After that I don't think there are any restrictions."

"You'll never know how much this means to me. A simple thank you seems so inadequate. If Mother goes through with this and is cured it will be so wonderful!"

Paul could see the tears welling in her eyes. Obviously, she had been contending with far more than he had any idea of. He noticed, too, that she never complained.

"I'm sure it would," he agreed, taking her hand and lowering his voice. "Would you just call me Paul? I'll call you Vivian. There's no cardinal rule that says we have to address one another as brother or sister. It's so unnecessary where you and I are concerned. Don't you agree?"

"Yes, I do. But we must not forget ourselves in Dad's presence; he holds to it religiously. If he found out he would accuse us of being pagans," she laughed.

"Then it will be our secret. By the way, would you like to go to a concert with me this coming Friday?"

"I would love to," she said.

"Then I'll come by for you at seven. The concert begins at eight. Goodnight"

When at last he had gone to bed he lay there thinking about what he should do about his relationship with Vivian. Now that he was firmly established and had saved a little money, he thought it was time to ask her to marry him. After all, George had promised him a raise in salary whenever he did get married. The thought brought a lightness of heart and an excitement like that of a child at Christmas waiting for Santa's arrival.

Arriving at the office the next morning he could hear Ethel already busily at work. He wouldn't know whether Adra would be entering a care center until he heard from Vivian after she had talked with her dad. He would go ahead and see what he could find so it would be ready whenever it was decided on. He was sure that Adra wasn't aware of how hard the treatment would be and hoped she wouldn't find out until after she had been admitted. Once admitted she would be closely watched, closely attended to, and closely supervised, especially during the first week.

When Paul reached the open highway he turned north and drove toward a beautiful home he had previously seen in a lovely valley tucked away between rolling hills. It looked so peaceful and quiet and the air so fresh and clean. He wasn't sure where he had seen it, or even if he could find it again. He felt he had driven for miles and hadn't seen anything that looked remotely like the place he was searching for. He was just on the verge of turning back when he rounded the next curve and there, spread out before him, lay the very place he had been looking for. It was the ideal place. It was secluded and very private and, as Vivian requested, not too far out.

He pulled onto the paved driveway, passed through a large white gate over which the words House of Hope were inscribed. He drove into the parking lot, parked, and walked to the main entrance. He entered a spacious waiting room with an impressive office. He went to the office window where a pleasant, middle aged lady greeted him.

"Good morning. Welcome to the House of Hope. May I be of service to you?"

"Yes. I'd like to inquire about a friend of mine being admitted here for treatment. She's an alcoholic."

"Then you need to talk with Mrs. Orell. Just go through that door there on your left. Her office is also on the left as you enter."

He tapped lightly on the door and entered the office. Mrs. Orell was a pleasant looking lady, dressed in a clean, light blue uniform. She, too, greeted him cordially with a warm smile. "Good morning. Welcome to the House of Hope. I'm Mrs. Orell. How may I help you?"

"Good morning, Mrs. Orell. My name is Paul Langley. I'm here on behalf of a very good friend of mine who is an alcoholic." He did not reveal to her that he was a minister. That would come in due time. "This looks like a nice place for her to get the treatment she so desperately needs. It has just the setting we have been looking for."

"Is is beautiful isn't it?" she said, picking up several sheets of paper from her desk. "Please be seated, Mr. Langley, and we will get the forms filled out for her admittance."

"I'm not sure when she will be admitted. You see, the decision for her to actually be admitted hasn't been decided as yet. I'm most sure she will be though. But I wanted to find the right place for her when it is decided that she will be admitted."

"I understand. However, we can get the paper work out of the way so that when she does come in it will all be taken care of. If she decides not to come we will simply destroy the forms and discard them."

When all the information had been dutifully collected and written down she reached him a brochure detailing the operation of the home and explaining the different stages of treatment. It also contained the cost for the service, room and board, and other pertinent information pertaining to the rules and regulations and visiting hours. The patient was expected to commit themselves to a ninety days of treatment to which an extended period could be arranged if needed.

"Would you like a tour of the home while you are here?" Mrs. Orell offered.

"Not at this time. I'd like to wait and bring the patient's daughter here to see what she thinks of the place. I'm sure she will love it as much as I do."

She shook hands with him and bade him goodbye. He drove straight back to give Vivian the news and the informative brochures Mrs. Orell had given him. He wasted no time in taking her to see the home. After they had given them the tour of the home, Vivian was delighted with it and very satisfied with all she had seen of the place. Even the patients spoke well of the home. "Oh, Paul, it's just what I hoped it would be! Mother will love it here!"

Their guide, Dr. Alfred Bernhauzer, was a noted psychiatrist and was in his mid-fifties. He had salt and pepper hair with a matching mustache and goatee, giving him a dignified look. He was lean and trim in build and had dark blue eyes. He had a pleasant disposition, a nice smile and beautiful white even teeth. They both liked him immediately. He took them back to his office and there asked Vivian a few questions.

"Will Sunday evening be suitable for Mrs. Blakely to be admitted? We like our patients to get a full night's rest before beginning their recovery."

"She will be here. She is prepared to come in at any time."

"We ask that she sign an admittance form indicating that she is willing to be admitted for treatment and that her husband sign the form as well. He can come in and sign the form or they can be sent to him and brought back in when it's convenient. They can even be mailed in. Whatever way you choose is all right with us."

"Then I will take them for him to sign and bring them back to you myself. Incidentally, we would appreciate it if this was kept confidential and handled as discretely as possible. I'm sure you understand our reason for this request."

"Of course, we understand perfectly. I must leave you now. I have a patient due for consultation shortly. Mrs. Orell will give you the required forms and I hope to see Mrs. Blakely in the very near future." He shook their hands, turned and walked briskly away.

Driving back to Blakeville Paul asked Vivian, "Do you think your dad will take your mother to be admitted?"

"I hardly think so. It will probably be left up to you and me to see to that."

He suspected that she felt the same as he did, that George was too proud for anyone to know that he was a minister with an alcoholic wife. Vivian was certain she would have no trouble getting him to sign the papers.

When they reached Blakevill, he took Vivian to her mother's and then decided to drive to the Stellar Club to check it out and see what kind of club it really was. George had been careful not to mention the club to him. He found out about it by chance having overheard two guys talking about it when he was at the Board of Elections. He had stopped by there to check to see if he was properly registered and happened to hear one of them say that the Mayor was having a big blow-out at the Stellar Club on the weekend.. He hurriedly jotted down the name right then and there so he wouldn't forget it.

When he entered the club he wasn't impressed as much as he thought he would be. Knowing George was involved with the club he expected it to have been much more elaborately furnished than it was. It could be best described as plain tacky—until you entered the inner sanctum, as he was to discover later. He wasn't long in finding out that it was also a private club. As he walked toward the door leading into the inner sanctum he was stopped from entering by a gruff voice somewhere in the back of him. He turned to see who spoke and found himself looking into the face of a man that could only be described as having once been a wrestler. His nose looked like it had been flattened several times, he had high cheek bones and dark brown eyes that were wide apart. He knew at once that he was undoubtedly the bouncer.

"Who are ya and what does ya want?" he asked in a stern, gruff voice. "Ya lookin' for someone special or sumpin' else."

"In a way I am," Paul answered. "I'm here by invitation of Mayor Adams. Would he happen to be in at this hour?"

"There are very few people here this early in the day. The place don't start rockin' 'til about four or five o'clock. Then really starts jumpin' about ten in the evenin."

"Then George Blakely wouldn't likely be here either, right?" He knew George wouldn't be there but he thought he might get a tad of information on George out of him. "He is a member here isn't he?"

"Youse know ole George? He's called the Preacher 'roun' here. He's not only a member, he owns half the joint. I don't think he does very much preachin' though. He's one fine man. Yes sir, a real fine man!" He went over and sat on one of the bar stools. "My name's "Tank" Gowdy. Wha'd ya say yer name wuz?"

"Langley. Paul Langley," he said, careful not to reveal that he was a minister. He suspected that if he found out he would not speak as openly to him and his purpose for being there would be lost. He shook Tank's hand and stood rubbing his own after a bone crushing shake. To keep the conversation moving along he asked. "What's the requirement for becoming a member here?"

"There's ain't none that I know of. But that room over there—the one I stopped you from entering—well, to go in there ya gotta be worth some dough."

"Sounds interesting. How much worth are we talking here?"

"How does twenty-five grand grab ya."

"Twenty-five grand! You're kidding! That certainly leaves me out. I'm surprised that the Preacher has that kind of money. They're usually the poorest of the lot."

"Not this preacher—he's loaded! I wonder where people like him and the mayor get that kind of dough." Tank got up and went behind the bar. "I'm gettin' dry. Care for a beer?"

"No thanks. I've got to be going. I was just passing by and was curious to see what the club was like; I've heard so much about it." He turned to leave, paused, then asked, "How do they manage to keep the ladies out? I assume they are kept out."

"They ain't allowed to belong to the club but they are invited as guests on the weekend. The Preacher is quite the ladie's man. He brings a different gal here quite often. He's generous with tips too. He has always treated me ok."

"Thank you for giving me the run-down on the club. I appreciate it," Paul said, taking his leave. "The first cool million I get hold of I'll be back."

"Yeah, I know whatcha mean. But, you don't have to have a million to be a guest. All you need is to bring a pass from your host."

"Sure will. See you later, Tank." Paul left, hoping he didn't run into anyone he knew. Now he knew why George had never mentioned the club to him and why he didn't want him to know he was a member. He was puzzled how George had accumulated such an enormous amount of money. The deeper Paul delved into George's affairs the more he was convinced that he was converting church funds and money from other schemes into his own personal account. If I could only find that ledger I once saw, he mused to himself, I would be able to better understand it. He would just have to keep searching for it; it had to turn up sooner or later.

George had finally gotten around to giving him an automatic gate opener. It was a lot less trouble not to have to get in and out of the car to open and close the gate. As he pulled into the garage he glanced at his watch and saw that it was nearing noon and decided to walk to the Beanery for the exercise and to get something to eat. He had become a regular customer there and had gotten well acquainted with the waitress, Rosie Taggert. He felt sorry for her and the way she was treated by some of the men. She could be such a lovely girl if only she had someone to show her how to dress and apply her makeup properly. Her auburn hair could be made to look very becoming if she would only take the time to fix it. She wore her dresses far to short and the bodices too low. She always flirted with Paul whenever he went there to eat. Her eyes were graygreen and could be made very attractive if only she would leave off so much eye shadow and all that mascara. He thought it made her look so cheap. He was sure that was why the men treated her as they did. They just didn't seem to have very much respect for her.

She was wiping off one of the tables when he entered. When he had seated himself at a table near the window she quickly came over and handed him a menu. He noticed she wasn't her usual cheerful self and knew something must be wrong.

"What's wrong with "Sunshine" today?" he asked. "It looks as though it might rain."

"What's with you, Preach? It's a beautiful day!" she said with brave bravado, reaching for a pencil stuck in her hair. Not asking how are you or anything. Just, "What will it be—the usual?"

"No, I'm not all that hungry today. How about a bowl of your delicious bean soup, a few crackers and a glass of milk for a change."

When Rosie returned with his order and set it on the table he noticed her engagement ring that she had raved so much about was missing from her finger. "How's the boy friend doing on his new job?" he asked, knowing she was dying to tell him about what had happened.

"He ain't and we ain't," she said. "It's all off! He's just no good. I gave him his ring back." She leaned over and whispered in his ear. "Now's your chance, Preach, while I'm fancy-free."

"Can you spare a minute and sit down? I'd like to have a little talk with you."

"Okay, but only for a couple of minutes." She sat down. "What's on your mind."

"Look," he began, "I know it's none of my business. But I think you're making a big mistake letting what's-his-name get away from you. I'm a pretty good judge of character and I believe he would take very good care of you. He would give you a nice home and I'm sure you would be a very good wife and mother to his kids."

"That's what I thought too, at first, until I found out differently. The big lug wants me to shuck my job and go to Alaska with him. Who, in their right mind, would want to go to a God forsaken place like Alaska? I sure don't!"

"It's cold there most of the time, I agree, but why not give it a try? It's possible you might even like it. I've been told it's nothing like we have been led to believe." He took a sip of his milk. "That is, if you really love the guy. If you don't, then it would best to forget him whether you went to Alaska or not."

Just then some other customers came in and Rosie got up to wait on them. As soon as she finished with serving the new customers she returned to finish her chat with Paul.

"I may change my mind; I do love the big lummox. But he has a good job here driving a truck."

"Maybe he's looking for something that would allow him to be at home more and not have to do so much traveling. Have you ever thought of that?"

"By golly, no, I never thought about that. I guess I was just thinking of myself. Gee, I'm glad I got to talk to you. I just might go to Alaska after all," she said and he could see the spark of happiness back in her eyes. She left to wait on customers.

He finished eating, paid his bill and left. He returned to his office and could hear Ethel busily typing away on some letters George was having sent out for a project that would never materialize. How he got away with such things he would never understand.

Just as he sat down, Ethel came to the door to tell him something she had forgotten to mention. "It almost slipped my mind. Some man called, he wouldn't give his name, and asked that you call him as soon as you came in." She took a slip of paper out of her pocket with the number written on it and handed it to him.

"Thank you, Ethel," he said, reaching for the phone. He was surprised to find out the caller was none other than Harry Stoddard.

"Good afternoon, brother Langley. I was wondering if you could meet me at the corner drug store. I need to talk with you about something I'd rather not talk about over the phone."

Already, Paul could detect a change in Harry's attitude. "Sure thing. I'll be there as soon as I can," Paul said, and left immediately.

He found Harry sitting in a secluded booth in the back where he could talk without being overheard. "How about a sandwich or something to drink," Harry said, calling the waitress over. "It's on me."

"Nothing to eat, thank you. I'll just have a coke." He noticed the lines of worry and the tired look in Harry's eyes. "What's on your mind, Harry?" he inquired.

"Thank you for coming brother Langley. I know it's a lot to ask of you, but I was wondering if you would stand as surety for David. It would give him another chance to rectify what he did and maybe prevent him from going to prison. He's so young!"

"Since I'm addressing you by your first name, call me by mine. As for David, I don't wish to see him go to prison, believe me, but I really don't know him that well. To stand surety for someone is a great responsibility. What if he should mess up again. He would ruin me financially and destroy my future. I could come to regret having stood by him."

"I don't think he will be stupid enough to do anything so foolish again. I honestly believe he has learned his lesson. Besides, I feel it's partly my fault to begin with. If I had been a father to him I should have been all along he would never have done what he did. I was greedy enough to think I wanted something I really didn't want at all. I kept getting busier and busier until I no longer had any time for him. We used to be real close—pals if you will—and he resorted to what he did just to get back at me."

"Why don't you get George to vouch for him? I'm sure he could accomplish more for him than I ever could."

Harry raised his head and look straight into Paul's eyes. "That's where you're dead wrong! It's because of George this has all happened to begin with. Do you think for a minute the court would release David to his care, knowing what I know about the man. No way! Now with you it's a different story and the people here know that. I've told David that I intend to be the father I once was to him and should have been all along. Incidentally, I have resigned from the board and will leave as soon as someone is appointed to fill my place."

"What's David's attitude about all this, and what does he feel his chances are of getting off?"

144

"I'll be honest with you. He's scared to death and doesn't think he has much of a chance at all. However, since this is his first offense, it's possible he may be released on probation. He is to be sentenced in just a matter of weeks now."

"I wondered when his sentencing was to be. All right, I'll stick my neck out on his behalf if it can keep him from going to prison. It would mean a lot to keep him from becoming a hardened criminal."

"Then will you be at his sentencing?"

"I'll be there, the Lord willing. You can depend on that."

Harry rose to go. "I thank you again and appreciate what you're doing on David's behalf. I'll see you at the hearing," he said, shaking Paul's hand. He turned and walked away.

Paul left the drug store and looked for a pay phone. He had an important call he had to make and had to be sure George didn't find out about it. If he did find out about the call he would dismiss him on the spot. He was calling church headquarters to inquire about the church's financial reports. To his dismay the person on the phone reported that everything seemed to be in order and that the reports were coming in on time. He hung up the phone throughly puzzled as to how this could be.

When he got back to the house he shaved, showered and dressed and left for his date with Vivian. He pulled up in front of the parsonage, got out and knocked at the door. Vivian came out wearing a stunning pink dress with matching bag and slippers and a white, cashmere sweater draped around her shoulders.

The concert hall was crowded, for the most part, and Paul was pleased to know there were others that enjoyed the same kind of music they did. They found their seats in the center aisle and shortly after they were seated the concert began. They enjoyed the concert so much that it seemed to have ended far too soon. Back in the car, Paul headed toward the outskirts of town to a restaurant he had seen earlier called the Embers. He hadn't told Vivian where he was taking her for dinner. It turned out to be everything he had hoped it would be. It was an ideal place for him to make his proposal and ask her to marry him. The lights were low, the music nice, soft and easy with an atmosphere made to order. They were seated at a table that gave them ample privacy.

Vivian leaned over and whispered to Paul, "Isn't this awfully expensive?" She knew she shouldn't ask but she didn't want him to spend money on her extravagantly. She was sure he really couldn't afford this.

He knew she was pleased and it pleased him to know she was concerned about not wasting his money. He was glad it turned out to be such a nice place. It had been far too long since they had been on a date such as this. He felt he was as happy as he could ever hope to be. He had it all planned: he would propose to her tonight and they would set the date for their wedding—that is if she accepted his proposal. After all, George had promised him a substantial raise once he was married, so there shouldn't be a problem.

The service was superb; the waiters very attentive; the food delicious. There was a trio playing softly and Paul arranged for them to play their song, "Stardust", while Vivian had gone to powder her nose. He had purchased a nice set of rings, relatively expensive but not overly so, elegant with a beautiful setting.

She returned to the table and he kept glancing at his watch. The trio was to start playing at five minutes after the hour. Suddenly they were playing Stardust and Vivian noticed it right away. "Oh, Paul, they're playing our song."

At that moment he reached over and took her hand and said, "Vivian, as a minister I don't have much to offer you right now but I hope to one of these days. I know you are fully aware of what a preacher's wife has to contend with, but…well…," he stammered. Then blurted out, "Will you marry me?"

"Oh, Paul, how I have longed to hear those very words! Yes, I'll marry you. I've loved you since I first saw you on the train."

He took the rings from his coat pocket and gave them to her. "I hope you like the rings I selected. I promise to get a more expensive set for you later on."

"Why, Paul, they're lovely!" she said, opening the box. "These will do nicely. Thank you so much." She took out the engagement ring and handed the wedding band back to him. Then she gave him the engagement ring and held out her hand for him to place on her finger. Now that they were engaged he breathed a sigh of relief. He was so afraid she might not want to be a preacher's wife.

It was getting late and he knew she had to work in the morning. He had to be getting her home but still he lingered, dreading for the evening to end. Two or three minutes later he was to wish a thousand times over that they had left. Had they done so she would have been spared the shame and humiliation that was soon to follow. He was just about to escort her from the restaurant when they both saw them at the same time. George came walking through with a young, attractive blond lady on his arm. He stepped back to allow her to lead the way to their table.

She was dressed very smartly in a powder blue dress, and appeared to be no older than Vivian. George walked behind her with self confidence and carefree abandonment. Vivian quickly turned her head away and a muffled sob of shocked disbelief escaped her lips. She grabbed her purse and hurried from the place. He knew she was very upset but couldn't follow her until he had paid the bill. He found her sitting in the car crying, as he expected she would be, and sought as best he could to console her. When she had calmed down he started the car and turned toward home.

"How awful! I don't know why it shocked me so much. I guess I'm embarrassed more for you than I am for myself. I have suspected all along he was having his affairs." She stopped crying and dried her tears. "Do you still want to marry me, knowing what you do about my family?"

"Of course I do. You're not responsible for what your parents do. We all are only human and subject to make mistakes. Try not to think too much about it; it will only upset you the more."

"I'm so sorry this had to happen!" She began crying again. "Everything was going along so beautifully. I knew it couldn't last! Why did it have to happen just at this time?"

"For us, we will make it last!" he said determinedly, changing the subject to her mother. "I can't wait for your mother to be admitted to the home and begin her recovery. She will love the place we found for her."

They drove along in silence for a while and he knew her mind was on how she would now get those papers signed should George try to balk at signing them. "When Mother is cured and has become her own sweet self again it will mean so much to me as well as to herself. I can't ever thank you enough for your help and encouragement, your love and understanding. I'm sure that's why I love you as I do."

"I'm thankful to be able to help in any way that I can. How could I do any less for the someone I love so much. Besides, it's nothing more than what a minister is for: to be ready to to give of himself unselfishly in any way he can and to be a blessing."

"That's a wonderful philosophy. If only others felt the same way." He knew she was referring to her dad. "You know, I hate to mention it but it just occurred to me. What if Mother should hear of this and change her mind and decide not to go in for treatment. What do we do then?"

"We'll cross that bridge when we get to it. I don't think you have anything to be worried about unless your dad refuses to sign the papers."

They reached the parsonage and Paul escorted her to the door. "Thank you so very much for a lovely and unforgettable evening—in spite of what happened. I'll always treasure the memory of it. And don't be concerned about Dad signing the papers. I promise you, those papers are as good as signed already."

He suspected what her motive was and cautioned her not to say anything to her mother about the incident. "I'm sure it would do more harm than good and cause her to change her mind mind for sure."

"No, of course not. You're right. She probably wouldn't see any reason to go through with it." She gave him a goodnight kiss, opened the door, smiled at him and said, "Goodnight, darling."

"Goodnight, my love."

She closed the door softly behind her.

CHAPTER 10

The middle of September came at last and those concerned about David Stoddard's life were gathered in Superior Court for his trial. The honorable Daniel Snow was the presiding judge. He called to order and the trial got underway. Most of the witnesses were the same ones that participated in Colby Warfield's trial. It didn't take long for the trial to come to an end and for the jury to begin their deliberation. It took them only an hour to reach a verdict. They informed the bailiff, who in turn informed the Judge. He sat behind the bench looking down on a fifteen year old contrite boy who stood with his head bowed and with tears in his eyes.

"Young man, you stand before this court today for which you have been found guilty of robbery and for the maiming of one, Jesse Latimer. You have shown a blatant disregard for the welfare of others and what you did was a rash act of imbecility. However, it appears you have come to regret what you have done and are sorry. I have reviewed the evidence against you and, as well as I can tell, what you did was done without malice aforethought and that the shooting of Mr. Latimer was solely an accident during the struggle for the gun. Although you did act recklessly in what was nothing more than a youthful prank to get your Dad's attention that got out of hand. Do you have anything you wish to say to the court"

"Yes, Your Honor. I just want to say how really sorry I am for the trouble I have caused. I admit it was a foolish thing to do. I ask for everyone's forgiveness and for mercy from the court. Thank you," he said, his tears overflowing.

"This being your first offense I'm inclined to be lenient with you and give you a lighter sentence. I hereby sentence you to five years probation, fifteen hundred dollar fine, and fifty hours of community service. You are warned that if for any reason you are ever brought before this court again you will be given a much sterner sentence. Do you understand that?"

"Yes, your Honor."

Judge Snow rapped his gavel three times and declared, "This court is dismissed." And then the court erupted with joyous shouts of jubilation with hugging and backslapping. Harry embraced David and hugged him tightly with tears running down both of their faces. "Thank God, son!" he exclaimed. "I hope you never try anything this foolish again." He then turned to Paul, hugging him also, and said, "Brother Paul, I can't thank you enough for what you have done for us. If there is ever anything I can do for you in return just let me know."

"I'm happy to have been able to help," Paul said, "and should I ever need your help I won't hesitate to let you know." He then hugged David and said: "I don't know you very well but I hope we can become the best of friends. If there ever comes the time you feel you need someone to confide in feel free to give me a call at anytime."

"Thank you, Mr. Langley, and for standing by me. I'll remember that."

Paul left and went straight to his office to catch up on the work he had let go while attending David's trial. There was nothing more he could do on Adra's behalf until Vivian got her dad's signature on those forms. A lot of calls had come in that would keep him busy for a few days so he would take care of them right away.

It was one of the hardest things Vivian had to do to pretend that she knew nothing of her dad's infidelity. She had been careful not to mention it to her mother and probably never would. At least, not until she had completely recovered from her illness. She was more determined than ever to get those papers signed and he dare not refuse. Having seen him at the Embers with that woman, she wouldn't hesitate to confront him with it if he showed the slightest inclination of refusing to sign them. She was in her mother's bedroom reading to her while she was resting when her dad stopped by on his way to his room probably to get dressed to go out again. She had the forms laying close by ready for his signature.

"What's going on here?" he asked.

"Just reading to Mother while she tries to get a little rest. Say, Dad, are you going to be here for awhile or will you soon be going out again?"

George, unaccustomed to being questioned about his coming and going, stood looking at Vivian curiously. "Why, who wants to know?" he asked snidely.

"I do," she said curtly. "Because if you are I have some forms for you to sign for Mother to be admitted to the House of Hope for treatment for alcoholism."

"Alcoholism!" he spat out derisively. "Do you realize what that would do to me? It would destroy my standing in the community and my reputation in the whole city! There's no way I will agree to that."

"I think you will," she said defiantly. "Step into the next room with me. What I have to say must be discussed privately between you and me."

He walked into the next room with her following close behind. "What is this; why are you acting so obnoxious? It's so unlike you."

"Be that as it may. But I'm determined that Mother is going to get well. All you have to do is sign the papers, the rest is taken care of. I know about your fooling around with other women. I saw you at the Embers with that blond hussy and it was totally disgusting. Mother must not hear anything about this until she has fully recovered. Sign or suffer the consequences."

"Why, this is blackmail pure and simple!"

"Call it what you will but it's Mother I'm concerned with here. Now let's go back and get those papers signed."

They went back into Adra's bedroom and he went over and sat down on the side of the bed next to her. "I had no idea you were this ill. When did you reach the decision to go in for a cure? Do you think you will be able to endure all this entails?" asked the cowed and loving dutiful husband.

"I just recently decided to go with Vivian and Paul's prompting. As for enduring it, that remains to be seen." She began to cry very softly. "I do so want to be well again; my life has become one long continuous nightmare."

"And what do you think people are going to say when they find out that the Reverend George Blakely's wife is an alcoholic?"

"What does it matter!" Vivian said angrily. "All that matters now is that she get well and be damned what the people say! Have you forgotten the trial and the humiliation she endured there? There's hardly anyone who doesn't already know by now. Besides, Mother is the only one we need to be concerned about at this time. Personally, I couldn't care less what other people think or say about it."

This unusual outburst from his daughter got him to thinking. She had never used that tone of voice with him before. Of course, now he understood the reason for her defiance. She was angry with him after having seen him with that young lady at the Embers. He thought he caught a glimpse of her across the room when he first entered but thought it highly unlikely that it was her. Evidently it had been her since she had so brazenly confronted him with it. He had no other alternative but to comply with her wishes. If he didn't he was sure she was certain to do something drastic. He knew she hadn't told her mother as yet so he was safe for the time being.

"All right, I'll sign," he said, sheepishly. "After all, I want to see Adra well and happy as well as anyone else."

Vivian handed him a pen and he signed with a flourish, which was naturally becoming to George, and handed the pen back to her. "Let me know when one is permitted to visit and I'll drop by to see how things are going." He rose and walked quickly from the room.

The first thing she did was to call Paul and tell him the forms were signed. Paul called George and informed him that he would be taking Adra to the home for admittance on Saturday evening.

Adra sat in the back seat of the car quiet and withdrawn. Vivian knew it was because she was apprehensive and nervous not knowing what lay ahead of her. George's words kept echoing in her mind—' ' "Will you be able to endure it…able to endure it." ' She shook her head to clear it. She wouldn't allow those thoughts to defeat her. To make matters worse, it was raining and that only added to the gloom. The rain was needed but she wished it could have come at a later time.

Paul sat driving, saying very little, not wanting to interfere with mother and daughter's last few minutes together. It was a sad time, to be sure, but once Adra was released from the home this all would be soon forgotten.

The rain had slackened by the time they reached their destination. Paul drove to the front entranceway to let them out to keep them from getting wet. They waited for him to park and when he got back to where they were they all entered the building together. When they entered the office there was another lady on duty but she had been fully informed about Adra's coming. "You are Mrs. Adra Blakely, is that correct?" she asked, checking to make sure she was the right patient. "I'm Myrna Jones. Please be seated while I get a wheelchair to take Mrs. Blakely to her room."

Myrna was soon back and seated Adra in the chair. "You will love it here once you get adjusted to your surroundings. Now, let me get your folder and we will be on our way?"

When they reached the hall where Adra's room was located, Myrna turned her over to Lucy Symthe, the halls senior nurse.

"Hi, I'm Lucy," she said, introducing herself as she pushed Adra down the hall to her assigned room which was about middle way down the hall. The room was painted light blue and had white curtains hanging at the double windows. From her window there was a nice view of an open field and a small lake just beyond the fence.

Vivian and Paul waited in the hall while the nurse got Adra ready for bed and tucked her in. She came out and told them, "You can go in now. Please don't stay too long for she needs to get as much rest as she can before she begins here treatment."

They chatted with Adra for a few minutes then Vivian said, "Mother, we must be going now. They want you to get as much rest as you can. Tomorrow will undoubtedly be a busy day so we will come back to see you as soon as visitors are permitted. Try not to worry and if you need anything call us and we'll come running." She leaned over and kissed her on the cheek.

"That's right," Paul chimed in, "we want you to hurry and get well. We'll be back at the first opportunity we have."

As they were leaving, the nurse came in and gave Adra a shot to help relax her and ease her withdrawal symptoms. They figured she would be asleep by the time they reached the car. When they were in the car, Vivian said, "It's best for her, I know, but I hate to leave her there all by herself. I feel as though I'm deserting her to the lions."

"I understand how you feel," Paul sympathized. "But, as you said, "'…it's best for her.'" Just think, in a few months she will be well and happy again. I can't wait for that time to get here."

They were nearing home when Vivian looked over at Paul and said, "I may be wrong in saying this, but I don't think Dad cares one way or the other whether Mother gets well or not." She looked straight ahead before saying, "I hate it that you had to get involved in our personal affairs. Do you think once Mother is well they will get back together again?"

"Let's not look too far ahead and borrow trouble. Remember what Jesus said: Sufficient unto the day is the evil thereof. Only time will tell. Just do the best you can and that first week will be over and done with and your mother will be on her way to a full recovery. Then you will be able to visit with her and see for yourself what has been accomplished."

It's strange, isn't it, how people get themselves into these predicaments believing at the time it's what's best for them. Generally, it always turns out to be the wrong choice—-oh, look, what a lovely rainbow!"

It was raining just enough for the sun to break through in the clouds and produce a rainbow beautifully displayed just ahead of them.

"I believe that's a sign that everything is going to be all right."

"I certainly hope so. Forgive me if I seem a little pessimistic; so much has gone from bad to worse lately."

He felt that once the rain had stopped and the sun had come out she would feel a lot better. Especially, once she had gone back to visit with her mother. They drove the last few miles in silence, comfortable in each other's company and words were not always needed. He pulled into the garage, walked her to her mother's house so she could straighten up the place before returning to her own apartment. She would let her dad look after himself.

Just as Paul unlocked the door and stepped into his house the telephone rang. He picked it up only to hear a strange voice and the conversation went like this: "Is this the Reverend Paul Langley's residence?"

"Yes it is. Who is this?"

"Brick, a friend of Rosie Taggert's. I understand you know her."

"Yes, I know her. She's a waitress at the Beanery—or was. Why, is something wrong?"

"Only that she has been stabbed."

"She has been stabbed you say?"

"Yes, that's right. She's in St. Mark's hospital."

"Thank you for calling and telling me. I'll get over there right away."

He rushed into the hospital and up to the information desk. He inquired about Rosie and was told she was on the fourth floor in room 461. He talked with a nurse on that floor about visiting Rosie in her room.

"I'm sorry," said the nurse, "but you've already missed her. She has already been rushed into surgery. If you will please be seated we will let you know as soon as she comes out of surgery and is in the recovery room."

"Thank you. I'm Reverend Paul Langley and a friend of Rosie's. I'd appreciate getting to see her as soon as possible."

He sat down in the waiting room and picked up a magazine to occupy his mind while he waited. The next thing he knew the nurse was tapping him on the shoulder to waken him. "Miss Taggert is out of surgery now in in the recovery room. You may speak with the surgeon if you like. He's at the nurses station and his name is Dr. Sturges."

He hadn't expected to fall asleep. He glanced at his watch and saw that he had been waiting a little over an hour. He found the doctor filling out his report.

"Excuse me, Dr. Sturges, for interrupting you. I'm Reverend Langley whom Miss Taggert had been asking for. How is she doing?"

"It's really to early to tell yet but I believe she will survive if she manages to make it through the first twenty-four hours. She came through the surgery just fine and is one lucky lady to be alive considering the nature of her wound. Her assailant barely missed puncturing the Vena Cava, the large vein that discharges blood into the right auricle of the heart."

"When will I be able to speak with her do you think?"

"It will be anywhere from twenty-four to thirty-six hours. She will be on the critical list until then and unable to talk to anyone. I suggest you come back late tomorrow after noon."

"I'll do that. Thank you, Doctor. If she asks for me again will you please let her know I was here."

"Of course, Reverend."

Paul returned home, ate a light snack and got ready for bed. Not until he lay down did he realize just how tired he was. As he waited for sleep to envelope him his thoughts drifted to Arno. It occurred to him that it had been sometime since he had last seen him. He would drop by to see him in the morning to see what had taken place since he last talked with him.

He was up before seven and had slept soundly throughout the night, leaving him feeling rested and refreshed. He had a cup of coffee and a sweet roll for breakfast then went to write a letter to his mother while he waited to go to Arno's. It had been quite sometime since he had last written to her and he had quite a lot to tell her. He finished writing it and laid it aside, he would mail it later in the day.

He climbed the steps and knocked at the door. He knew Carl was back in school and he expected Arno to answer the door. He was surprised when Miss Minna opened the door instead.

"Why, brother Paul, what a pleasant surprise. Come in." She could tell by the look on his face that he was surprised at seeing her there and was probably wondering what she was doing there so early in the morning.

Paul was so taken aback he just stood where he was. "Is Arno in or has he already left for work?"

"Yes, he's here. He was just getting ready to leave. Come on in," she said again.

"I haven't seen any of you for a few days and was wondering how all of you were doing. I have been so busy for the last few days doing one thing or another," he said as Arno walked into the room. "I just attended David Stoddard's trial, poor kid, and he's lucky he got off like he did. What have you guys been up to?"

"Nothing much. Just the things we usually do. We're all doing well, especially since Minna and I have gotten married."

"Married! You got married and didn't invite me to the wedding," Paul said. He was surprised and a little hurt that he hadn't been asked to marry them.

"We had a simple wedding and was married by the Justice of the Peace with only his wife and one of my friends as witnesses," Minna informed him. "Otherwise, you would have been first on the list to marry us. Anyway, I'm no longer Miss Minna, but Mrs. Arno Holseman now. Just plain Minna to all my friends."

"I hope our decision to be married by a JP hasn't offended you. We neither one wanted a church wedding and thought this would be the best solution for us." Arno explained.

"I understand. It's just that I thought I should have been the one to perform the ceremony. I don't blame you at all. In fact, I'm very happy for both of you. I'm glad Carl now has someone to devote more time to him. How is he?"

"He's doing great and seems to be his old self again," Arno said. "Our biggest problem is keeping him away from George. We let him ride his bike to the Warfields to play with Perry on the weekends. That helps a great deal.,"

"Could I get you something to drink?" asked Minna.

"No, thank you. What I really came by for was to see if Carl could be our mystery guest at the Halloween party that's a litttle over a week away."

"We will ask him when he gets home this evening. I'm sure he would love to," said Minna. "Do we need to get a costume for him to wear?"

"No. I'll take care of that. I plan on having a contest and charge five cents for anyone who wants to guess who he is, a prize going to the one who guesses correctly. And he gets to keep the money from all who pay to guess."

"With a deal like that what has he got to lose. He will be anxious to do it." Arno opined.

"I've got to go. Have Carl come by the recreation hall this Saturday to see about devising a costume for him."

Minna saw him out, already at home as if she always lived there. "Come back when you can find the time. We're always glad to have you."

"Thank you, I will," he said as he descended the steps.

Paul returned to his house to make sure the doors were all secured then went to his office. He didn't hear any commotion coming from Ethel's office so he assumed that she hadn't come in yet. Finding there were no messages that needed his immediate attention, he decided to go to the Skyroom to look once again for that ledger he once saw, and anything else that could be used as evidence against George when the need for it arose. He checked the garage to see if George's car was there or not. It wasn't, so that meant he wasn't anywhere around, making it safer to do his searching.

He entered the Skyroom, which he was now rather familiar with, and began his search in the middle drawer which he thought was the one he remembered seeing it in. There was no ledger to be found there so he moved to the next drawer. If only I could find that ledger, he thought, it would simplify matters considerable. Where ever it was it was well hidden.

How George managed to conceal the things he had been doing for so long was more than he could understand. Surely someone knew about his chicanery but were more comfortable turning a blind eye toward it in order not to get involved. In one of the side drawers he found a bill from a pediatric clinic located in Covington, Kentucky. If he wasn't badly mistaken this would be the place where he would find Nora Letty, hidden away there by George until she had the baby. He was almost ready to give up his search when he glanced at the top of the desk and caught sight of a piece of paper just barely visible sticking out from beneath the desk pad. He pulled it from beneath the pad and saw that it was a deposit slip from a bank in Switzerland. He quickly copied down the telephone and account number then replaced it just the way he had found it. He left in search of a pay phone so this call could not be traced to him.

"Operator, I'd like to place a call to the International Bank of Switzerland," He gave her the number and waited. Soon he was talking with one of the tellers and after requesting the information needed he was surprised it had been so freely given. Now, at least, he knew that an account existed there. He felt like a traitor, yet it was something that he had to do. Obviously, there was wrongdoing going on here that had to be rectified.

He went to the Beanery for lunch but it didn't seem the same without Rosie being there. The waitress filling in for Rosie wasn't as friendly, but she was efficient. He finished his meal and left to go shopping for the things he would need for Carl's disguise. After purchasing what he thought he would need he took it to his house to make sure no one saw any part of it. It was very important that no one saw a single item Carl would be wearing in order to make it more difficult for anyone to identify him. If he didn't forget and say something and give himself away by his voice he was sure they could pull this off.

Ethel was gone when he got back to the office. She had probably gone out to lunch. He hadn't been in his office but a few minutes when the telephone rang. It was the hospital calling to tell that Rosie was still in ICU but was alert and asking for him again. He got up and left immediately to go and see her. He asked what room she was in and found here sitting up in bed propped up among a bunch of pillows watching a soap opera.

He knocked lightly on the door, stuck his head inside and asked, "Is it all right if I come in?"

He knew right away that she was doing okay but she didn't act very friendly toward him for some reason. He suspected she was pouting over something.

"Rosie, first off, how are you feeling?" he asked, stepping up to the foot of the bed.

She turned off the television before answering him. "I think I'll survive. But, before we go any further, tell me why you didn't show before I went into surgery?

There it was. He knew she was peeved with him about something. That was one of the things he liked about her, she was straight-forward and openly honest.

"Do you mean to tell me they didn't give you the message I left for you? I specifically told Dr. Sturges to tell you I was here. However, by the time I got word about your near fatal accident and got to the hospital you had already been taken into surgery. They wouldn't allow me to see you until twenty-four or more hours after your surgery. I'm sorry I didn't make it in time and am doubly pleased that you did."

When Rosie saw that I hadn't forsaken her or forgotten her, she readily became her old self again. "Then you're forgiven," she said, "but I was just teasin' anyway. I knew something had happened to prevent you from comin'. Come stand beside the bed closer to me. I can't talk very loud."

He did as she asked, knowing she hadn't gained back much of her strength yet. "Isn't this going to the extreme," he said jokingly, "just to get a little rest? Seriously though, what really happened anyway?"

"Nothing more than can be expected livin' in the ghetto as I do. Some punk grabbed my purse and when I wouldn't let go of it he stabbed me. I let out a piercing scream and he high tailed it leaving my purse intact. I had my week's pay in it and I wasn't about to let him get away with it."

"Could you identify him if you saw him again, or has he already been apprehended?"

She looked up at the ceiling pondering the question. "I saw him well enough but the shock of being stabbed seemed to have erased his likeness from my memory. I doubt if I could identify him." She paused a few seconds then went on. "No, as far as I know, he hasn't been caught—that degenerate!. Excuse my French. He probably never will be. The police don't take this sort of thing serious enough."

"Why didn't you just turn loose of the purse and let him have it. It wasn't worth taking a chance on your life. Your life's worth more than a weeks pay."

"Maybe so. But I work hard for my money and I didn't intend to let him get away without a fight. It has certainly helped me to see that Alaska has to beat this place all to pieces. As soon as I have completely recovered, Jack and I are out of here headin' in that direction."

"I'm so happy to hear that you have patched thing up with him."

"Sure as the sun sets in the west," she said, holding out her hand so I could see the ring was back on her finger. "It wasn't that I didn't want to go to Alaska. I just didn't think Jack really loved me. I was wrong, I know that now."

"Rosie, no one could wish you more happiness than I do. I sincerely hope it works out for you both. We will miss you and I'm so thankful your going to be all right. May I pray for you before I go?"

"Please do," she said solemnly.

After a short prayer he made ready to leave. "I must get out of here before I overtax your strength and end up doing more harm than good." She reached out her hand and Paul took it and held it warmly in his.

"Thanks, Preach, for comin' by and for bein' so nice to me." She smiled broadly at him. "If you're ever have an occasion to be in Alaska, be sure to look us up."

"I don't know if I'll ever be going up that way or not, but, if I ever do, you can be sure you'll be the first one I'll look for."

Paul made his way to the car and while driving back to the church he thanked God for sparing Rosie's life and for having had the privilege of knowing Rosie and could count her as a dear friend.

CHAPTER 11

Nora "Thompson" Letty stood at the window of her room looking out over the well kept grounds of the home for unwed mothers. Named "The Other Home", it was here that George had committed her under the alias of Nora Thompson. He wanted to make sure she was far enough away where she would be less likely to run into anyone he or she knew. Also, not to have to travel very far to visit her. She couldn't help but recall the events that had led her to be at a place such as this. She was thankful that he had chosen a place as nice as this instead of one of those shabby, run-down places that she couldn't have coped with at all.

The Other Home was made to be as comfortable as a home away from home could be. It was an old two story farm house that had been remodeled throughout and surrounded with a white picket fence. The exterior was painted white and the interior featured a color scheme for babies. Each room was painted in soft pastel shades of Lemon Yellow, Robin Egg Blue, Canadian Pink, and Mint Green. The home's success was credited, to a certain extent, to being selfsustaining. They raised most of their own food and vegetables, had their own cow, and enough chickens to supply them with fresh eggs.

The owner and operator of the home was Mary Blaume, a woman in her late fifties, a short five feet tall and rotund. She wore her hair, already completely gray, in a bun at the nape of her neck. She had a warm, ready smile for everyone and was sweet tempered. She had lost her husband to a massive heart attack two years earlier and, needing additional income, decided to transform her home into a home for unwed mothers. The money from her husband's insurance paid for the remodeling.

The fact that she, too, had been born illegitimately was a deciding factor in her decision. She remembered how difficult it had been for her mother and she wanted to help in some small way those unfortunate ones whom suffered from the same fate. She sincerely tried to be, as best she could, a "mother" to all the girls that came under her roof. She was affectionately called "Mama" Blaume and it didn't take long for any new girl coming in to realize her love for them and that she had their best interests at heart. Nora turned away from the window and looked about her room. Although it was of medium size it was adequate and permitted her to be all to herself. And right now that suited her just fine since there were so many things between her and George that were yet to be resolved. Once again her mind dwelt on the beautiful church wedding she had always dreamed of having and caring for any children she may have. She could almost see the nursery all done up in yellow, her favorite color, and of course the baby would be a girl....

She couldn't restrain the tears that spilled over each time she got to thinking about it. She forced herself to put those thoughts aside and concentrate on changing her way of thinking, realizing that reality was far different from what dreams could ever be. Needless to say, she had done a lot of crying lately and wasn't sleeping any too well. She believed that after she had a talk with George around the middle of November, he said he would be by about that time, that most of her problems would be solved or eliminated entirely. She couldn't wait to see him and looked forward to his visit, hoping it would bring about some sort of order and stability to her now disordered life. She still had complete faith and trust in him and was anxious to find out what he had managed to resolve concerning their getting married.

She checked the calendar and her spirits were lifted somewhat on seeing that it was now the later part of October. A little more than two more weeks and he would be here. Looking back to the time she came to the home she found she had been there only six weeks. Already it seemed a life time ago. She would have to find something to occupy more of her time. Then she got an idea; she would get a job somewhere nearby. She found the idea very appealing. "Why not" she said aloud to herself. George was presently sending the money she needed but what would she do if, for some reason, he should suddenly stop sending it. The possibility of that happening nagged at the back of her mind. She decided to talk with Mama Blaume about it just in case. Perhaps she might know where she could find a job close by.

She went in search of her and found her in the kitchen helping the cook prepare the evening meal busily making the biscuits. Mama Blaume looked up and saw Nora coming toward her as she wiped the hair back from her eyes.

"Mama Blaume, could I speak with you for a few minutes?"

"There isn't time right now dear. I must finish with these biscuits. Can it wait until after dinner?"

"Sure. No rush. That'll be fine." She turned to go and as an afterthought asked, "Could you come to my room so we could talk alone?"

"I'd be glad to," she said.

The meals were served buffet style, each person taking only what they could eat. It was also a rule that each one take their dishes to the kitchen when they had finished eating, cutting down on the work for the dishwasher. Nora finished her meal and went to her room to wait for Mama Blaume. She sat crocheting while she waited.

Mama Blaume was taking her dishes to the kitchen when the door bell rang. "I'll get it." she called out and went to the door.

"Telegram for Nora Thompson," he said, "sign here please." He handed her the clipboard for her to sign.

She stuck the telegram in her apron pocket and went to Nora's room. She tapped at the door and let herself in. She went over and sat down on the side of the bed. "Before you tell me what you wanted to talk to me about here's a telegram that just came for you."

Nora took the telegram and sat staring at it. They always made her nervous. Before opening it she looked at the address and noticed it was addressed to a Nora Thompson. "This isn't mine. It's addressed to a Nora Thompson, My last name, as you know, is Letty."

"Yes. I know. Thank you for being honest about it. I like it better than Thompson. Most of the girls here are ashamed for anyone to know their real name. Weren't you told that you were registered here under the name of Thompson?"

"No. Evidently George forgot to tell me he had registered me under an alias. So I'm a Thompson now. I must remember that. Excuse me," she said, stepping aside to read the telegram.

Nora,
Unexpected business matter has arisen stop
Will see you Thursday, following week stop
Until then take care.
GB

She replaced the message in the envelope and sat down beside Mama Blaume. The terse message contained not one word of endearment, leaving her a little stunned.

"I hope it wasn't bad news."

"No. Nothing like that. Just George, my benefactor, letting me know he won't be here as previously planned. It's because of things such as this that as made me realize I need to have an income of my own in case he should decide to stop sending me any money at all."

"I understand your concern and well you should be. What was it you wanted to speak with me about?"

"This may sound ridiculous, considering my condition, but I need to find a job. I was wondering if you could help me find one. It would have to be close by as I would have to walk to and from work. I love anything to do with children and I've done secretarial work and…"

"Here, here, not so fast." Mama Blaume interrupted. "You say you have done secretarial work?"

Nora felt herself blushing. She got carried away for a minute. "I'm sorry. Yes. I've done secretarial work."

"Then I may be able to help you. As a matter-of-fact, I may be able to get you a job where you can combine your secretarial skills as well as looking after children."

"Oh, Mama Blaume! Do you really think so? I…"

Again she interrupted. "Now wait a minute. Don't get your hopes up too quickly. I said maybe," she cautioned her. "I did know someone who had such an opening but it may have been filled by now."

Nora felt tears of gratitude fill her eyes and she was so relieved. She breathed a prayer that the job would still be available and somehow felt it would be.

"You're so kind. You'll never know how much this means to me and how much I appreciate it! If I do get the job, and I believe I will, somehow I'll repay you." Here the tears came again trickling down her cheeks.

"Let's wait and see if this comes to fruition first before we make and promises. Besides, you won't owe me a cent. I'll call first thing in the morning and let you know." She rose to go and Nora walked to the door with her.

"Thank you for being so sweet and kind. I love you, Mama Blaume. Goodnight."

***

Due largely to Mama Blaume's efforts, Nora got a job at a children's orphanage. It was called "A Doll and Dude Ranch" and was about three fourths of a mile just down the road from the home in which she was staying. She would be working part time until after the first week in November, which was when the lady she was relieving was leaving, then she would begin working full time as long as she could and then go back to part time again. She hoped to work until the middle of January then take a leave of absence until the birth of her baby. According to the doctor, she was due for delivery the last of February.

Her boss had agreed she could be off from work when George was to come for a short visit. He usually stayed only an hour or two and was gone. Sometimes she wondered why he bothered to come at all. She didn't want him to know that she was working; she feared that if he found out he would stop sending her the money he was presently sending. She always returned to the job as soon as he left. So far, so good. He was not the wiser. Fortunately, he always let her know when he was coming so she was able to be at the home when he arrived.

He arrived punctually on Thursday as he said. He stood staring at her, making her feel uncomfortable. "Why are you staring at me—is something wrong?"

"No. Nothing's wrong. But there seems to be something different about you. I keep trying to figure out what it is."

"It's just your imagination. I haven't changed at all. I just keep getting bigger is all."

He seemed to be more concerned about how far along she was and when the baby was to be born. Lately he seemed to be getting a little more distant with each one of his visits. He certainly wasn't as affectionate as he once was. To her it was obvious that he wasn't as pleased to see her as she was to see him. "I still say there's something different about you."

"It's probably my hair. It's cut much shorter than I usually have it cut. One of the girls here cut and styled it for me. Don't you like it?"

"It's okay I guess. Just…different." he said again, making no attempt to embrace her.

She had made up her mind that she wasn't going to beg him for his affection. But in spite of herself, before she knew it, she blurted out, "Aren't you going to kiss me?"

He kissed her, but it wasn't the same as before. There was a stiltedness in his kiss and she knew something had changed. He let go of her and went over and stood looking out the window. She didn't quite know of what to make of the way he was acting. As she stood watching him she saw him sort of stumble and grab hold of the window sill to steady himself. She rushed over to where he was.

"Are you all right?" she asked, a little alarmed.

"Yes. I'm okay. I just felt a little weakness in my knees."

"Come over and sit down for a few minutes until it passes." She helped him to the chair.

His next words disturbed her even more. "What if I can't get a divorce? What will you do then?"

"What else could I do but have the baby and try to make it as best I could." She sat down on the side of the bed.

"If only you had aborted the child. I would have made matters so much simpler."

The way he spoke of the baby as "the child" sent a slight chill down her spine. It sounded so cold and callus.

"It might have simplified matters, but I couldn't think of deliberately doing away with my baby. I want this baby whether you do or not."

Then he suddenly changed back to himself again. It was the first premonition she had that he could possibly be ill in someway; that something wasn't exactly right.

"Forget I ever mentioned it. It's too late now anyway. But I still think it would have been the best solution for both of us. I was just grabbing at straws trying to find a way out of our dilemma." He went over and sat down next to her on the bed. "I've been thinking. Would you consider giving the baby up for adoption?"

"Absolutely not! It may solve a lot of things but it is out of the question. I don't want to hear another word about my baby being adopted. I'm having this baby and I'm keeping it and that's all there is to it!"

Their quarrel was the worse one they had ever had yet. She surprised herself by defying him. She had never done that before.

"Have it your way. After all, it's you that will have to suffer the consequences."

"That may well be. But what do you think of my getting a job close by here somewhere?"

"A job! what do you need a job for? Isn't the money I send you sufficient enough to cover your expenses here?"

"It isn't that. I need something to help me pass the time and not be shut up here in this room all day alone."

When she first mentioned about a job it shook him up a bit but after thinking about it for a minute or two he felt it wasn't such a bad idea after all. It might ever save him a little money. "You know, I've given some thought about the job situation and I don't think that's such a bad idea at that," he said. "What sort of job do you have in mind?"

"Oh, I'll find something," she said, not telling him she already had the job, "Anyway, I may change my mind and forget about the whole idea."

"That's a woman's prerogative. Anyway, I've got to be going." He got up to leave. "Call me if anything comes up you can't handle."

She watched him until he disappeared from sight. She then lay down on the bed and cried until she fell into a fitful sleep. When she awoke it was nearing time for the evening meal. George had so upset her that she that she didn't want anything to eat. With the way he had been acting lately she was sure he wouldn't be there for her when the time came for the baby's birth. She was getting more and more to the point where she was altogether losing her confidence in George. She was so thankful that she had a job now and did not have to be totally dependant on him.

***

There always seemed to be some kind of activity going on at the Recreation Hall to keep the youth occupied and busy. Carl made his way there to meet with Paul as he had been requested. He was so excited with the prospect of being the mystery guest and the promise of getting all that money. The first thing he planned to do with it was to buy a nice Christmas present for his dad and Minna. He entered the hall and went to where Paul sat at a table waiting for Vivian to return with his drink.

"Carl, I'm glad you could come. Did your dad or Minna tell you what I wanted you for?"

"Yes. They told me and I'm so excited! Do I really get to keep <u>all</u> the money that's paid to guess who I am?"

"That's right. Every penny of it."

"Really! Wow, I'll be rich!

"You've got to be very careful not to say anything that would give your identity away. A lot of them will recognize your voice if they should hear it so you must not say a single word. If you slip and give away your identity away you won't make much money. Do you think you can keep from talking?"

"I think so. I don't care what you disguise me to be except an ole girl. I ain't going to be any ole girl!"

Vivian returned with Paul's drink and brought an extra one for Carl. She figured he would be there by the time she got back. "Who isn't going to be an ole girl?" she asked.

"Carl was telling me what he would and would not be and a girl was one of them."

"What's wrong with girls; don't you like girls?" teased Vivian.

"Well, not really. I like you and Minna though," Carl said in their defense. He adored Vivian because she always gave him so much needed attention.

"How about a costume of a hobo-clown. Would you like that?" said Paul.

"Cool!"

"Whatever you do you must be sure not to tell a single soul who you're going to be. Not even your best friend Perry. I has to be a secret just among the three of us," Vivian cautioned him.

"I haven't been able to keep up with your dad. What's he into now?"
"He says that since he has married Minna his life has become more orderly and has more time to devote to his hobby. I don't know what they are so excited about but Minna says she believes Dad will soon develop a new rose—a blue one. Who ever heard of a blue rose."

"Say, that would be something!" Paul said, realizing what this could mean to Arno <u>and</u> the church if his experiment proved to be successful.

"I think he has done a tremendous job on the roses at the church this past season. They were beautiful!" Vivian enthused. "But, Carl, I don't think your Dad would want you to mention the rose to anyone until he has perfected it."

"Is it something real important? Please don't tell him I told you guys. Gosh! Maybe he will make a million dollars."

Paul pulled Carl over close to him and gave him a hug. "It is something real important and could turn out to be a very big event. I don't expect he will make a million on it but it could make him famous."

"I won't mention it to anyone ever again. I promise."

"Neither shall we," Vivian promised too.

"In just a few more days the Halloween party takes place," Paul said to Carl. "You have to slip over to my office so we can get you into the costume without anyone seeing us. Be sure no one sees you come in. Okay?"

Carl nodded his head that he understood.

"We will tell Minna, or your Dad, when you are to come to the office. We will see you then," Paul said.

Carl ran all the way home as excited as if he was going to be rich.

"I've got to be getting back to my apartment. It's a mess. I've got to get it cleaned up for Thanksgiving. I plan to prepare a nice dinner for the two of us—unless you have other plans that is," she added.

"That's wonderful. I'd love it. No. I don't have anything going on at that time."

"It's a date then," she said as she turned to go. "Goodbye now. I'll see you shortly."

"Bye, dear. I look forward to it."

Paul busied himself with preparations for the Halloween party and setting things up in the rec hall for the children's enjoyment. He was satisfied with his endeavors and trusted that everything worked out. His biggest concern was for Carl. He hoped it all went well for him.

Then before he knew it the day for the party finally came and everybody had a wonderful time. Paul was really pleased with its success. So much so, that he was already looking forward to the next one. What pleased him most was that Carl fooled everyone and never uttered a single word. When they counted the money he had twelve dollars and seventy-five cents. He couldn't believe that no one guessed who he was.

Vivian helped all she could since she now had Saturday and Sunday off at work. She liked it much better being off Saturday instead of Monday. So many more things took place at the rec hall on Saturday.

It was late by the time they got the place straightened out and back in order. She got ready to leave to go back to her apartment and went to tell Paul she was leaving.

"I'll see you in the morning at Sunday school, Lord willing. Goodnight,"

"Goodnight, my love," he said, blowing her a kiss.

CHAPTER 12

It seemed to him that he and Vivian were always telling each other goodbye or goodnight. He looked forward to the day they could be married and go home together. He meant to make that happen in the very near future. It suddenly dawned on him that he didn't believe that he or Vivian either one had told her mom and dad that they were engaged.

In the meantime, George was making his way to the airport after having visited his paramour whom he has hidden away in a home for unwed mothers. He had a lot on his mind, personal and otherwise, and it made it difficult for him to concentrate on any one thing. Trying to sort it all out caused his head to begin throbbing. He searched his pockets to see if he had anything that would deaden the pain until he reached the airport. He found a couple of Aspirin and, fortunately, since he always carried a bottle of water in the car for such an emergency, he swallowed them and felt some relief, although the aspirin wasn't strong enough to completely deaden the pain. The headaches were coming more frequently now, still he hadn't taken the time to see a doctor. Maybe he could find the time soon after he got back.

***

His mind went back to a further conversation he and Nora had had before he left and he was aware how they had skirted around the real issues that concerned them both. He recalled how she had asked, '"When do you think you will be coming back again? I wish you wouldn't stay away so long and would come by a little more often; it gets so lonely here." '

' "Right now I really don't have any idea. I'm kept pretty busy but I'll let you know when I can make it." '

When it came time for him to leave she walked to the car with him. ' "I'll be waiting to hear from you." ' she said, leaning down to kiss him on the cheek. ' "I love you," ' she said, hoping he would tell her the same. But he didn't. Before he pulled away she said, ' "I don't mean to nag but the baby will be born in about four more months, more or less, and I'd like very much for her to have a name. It would mean more to me than anything." ' Of course she didn't know if the baby was going to be a girl or a boy, but she was hoping for a girl.

He sat gripping the steering wheel, the whiteness of his knuckles showing as he looked straight ahead. He relaxed and released his grip and turned to look at her. ' "I'm doing the best I can. After all, I can't force the issue. By the way, you never mentioned anything about your physical condition. What does the doctor say are the chances of the baby surviving?" '

She had laid her hand on his arm before saying, ' "I'm sorry. I thought I had told you. He says I'm doing fine and that everything is coming along nicely—barring no complications. He wasn't expecting any problems with the delivery." '

With no further word he said, ' "Bye now. I'll see you later," ' and drove away without a backward glance.

He had left her with the impression that he hoped she would lose the baby, somehow by the way he kept asking what were the chances of its survival. She had stood looking after the car until it was out of sight.

***

He reached the airport where he returned his rental car then boarded the plane for Blakeville. He waited until they were airborn then asked the stewardess for a glass of water. He took a quaalude, the only thing he found that would wipe away the pain completely. As he sat waiting for the pill to take effect, his thoughts went back to Nora's last words just before he drove away. He couldn't seem to get them out of his mind. They kept reverberating over and over ' "...the baby to have a name...the baby to have a name." ' She's trying to put pressure on me and I don't like that. If I could think of a way to rid us of that child it would solve my biggest problem, his thoughts continued, but that's out of the question. By the time the plane reached its desired altitude and leveled off the pain was gone.

The next time the stewardess came by he ordered a scotch and soda although he knew he wasn't supposed to mix alcohol with the "quads". He sat sipping his drink and by the time he finished it he was ready for a nap. The next thing he knew, the stewardess gently shook him awake to tell him to fasten his seat belt, they would be landing shortly.

On the way to his car he noticed he had a tendency to stagger a little. He felt it was due more to the quads than the alcohol. He would have to try and cut back on his use of them. He left the airport and drove to the institution where Adra was being treated. His main reason for doing so wasn't his concern for her treatment but primarily to ask her for a divorce. First he would see how much she had improved before he mentioned it to her.

When he entered the parking lot he was impressed before even going inside. The place was nicer than he had expected. He was sure it was going to cost a fortune. He didn't mind as long as he got the divorce he wanted. It was his first visit and, in all likely hood, it would probably be his last if she consented to a divorce. He wondered what the staff would think of him for not visiting before now. He had lost track of how long she had been in there. He judged it to be about three weeks. Actually, she was nearing the end of her fourth week.

He walked into the office and was greeted by Mrs. Orell. She gave him a friendly smile. "May I help you?"

"Yes, thank you," George said politely. "I'm the Re...er...I'm George Blakely. My wife is a patient here. I'd like to see her if I may." He didn't want them to know he was a minister; he was embarrassed that his wife was there. His attempt to hide his profession was unnecessary, for they knew all there was to know about him.

"We are so pleased that you could graciously find the time to come visit your wife. We believe visits from family and friends bolster the patient's moral. She's in room 210. We trust you will find her much improved."

He detected a touch of sarcasm in her voice and knew the had been gently reproved. But that didn't bother him. He didn't let the likes of her faze him. He would do as he pleased. He walked away without a word. He found her room and tapped lightly on the door, opened it and walked in.

Adra was sitting next to the window reading a magazine. He saw at once that she was indeed much improved. She looked up and saw it was George who had entered. She laid aside the magazine to greet him, glad to see him in spite of her resolve not to show it.

"Oh, it's only you, George. I'm humbled that you could finally find the time to spare to come and visit me," she said indifferently, not caring one way or the other that he had come at such a late date.

"Why is everyone being so sarcastic? I get it from the gal in the office and now you. Anyway, she said I would find you much improved and you look as if you have."

"I'm over the worst of it and believe I'll make it after all—with no thanks to you. Why have you waited so long before coming by?"

He went to a chair, pulled it over next to her and sat down. He had to be careful not to make her angrier than she already was if he expected her to consent to a divorce. "I'm sorry (he wasn't, really). I simply couldn't get here before now. I haven't been feeling well myself

180

and with having so many things to take care of it was impossible for me to get here any sooner. He made no mention of the time spent in getting Nora settled in that establishment in Kentucky. "How much longer do you think you will be here?"

"It all depends on how well one progresses in their recovery. They seem to be pleased with my progress. I feel better than I have felt in a long time. I've come to believe I'll recover completely, thanks to Vivian and Paul."

There it was: another put down. He ignored it. "You may think I'm being facetious, and you may take this for what it's worth, but I believe you're going to make it too," he said, to soften her for the real reason he came.

"Why the sudden change, George? You should know I'm well aware of your tricks and persuasive power. I don't believe you! You could care less about me or whether I get well or not." She looked him straight in the eye and said, "What is it you really came by here for? I'm sure it wasn't for my benefit."

He got up from his chair, walked over and stood looking out the window to get away from her penetrating gaze. "All right, I'll tell you the real reason why I came here! I want a divorce."

His words both surprised and shocked her. She hadn't expected it to come to this. She realized their relationship had deteriorated and they had grown apart. Yet, actually hearing him ask for a divorce hurt her terribly and filled her with dismay. She had hoped by committing herself to be cured it would bring about a change in their marriage and draw them together once again. But she had evidently put off her treatment too long and now it was too late. She began to cry softly, tears of remorse overwhelming her.

George waited until she had done crying and composed herself, untouched by her pain and suffering. "Well, do you consent to our getting a divorce or not?"

As she dried her eyes she said, "I'm sorry. I had hoped it wouldn't come to this, that we would see what we were doing to each other and try to correct it. I guess it was foolish of me to think we could recapture the love we once had for each other. Apparently, I didn't make amends soon enough."

"It isn't all your fault; I'm guilty too. However, I'm as sorry as you are believe me. But we couldn't possibly pick up where we left off. Too many things have transpired for us to try and do anything about it now."

"Are you sure this is what you want? It's not what I want," she said. "If you are certain this is what you want I must have time to think it over before deciding what to do."

"Yes, I'm certain," he said, without hesitating, not quite believing she was acquiescing so meekly. He turned from the window and stood next to her. "This may or may not come as a surprise to you, but I have fathered a child by another woman and she desperately wants the child to have a name."

He didn't know why he had the need to further humiliate her, but he guessed it was because of the humiliation she caused him when she admitted publicly of being an alcoholic.

She rose from her chair and faced him, the anger clearly visible in her eyes and voice. "You are so disgusting! How could you do such a thing! But, you're right, it doesn't surprise me. I've suspected that you were being unfaithful all along. I was willing to overlook your faults, up to a certain point, but this I can't abide. Now, get out of here!" she said vehemently. "And I want you out of the house by the time I'm released from here."

"Don't you worry! I'll be only too happy to get out!" He stormed out of the room about as angry as he could get.

He had barely got out of sight when nurse Lucy entered Adra's room with a dose of her medicine and found her crying and greatly upset. "Mrs. Blakely, what's wrong; what has upset you so much?" she said with alarm.

Through her sobs she managed to tell her a little of what had taken place. Lucy could see that she was trembling and badly in need of a sedative. She coaxed her back to bed. It was unfortunate, but what had happened had almost destroyed what progress had been made. She returned and gave her the shot then went to enter a report on her chart of her condition.

When George reached his car he sat for a minute trying to figure out what had caused him to go so far as to reveal his pending fatherhood. He was sure she would attempt to take him for all he was worth out of spitefulness and revenge. "How could I have been so stupid?" he said aloud to himself. He started the car and headed straight for the club. As he drove along he began to go over the course of events and concluded that he wasn't so stupid after all. What does it matter whether I get a divorce or not, he thought, I can have a good time with the ladies married or not. He had no intention of marrying Nora, regardless of what the outcome may be.

It was still early in the evening when he reached the club, and, since Adra had ordered him out of the house, he would make the club his permanent residence since he already had a room there anyway. Being a third owner of the club didn't hurt either. The other two partners in the venture were none other than mayor Josh Adams and judge Daniel Snow. So far they had managed to keep their ownership from been known by buying the property under the title of the "BAS Enterprises." They were well aware that if they were ever discovered they would be defrocked, dethroned, and demeaned. Named the Stellar Club, only the influential and well-to-do were admitted for membership. It was an all male club and females were only permitted entrance on the weekend as guests of members in good standing. Even with stringent rules the club had been a success from its inception.

George entered his room, turned on the light and checked to see that everything was just as he had left it. Satisfied that nothing had been disturbed, or was missing, he went to the dining area for a sandwich and a drink. While he sat eating, a young man whom he did not recognize, approached him and said, "Hello, George. It's nice seeing you again. Mind if I join you for a few minutes?"

"Not at all. Have a seat," George said, taking a bite of his sand-wich while trying to remember where they had met. He drew a blank. "Obviously, you know me, but I'm afraid I don't remember you or your name."

"The name is Cranston. Frank Cranston. I was a guest here a few weeks ago and played a round of golf with you and some of your friends. I'm a reporter with the Morning Star."

"Oh yes, I remember you now." The fact that Frank was a reporter made him rather nervous. He wondered what he was snooping around for or what he might be on to. He saw his face light up slightly with a smile by his remembering him. To put him at a disadvantage he asked, "Are you still in dirty journalism?"

The smile left his face. He would have to be very careful what he said while Frank was around lest he slip and give things away. If he got hold of the slightest bit of information of his ownership in the club, or his possible divorce, it would mean his downfall and financial ruin. To keep ahead of him, he made mention of an article Frank had writ-ten after Adra's appearance in court. Bordering on sensationalism, the headline read: "Minister's Wife Admits Being Alcoholic".

"Do you call up front, straight-forward journalism dirty? I prefer to think of it as…well, you know, telling it like it is." He pulled a pen and pad from his coat pocket before going on. "What I really want to talk about is a tip I recently received—anonymously of course. It seems that you have an interest in…" here he paused for dramatic effect before continuing, …say this club for instance, among other things. I know it sounds far out; but who ever heard of a minister owning a club? Anyway, that's what my informant said. Any comment?"

"That's the most asinine, outlandish, ridiculous thing I've ever heard!" George exclaimed as innocently as he knew how, being careful not to concede to the accusation and getting more nervous as the conversation continued. He had to think of some way to get rid of this guy—but quick. While he tried to think of just the person to send him to he asked, "Are you sure you can't give me the name of the bearer of this bit of gossip? It could be someone I know."

"A tipster never ever, if at all, give their name. They just slip one the tip and let you take it from there," Frank replied. "I've noticed you hang around here a lot, and that's your business, but isn't that a little peculiar?"

"Not in the least. Especially when the food is good. And I have to stay somewhere and this place is as good as any other."

"Then am I to assume that you and your wife are getting a divorce?"

"You may assume no such thing!" George said, getting a little hot round the collar. "At the moment we're just estranged." Then it came to him how to get rid of this guy. "Listen, I'm not the man you should be talking to. You need to talk to William Engleton, the manager of this place. Come along, I'll take you to his office and introduce you to him."

"Now we're getting somewhere."

William Engleton, "Bill" to his friends, was a man of considerable size and no one tried to push him around. He had once played quarterback at one time on a now long forgotten team and had been sought out by the owners of the club to act as its owner-manager as a front for them. He was accustomed to facing the press and adept at giving evading answers. George tapped on the door, waited until he heard Bill call "Come in", then ushered Frank into the office. George introduced them. "Bill, this is Frank Cranston, a reporter with the Morning Star. Frank, Bill Engleton." As they shook hands, George went on, "Frank has a few questions he'd like to ask you. It seems that someone has led him to believe that I own this club."

Bill laughed. "Very funny," he said. "Have a seat Frank. I think I can answer your questions without too much difficulty."

George made a hasty retreat knowing Bill would answers Frank's questions, yet, at the same time, being careful not to give him any substantial information of actual fact. Once clear of the office and the reporter, George stopped in the hall and took several deep breaths while circling both elbows back as far as he could to relieve the tension between his shoulder blades. On his way back to his room he caught sight of the mayor who, in all likelihood, was headed for the bar. He hurried to intercept him.

"Quick," George said, grabbing hold of his arm, "let's go to my room. I'll explain when we get there."

Once in the safety of George's room, the mayor stood puffing from the exertion of climbing hurriedly up a flight of stairs. "What is all this cloak and dagger stuff about?" he queried, sitting down in the nearest chair.

"Would you happen to know a Frank Cranston, a reporter from the Morning Star?"

"Yes. It so happens that I do. Why?"

186

"Well, I didn't at first. He's in Bill's office talking with him right now. He has been asking questions—prying is what he's actually doing—trying to find out who the owner of this club is. It seems there's a fly in the ointment. Someone has tipped him off that I own the club and I have a pretty good idea who that someone is. In my opinion it has to be Harry Stoddard, although I could be wrong. He has just recently resigned from the board and possibly could be holding a grudge about something."

"We could find out easy enough," Josh said. "I'll have two of my men pay him a "social" call and warn him of the error of his ways. I don't think we would have any more trouble with him. By the way, I'm glad you spotted me and let me know that reporter was here. I would have one whale of a time trying to explain my presence here at this time of the day. He would have been able to put the two of us together and come up with quite a tidbit."

I suggest you wait until we see if we can find out who actually tipped Frank off about the club before we say or do anything to anyone. We could get into a lot of trouble should we accuse the wrong man."

"You're right at that. I'll wait."

"It wouldn't do for any of this to get out. I don't mind telling you—I asked Adra for a divorce today and if she should happen to get hold of it she would take me to the cleaners." He sat down next to the phone. "Do you think there's any chance of Dan showing up here this afternoon?" George was one of a few who called the judge Dan.

"It's possible. Do you have his number? Just call and tell him to stay away from here until after Frank leaves."

As he reached for the phone it rang. "Hello...uh huh...I see. He's gone did you say? ...you are sure...all right, thanks Bill." He relayed the message to Josh. "That was Bill, of course. He said Frank has left and he would fill us in with the details later. Are you going to be around here for awhile or do you have to get back to City Hall?"

"No. I'm finished there for the day. I told them I was off to a ribbon cutting ceremony. Why, what do you have in mind?"

"I was wondering if, after I have taken care of some business with my broker, we could call Dan and ask him to meet us here, then we all could go to Madam Suzette's this evening for a little fun and relaxation. I'm sure all of us could use a little French atmosphere."

"Say, that's a great idea!" Josh agreed, rising to his feet. "To tell you the truth I'm here to meet a guy about a business deal myself. You call Dan and if he wants to go you can come by the bar for me." He went to the door to leave. "I'll see you guys there."

By the time they all had taken care of personal business deals and were ready to leave for Madam Suzette's, they had had several rounds of drinks and were feeling far younger than their years. They left the club arm in arm, George between Josh and Dan to support him. It turned out that Josh was the soberest of the three so it was left up to him to do the driving although he wasn't in the best shape to do so either. They were laughing and singing and carrying on in happy anticipation of their intended destination. Since Josh was doing the driving they took his car to get there. George chose to sit in the back by himself.

Dan turned to George and said, "Why do you want to sit back there all by yourself? You should have gotten up front with us."

"I thought it would be a little too crowded. I don't like close quarters."

Dan figured that George had drank far too much as he detected a slur to his speech. He obviously had drank more than they had thought he had. Josh turned on the radio, since their conversation had dwindled down next to nothing. And when they turned onto the street that would take them the last few miles to Madam Suzette's, neither one of them had noticed George slip down on the seat and stretch out. By the time they pulled into the parking lot George was not to be disturbed.

"Well, men, we're here," Josh announced, turning to look at George. "I want you to look at that!" he exclaimed to Dan. "I do believe he has passed out on us."

They got out of the car and tried to rouse him, but to no avail; he was out like a light.

"Can you believe this? He was the one that suggested we come here in the first place," Josh said. "About the only thing we can do is leave the windows rolled down a bit and let him be."

"Come on. Let's the two of us go and soak up some of that French atmosphere he was talking about," Dan said. "He probably doesn't need any French atmosphere anyway."

They spent the better part of an hour enjoying themselves and left to return to the car. There they found George still sleeping as soundly as they had left him. They got in the car and Josh headed back to the club. They had been driving for about five or ten minutes when they heard George stirring and then sit up in the seat.

"Aren't we just about there?" he asked. "I can't believe it takes this long to reach Madam's place."

Josh and Dan both burst out laughing.

"Man, you missed out on the whole thing," Dan told him. "We got there only to find you had passed out and we couldn't rouse you. We're on our way back to the club now."

"You've got to be kidding me! It's a joke, right?"

"No, seriously, we're not kidding," said Dan

"Say guys, don't you give me away on this. I'd never be able to live it down."

"Would we do a thing like that to you?" Josh replied and they both started laughing again.

Chapter 13

The ringing of the phone wakened Paul. As he reached to answer it he glanced at the clock. It was only six o'clock. Who could be calling this early in the morning he wondered.

"...Yes, this is he...my father has had what...a stroke!...yes, I understand. I'll come as soon as I can get there...Yes, thank you. Bye."

It was hard for him to believe that his father had had a stroke; he was only fifty years old. He immediately called the club and left a message for George to call him at his earliest convenience. While waiting for George's call, he began packing a few clothes he would need for the trip. Just as he finished packing, the phone rang. It was George.

"I got your message and called as soon as I heard. I'm sorry to hear about your dad. Take all the time you need and we'll do our best to keep things moving along while you're gone. Is there anything else I can do for you?"

Paul was surprised that George was being so nice. "No, thank you. I'll call you when I get back and let you know when I've returned."

As soon as he finished talking with George, he called Vivian. "Sorry to call you so early, but my Dad has had a stroke and I'm getting ready to leave right away."

"I'm so sorry to hear that. I'll be praying for him, and you be careful."

"I will. Don't worry. I'll call and let you know when I get back. Bye, sweetheart."

Paul decided to go by bus, rather then by train this time. When he arrived he found that everything still looked the same. He took a taxi to the house and would drive his dad's car while he was there. He went straight to the hospital where he found his mother sitting alone in his dad's room. She looked tired and seemed to have aged so much. It was probably caused by the strain of his dad's illness. He would do what he could to help ease her burden while he was there. She rose and greeted him with a hug and kiss and then began to cry again.

When she regained her composure she said to him, "I'm glad you could come. This has been such a shock! It happened so unexpectedly. He's been asking for you."

"I got here as soon as I could. You take it easy and try not to worry too much. How is he doing?"

"He's doing a little better. At first I didn't think he was going to make it."

He stood by the bed and looked down at his dad and was surprised how much he appeared to have aged. He was on oxygen and his complexion was so gray looking. His mouth was slightly drawn down on the left so he knew the stroke had affected his left side. He took hold of his right hand and kissed him on the forehead. He opened his eyes and tried to give him a smile, pleased to see that he had come, but was unable to do so.

"We want you to hurry and get well and not worry about a thing. I'll see that everything is taken care of while I'm here," he assured him.

He felt a light squeeze on his hand and knew he understood. He stayed for a few minutes more than left, taking his mother home so she could get a little rest. When she reached home she went straight to the kitchen to prepare them something to eat.

"Are you hungry? What would you like for me to fix you?"

"I'm starving. If it isn't too much trouble, how about some of your delicious fried chicken, with biscuits and gravy. I haven't had a meal like that since I left."

"No trouble at all. You go sit down and rest a little while I get it ready."

Paul sat down in a comfortable chair, picked up a magazine laying close by and had hardly glanced at it before he was asleep. A light tapping on his shoulder awakened him.

"It's ready, come and eat. I hated to waken you; you were sleeping so peacefully. I know you must be very tired."

"Some. That bus ride did me in. It's rougher than riding the train."

He enjoyed the meal, it was delicious. He got up from the table and started gathering the dishes to take to the kitchen in order to help her with them but she would have none of it.

"You go sit down and relax. I'll do them."

"Where do you want me to sleep?"

"Why, in your own room, of course. I've kept it just the way it was before you went away."

"Then I'll go lie down for awhile. But, before I do. I've got to call Vivian and let her know that I arrived safely."

He told her he expected he would be back by the end of the week. He judged his dad would be out of the hospital and back at home in a couple more days and was doing as well as could be expected. The doctors were predicting a full recovery. After he hung up from talking to her he called George as he had promised. George was being so solicitous he couldn't help wondering what he was up to now.

After his nap he got up and they returned to the hospital. He couldn't keep his mother away for very long, she was spending every spare minute she had there. He had to have a talk with her to find out if there was anything she needed any help with, or anything he could take care of for her that she couldn't take care of herself. Now that she couldn't depend on her husband until he had fully recovered, she would have to learn to take care of things on her own.

Paul was in bed by nine o'clock and was still asleep at eight o'clock the next morning. He couldn't believe he had slept so late. He dressed and went to the kitchen where his mom was preparing bacon and eggs, gravy and biscuits for him.

"I can't believe I slept as late as I did. I'm always up by six, no later than seven, at my place. What do you think made the difference?"

"You were probably more tired than you realized. Will you be going back to the hospital with me today?"

"I thought I would drop you off at the hospital, then go on to the mall to see if I might run into someone I know. Then go by for a short visit with Dad and then take you home when you're ready to go."

At the mall, the first person he ran into was his former girlfriend Sueann. He exchanged a few pleasantries with her then moved on. She was a sweet girl, but nothing compared to Vivian. He wandered around a little while longer then left to see his dad.

The hospital released him the next day just as he thought they would. Paul helped his mom arrange for a nurse to help her care for his dad, then got ready to return to Blakeville. He would drive himself to the bus station in his dad's car and his mother would drive it back.

She hugged and kissed him then bade him goodbye. "Be sure to call and let me know that you arrived home safely. Also, be sure to write me and let me know how everything is going. Goodbye, my son. I love you."

He arrived home without any mishap and found things just as he left them. To his surprise, the preacher had taken care of all the messages, or had someone else to take care of them, and for this he was grateful. He called Vivian to let her know he was home and, while talking to her, made plans to take her out to dinner at their favorite restaurant, The Embers. They hadn't been back there since the episode with George and his lady friend.

November was now gone, taking with it Thanksgiving and the wonderful service they had had. It was now the middle of December and he was putting on a play with the children who were busy practicing their parts. He really enjoyed Christmas; it was his favorite time of the year. He loved everything about it. The color, the sparkling lights, the love in everyone's heart, making them so kind and friendly, and the giving of gifts. He was also anxiously looking forward to June. He and Vivian had set the date for when they would be married. He hoped his mom and dad would be able to make it to the wedding.

He was in his office sitting at his desk. He pressed the intercom button to Ethel's office and could hear her busily at work. He tried the preacher's office and found, to his surprise, he was in his office too. He wondered why he was in so early this morning. He usually didn't show up before eleven at the earliest. He checked his calendar to see if there were anything that needed attending to. He wanted to get all the loose ends taken care of so he could devote more time to the children with their practicing. The intercom begin to buzz. He answered it, it was the preacher.

"Paul, could you come to my office for a few minutes? I'd like to discuss a private matter with you."

"I'll be there shortly." He switched off the intercom and wondered what he did or did not do. He tapped on the door and went in. He caught a glimpse of the preacher locking something away in one of the desk drawers.

"What is it you wanted to talk with me about?"

"Have a seat. I have a proposal I'd like to make to you."

Paul let his breath out slowly, relieved that he hadn't been caught with his pants down after all. He sat down and waited for him to continue. Sitting this close he noticed how much grayer his hair had become and the dark circles about his eyes. He looked tired and Paul suspected he wasn't sleeping very well. Paul was unaware of it, but George had become suspicious of him since having discovered him in the Skyroom with a flashlight. This had got him to thinking. He had no reason to doubt Paul's explanation why he had used the flashlight rather than the overhead lights. It had sounded convincing at the time. Nevertheless, it made him consider the threat he could be. It occurred to him that if Paul was plotting to undermine him by scheming to win the people's trust and admiration, he could wrest control of the church from him without a struggle. It was the same ruse that David's son, Absolom, had used. It was the possibility of this happening that he set about devising a plan. He would try to induce Paul to join his inside group and become a member of the Stellar club. Knowing how devoted Paul was to his ministry, he knew he would have to use the subtle approach if he were to draw him into his web—and it would have to be done very insidiously.

"I've been thinking," George began, "you have been my partner for quite some time now. (Partner, Paul thought, what happened to assistant?) You have shown that you are capable of handling almost any situation, and we are very fortunate to have you. So, before someone comes along and lures you away with a more lucrative offer, I've decided it's time you were given a substantial raise in salary."

"Thank you. That's very considerate of you," Paul enthused, pleased with the added windfall and what it would mean to him in terms of his relationship with Vivian. "As for a more lucrative offer, I doubt that ever happening."

"Wait, that's not all, there's something more I'd like to tell you. Do you remember meeting the mayor at the picnic and his mentioning the club?" Paul shook his head yes, and George continued. "Well, I think it's time you became a member and enjoyed a lot of the fringe benefits it has to offer. You need to get away from the pressure of this place and relax a little."

George was careful not to mention that he was part owner of the club and hoped to keep that concealed until a more appropriate time. He didn't know it, but Paul already knew that he was part owner there. Paul couldn't outright refuse to join, so he would use evasive tactics.

"One is under a lot of pressure here, that's true, and I appreciate you asking me, but I'll have to give this some serious thought whether to join or not."

George got up and put his arm around Paul's shoulders. "Sure, I understand. Take all the time you need. There's no rush. Just let me know when you have decided. I would like to personally introduce you around."

He removed his arm from Paul's shoulder and Paul rose from his chair to return to the office. "Fine. I'll let you know as soon as I make up my mind."

Back in his office he resumed his planning. In addition to the play he wanted to have a nice Christmas tree where they would pile all the presents. Also, he wanted to have the children draw names and exchange presents. Suddenly, in the midst of his planning, it all hit him! He wondered what his ulterior motive was. He was a sly one for sure. George never done anything unless it was to his advantage. All that talk about being so deserving of a raise; of someone enticing him away with a more lucrative offer; the subtleness of his invitation to join the club. It was all presented with sheer perfection. For a moment, Paul thought, I almost fell for that line of his. He knew George was an expert at persuasiveness for he had seen him use that talent many times. For example he recalled the mob incident at the jail. He was also familiar with his method: first, one's ego is inflated, then one is made to feel they are special and it would be an honor to have you become one of them.

Now what could he be perpetrating? Paul wondered. He was sure he was up to something. But what? He would just have to keep alert and play along with him as far as he dared. However, he would gladly accept the raise in salary. He would have to string him along about joining the club without actually joining it, Paul concluded, and wondered what he had done to arouse his suspicion and was trying to entrap him by getting him involved in his nefarious conduct.

Paul looked at his watch and saw it was nearing twelve o'clock. He would go back to see George about getting the supplies he would need for the children's costumes and decorations for the tree, while he was still in his office, and then go to lunch. George sat with his elbows on the the desk and his head between his hands, a look of pain on his face.

"Are you all right," Paul asked. "You look tired and in a lot of pain."

"That says it all, I am. It has to be these awful headaches I'm having. Would you care to get me a glass if water?"

Paul returned with the water and George took one of his quads. "Perhaps you should have Doc McPharson give you a checkup. He seems to be a good doctor."

"That ole reprobate! He might be if he stayed sober long enough. You're right about the checkup though. I'll find a reputable doctor and go in for one soon."

"I came to get your approval for some supplies. I need things for the costumes and such."

"Get what you need. You're doing a great job with the youth. I've noticed a significant change in them."

Paul didn't know what kind of pill George was taking, but there was a noticeable change in him.

"You know how the youth are. They have to always be doing something. I'm on my way to lunch, so I'll see you later." he said, taking his leave.

***

The Botanical Garden's award for developing the most beautiful rose was won by Arno. He had successfully created a blue rose that closely resembled velvet, therefore, was called "Blue Velvet". When he was presented with a blue ribbon and no money, Carl was vastly disappointed. Paul managed to make it to the blue ribbon presentation in order to promote the church.

"Congratulation, Arno. I'm happy that you won. Your rose is splendid," Paul said to him.

"Thank you, brother Paul. It was a long, drawn out process but worth it."

"I've got to go. I'm meeting Vivian at the rec hall. We're going to decorate the hall for the Christmas festivities. Talk to you later."

They had just finished putting up the last garland, and Paul left to get them a Coke to drink while they took a break, when Arno came rushing in.

"Sister Blakely!, Sister Blakely!"

"Yes, Arno, what is it?"

"Sister Blakely, I'm sorry to disturb you, but there's a young man outside from the House of Hope looking for you. He wants to talk with you alone. He says what he has to tell you is strictly private, that they were unable to reach anyone by phone."

Paul returned with the Cokes and handed one to Vivian. "What's going on?"

"Oh, Paul, there's a young man here from the House of Hope. I say it's something concerning Mother. Wait here while I go see what he wants."

She went up to the young man and said, "I'm Vivian Blakely. Has something happened to my mother?"

"That's what I wanted to talk with you about. I'm an attendant at the House of Hope. We tried reaching you by phone but with no success. They sent me to inform you that she has run away. They would like for you to come to the home as soon as you possibly can. They will explain what has happened, as they know it at this point, when you get there."

Vivian stood dazed with disbelief, unable to grasp the reason for her mother's behavior. What could have happened to cause her to do something like this? she wondered.

"Thank you for coming. Tell them Paul and I will be there as soon as we can."

As soon as he left, she ran back to where Paul stood and told him, "Mother has run away and they can't seem to find her. They want to see me right away. I told the attendant to tell them you and I would be there as soon as we could."

"Come along then," he said, "we'll leave at once. We won't mention this to your father, just yet, until we have talked to them and find out what could have caused this, and what we can do about it."

He didn't know why, but he felt strongly that George had something to do with it.

Paul drove Vivian to her apartment to get her coat for it had turned rather chilly. They then headed for the "home" driving as fast as they dared to. Vivian was so upset that neither one of them felt much like talking. They couldn't imagine why she would do a thing like this when she was doing so well with her recovery. It would have been only a few more weeks until she would have been completely recovered. What ever happened had to have been very traumatic for her to do something as drastic as this. He looked at Vivian and could see tears in her eyes and felt so sorry for her. He reached over and patted her hand.

"Please try not to worry, honey. We will find her and bring her back. Hopefully she will take up where she left off."

She looked at him and smiled ruefully through her sorrow. "The more I think about this the more I'm convinced that Dad stopped by and done something to cause this."

They reached the "Home" and pulled into the parking lot and Paul got out to help Vivian from the car. He looked up and saw the sign, House of Hope and thought, how ironic. And here they were seemingly left with no hope at all. They were taken immediately to Dr. Bernhauser's office and were seated, that the doctor would be with them shortly, as he was presently with a patient. They sat together and Paul held her hand. She had now regained her composure and was bearing up under the ordeal admirably. Knowing her mother's condition was reason enough to be concerned, but the uncertainty of not knowing where she could be had to be very disturbing. They had been waiting about five minutes when Dr. Bernhauser came in, a look of deep concern on his face.

"I'm terribly sorry this has happened and I'm as perplexed as you are over it. As it now stands, we have no idea what has prompted her to do this. Evidently, something very traumatic has happened to bring this about. Although it's a common occurrence, when it does happen we seldom find a patient smart enough to carry it off. We don't know how she managed to get away without being detected, but she has now been missing for approximately six hours."

"I assume you've checked all the bars close by haven't you?" Paul inquired.

"Yes, among a lot of other places. Even so, we haven't been able to locate her. We are inclined to believe she must have had an accomplice to enable her to pull this off so successfully. And whom that could have been is a mystery."

"Then we must begin at once to help search for her," Vivian responded, rising to her feet. "If she has been gone only a matter of hours she can't be very far away. I don't think she had very much money so she couldn't get very far."

"If you should happen to find her, and I hope you do, please let us know at once," Dr. Bernhauser said. "Again, allow me to say how much I regret this happened. The sad part about it is, she was doing so well and had completed the worse part of her treatment."

"We regret it too," Paul said. "If we do happen to find her should we bring her back here?"

"Yes, by all means. But don't mention that you're bringing her back here or she may refuse to return. It would be better for her to return, for she could still complete her treatment without too many complications."

They walked to the car, both very dejected, hoping they could find her before any harm came to her. "There's no need to search this area since it has already been searched," Paul said. "Let's try to think the way she would. Where do you think would be the most logical place that she would likely head for?"

"I have no idea. I can't be sure, still I don't think she had very much money. The only place I think she would likely go to would be her home. I bet that's where we'll find her—in bed asleep."

With that suggestion, Paul wasted no time heading in that direction. If she was there they would soon know. They got there, rushed inside, but Adra was no where in sight. Vivian began to cry out of frustration. She was so sure they would find her at home. Now she didn't know where she could possibly be. They went to the car and sped off again, heading back to the area near the "home".

When driving back they passed through a section where the derelicts hang out. Sitting on the curb was a woman taking a swig from a bottle. At first glance, Vivian thought she recognized the woman as her mother. "There she is! Oh, Paul, stop the car, I'm sure that's her!"

She jumped out of the car and ran back to the woman, crying out as she ran, "Mother! Oh, Mother!" She took hold of the woman's shoulder, "Mother, we found you at..." her words trailed off into a gasp as she realized her mistake. It wasn't her mother after all. The woman took the bottle from her lips and stared at Vivian. "Whasha wan...you tryin' to take my bottle? Go get ya own," she said, her head dropping to her chest, as she returned to her own pitiful world.

Vivian drew back, shocked that she could have mistaken this person for her mother. She bit her fist to stifle a sob and cover her disgust. "I...I thought..." she stammered, turned and ran back to the car.

"Oh, Paul, how revolting! Now we've got to find her more than ever! I can't bear to think Mother might end up like that."

Paul drove beyond the area of the "home" to where he found a few bars, a restaurant or two, and a couple of motels. He couldn't help but believe that they would find Adra in a bar somewhere. "I may be wrong," he said to Vivian, "but she has to be in some bar within a few miles of this place."

He drove to the nearest bar, parked the car, and went in to see if his hunch was right.

CHAPTER 14

Adra stood at the window of her room looking out across the field. She could see the road in the distance and the cars passing by. She had gained a lot of her strength back and was a lot stronger than she was. She went back to her chair and sat down. There she remained sitting long after George had left, alternately crying, then feeling sorry then angry with herself. Perhaps she had been foolish to think that going through this and taking the cure would make a difference to to him, she thought bitterly, It had now come to what she most wanted to avoid—a divorce. She had hoped he would see the difference the treatment had made and they could find, once again, the happiness they once knew. Her mind drifted back to the time when they first met. She could remember it all so clearly, as though it were only yesterday. It all began at her home church.....

They were having an all day meeting, and afterward dinner on the ground. She had just finished helping her mother put the food on the table. Her mom had wandered off in search of her dad, leaving her alone. A young, handsome man, whom she did not know, came strolling up to her. She was immediately attracted to him. She could still recall how her heart fluttered at the sight of him.

"Hello, young lady. My name is George Blakely," he said, brazenly, introducing himself. "Wait a minute, don't tell me your name let me guess—providing my mystic powers are still working." He closed his eyes, rubbed his temples, and said, "Yes...yes, it's coming! It's...It's Miss Adra...Miss Adra Myers!" he exclaimed triumphantly.

"That's very good, I'm impressed!" she said. "Now, can you tell me whom I'll be having lunch with?"

"That's easy. I don't have to use my mystic powers for that. It's me, myself, and I. And, next Sunday we're going on a picnic, then we're going boating, just the two of us, and…."

She found him very appealing, and amusing, and with a wonderful personality. She was also taken with his novel approach.

"I'll fix you a plate, Mr. Blakely. What would you like to eat?"

"The name is George. Please call me George," he said, seating himself at one of the tables. The moment he set eyes on her it was love at first sight. He was smitten with her and instantly and totally in love.

"Then you must call me Adra," she said. "And now, what would you like to eat?"

"A sandwich would be nice and something cold to drink. Anything will do."

She made him a chicken salad sandwich and a glass of sweetened ice tea. She had the same and sat down next to him. "Seriously, I'm curious to know how you knew my name?"

"Well, to be perfectly honest, I almost didn't. I asked several of the guys around here and they didn't know it either. A young boy heard me asking who you were and told me your name. It happened to be your little brother."

"He's a brat. Sometimes I could choke him."

Her mother returned with her dad in tow and she introduced them. "George, these are my parents, Bertrand and Mary Myers. Mom, Dad, this is Mr. George Blakely."

George got up from his seat and shook hands with both of them. "I'm pleased to meet you. And, may I add, you have a very lovely daughter."

Adra smiled, shyly dropping her head as a slight blush touched her cheeks.

"Thank you. We think so too," her dad said. "Your name sounds a little familiar to me. What do you do for a living?"

He was embarrassing Adra with his questions. But she knew fathers always had to know what a prospective husband's occupation was.

"I'm a minister. You may have seen my name on the list of speakers for this afternoon."

"Perhaps that's it. I knew I had seen it or heard it somewhere. How long have you been in the ministry?"

"A little more than a year now. I'm the pastor at the Victory for Christ church. Are you a minister too?"

"No, I'm in the hardware business: Myer's Hardware and Farm Equipment Company." George saw his chest swell with pride when he added: "...and doing quite well at it too."

"Now, Bert, I'm sure Mr. Blakely isn't interested in business right now," Mary said, knowing where his real interest lay at the moment. "Adra, it's such a lovely day, why don't you take Mr. Blakely over to the display room and show him the quilt you and I made."

Bless you, Mother, she thought. "That's a wonderful idea."

Mary stood watching them as they walked away. She prayed a silent prayer for Adra, that the man she chose to marry would be faithful to her. They hadn't allowed her to date until she was sixteen and was probably a little over protective of her. She was now eighteen and would make her own decision of whom she would marry.

As they drew near to the building, and out of sight of her parents, Adra took hold of George's arm and said, "We don't want to go look at a silly quilt. Let's go wading in the creek instead."

George hesitated, concerned that the men of the church might think he was being undignified.

Adra ran ahead, calling out to him, "Come on, don't be an old stuffed shirt! It will be a lot of fun."

It was at that very moment that George made the decision not to let his life be governed by what others might think. He ran ahead, hung his jacket on a tree limb, took off his shoes and socks, and joined Adra in the middle of the stream. It was the middle of summer and the water felt so cool. They waded hand in hand feeling like two unruly kids. Adra stepped on a slippery rock and almost fell, letting out a girlish squeal. They were both laughing and George had caught her. Before either one of them knew what was happening, George drew her close to him and kissed her. The world was momentarily forgotten as they found the love that only the heart can know....

"Are you ready for your exercise, Mrs. Blakely?" the attendant asked. Getting no response from her, she became alarmed. "Is anything wrong; are you all right, Mrs. Blakely?"

Adra had been so engrossed in her reminiscing she didn't hear the attendant until she gently laid her hand on her shoulder. Adra looked up to see who was talking to her. "I'm sorry if I scared you," she said, wiping the tears from her eyes. "No, nothing's wrong. I was just reminiscing about an episode in my life that happened many years ago. I'm just a sentimental fool!"

"You did scare me a bit. I'm no doctor, but if thinking on the past is going to depress you, I wouldn't dwell on it too much if I were you."

"Perhaps you're right. It doesn't help one cope with this present world," Adra admitted, and knew the front office would get a full report on the incident.

"That's for sure. Now, let's get that exercise taken care of and out of the way."

Back in her room, Adra lay on her bed feeling rather tired. The exercise sessions were supposed to build up one's strength but to her they only succeeded in leaving her feeling weaker. If only she could get George off her mind and the reason he came to visit her. It was then the thought of getting out of this place came to her. After all, what's the use of one going through all of this torture if it did nothing toward salvaging her and George's marriage. She began at once to plot her escape. She saw no purpose in continuing with the treatment. Besides that, she was bored with all of it, depressed, very lonely, and felt she didn't have a friend in the world.

It was at this time she began to take note of their routine. When they were in and out of her room to give her medicine; when the exercise scheduled, and when they were all taking lunch. She now knew just the right time to make her move. Suddenly she had the strongest craving for a drink, and couldn't wait to get to a bar where she could get one. She began saving every nickel and dime she could get hold of. She would wheedle a few dollars from Vivian on her nest visit.

She waited until after lunch, when she would have close to an hour before she would be checked on again. She slipped on her shoes and went to the door and peeped out. She saw a man with two little girls coming down the hall and quickly put a scarf over her head to hide her face and hair. She fell in behind them as if she were the man's wife. When she had safely reached the elevator she breathed a sigh of relief, averting her face from the girls who kept looking at her curiously. She reached the outside, forcing herself to walk slowly. She prayed that no one would see her as she crossed the open field making her way to the woods. When she reached the woods she hurriedly walked in among the trees and disappeared among its shadows.

It had been a drain on her strength forcing her to rest for a minute or two. She finally reached the highway and thumbed a ride. By hook or crook, she had managed to save a few dollars, enough to buy several drinks and get something to eat. The first few cars passed her by, then a van pulled over and she climbed in. The driver was a young man in his early twenties. He had long dark brown hair and a beard to match.

He pulled back onto the highway and asked, "Been walking far?"

"About a mile I guess." To keep him from getting suspicious about her being out on the highway alone she told him, "I ran out of gas and was going to try and find a phone to call my daughter to come get me."

"I noticed a red Pontiac parked beside the road some ways back there." To her surprise, she heard him say, "I've got a gas can back there somewhere. Want me to stop at the next gas station for some gas, then take you back to your car?"

She had the preconceived opinion that anybody with long hair and a beard were dope heads and concerned only with themselves. She couldn't believe he was being so obliging.

"Thank you, but that won't be necessary. Anyway, my daughter will take care of it as soon as I can give her a call."

They made small talk about the weather and such. Her heart was touched when he disclosed that he had just recently lost his mother. "I enjoy doing what I can for elderly people—not that you're that old—but you are a mother. I'd like to think someone would have done as much for mine."

"That's sweet of you. There should be more young people like you," she said sincerely. Hereafter, she would refrain from judging people by the way they looked or how they dressed. They drove along in silence for some minutes when up ahead Adra saw a sign with the name Sunset Bar and Grill. "Drop me off there at the Bar and Grill, if you would, please."

He pulled off to the side of the road and let her out. "Take care now," he said as she stepped to the ground.

She smoothed out her dress as best she could, gave her hair a few pats and went inside. She chose a booth near the back, where she would be less conspicuous, and slid into it. The waitress came to take her order.

"I'm Red. What will it be for you tonight, honey? We have some delicious French Onion soup and our coffee is good and hot."

"Thank you, no. I just want a scotch and soda. I ran out of gas up the road from here and a nice young man gave me a ride and let me off here. I thought I'd have a drink before calling my daughter to come and get me." Adra figured a word of explanation would keep Red from getting suspicious.

"Are you sure you won't have a sandwich? You look like you could use a little nourishment to me," She said, pushing back a red curl from her eye.

"Thank you for your concern, the drink will do nicely for now."

"One drink coming up."

Adra waited until Red went for her drink before getting her money out of her shoe. She returned with the drink and said, "Enjoy your drink, honey."

Again, Adra waited for her to leave before attempting to pick up her drink. The liquor trickled down her throat and became a roaring fire. She got a buzz from it as soon as it hit her empty stomach. She felt a shiver travel up her spine then course back down. Her nervousness began to disappear and the tension melt away. Soon she began to hum softly and felt that life wasn't so terrible after all. She finished her drink and ordered another one.

Then another…and another….

An hour had gone by and she was feeling no pain, no guilt, no nothing…until her jubilation turned into a pity party and the tears began to flow.

After Red had served her fourth drink she expected she was going to have a drunk lady on her hands. She had no intention of selling her another drink and asked her, "Don't you think you should be calling your daughter? I'm sure she must be getting worried about you by now."

"I've schanged my mind," Adra said, slurring her words. "He couldn't care lesh. You know wha' he did? He ashed me for a divorsh—a divorsh!" she repeated, unaware that she had changed from a daughter to a husband. "And after all thesh years."

Someone started the juke-box playing and Adra got up and stepped out on the floor and began swaying to the beat of the music, now free of any inhibition. It was during this display that Paul and Vivian walked into the Sunset Bar and Grill and found her. Vivian took her to the car, while Paul talked to the waitress and did a little explaining about Adra, then went to the pay phone and called the House of Hope as he promised to do. He then went to the car and could see that Vivian had managed to get Adra into it, putting her in the back seat. He started the car and turned it toward "home".

When Vivian first tried to get Adra to get into the car she wouldn't get in. She insisted she was going back into the bar for another drink. Vivian told her they would find another one and she got in. She was in no condition to object and sat in the back seat swaying back and forth with each curve, mumbling incoherently, until she fell over in the seat and passed out. They drove most of the way in silence, Vivian so embarrassed she could hardly look Paul in the face. She could feel the tears stinging her eyes and the constrictive pain in her throat from the sobs she kept trying to suppress.

Paul knew she was struggling to control her emotion. He reached over and pulled her next to him. She lay here head on his shoulder and began to cry softly, unable to restrain the tears any longer. He patted her on the shoulder to comfort her and waited for her tears to subside. He gave her his handkerchief and she wiped her eyes, blew her nose and stuffed the handkerchief in the coat pocket of his suit.

"I'm sorry to be such a big cry baby. I simply can't understand what has caused Mother to resort to this. She was doing so well. I hope she is able to recover completely from all of this."

"Of course, you're not a big cry baby. Everybody has a breaking point and their emotions can only take so much." He removed his arm from around her shoulder. "Whether you know it or not, I understand what you are contending with. As for your mother, I hope we can find out what caused her to do this. She must have reached the point where she felt she just couldn't cope with it any longer and just ran away."

They both were to be surprised and shocked when they would later find out what really caused Adra to do what she did.

"They will undoubtedly keep a closer watch on her after this. As for Dad, I think he is acting rather peculiar. He's taken to doing things he wouldn't have thought of doing a few years back. He staying at the Stellar club now and never comes by the house at all."

"As for your dad, obviously, he is very sick in some strange way. He has been complaining of terrible headaches. I've been trying to get him to go in for a check up, but he keeps putting it off for some reason."

"Do you think it could be something fatal?"

"It could be. But, then again, I don't know. It could have something to do with his bazaar behavior. If he keeps refusing to go to the doctor, then I suggest you have the doctor come to him."

"By golly, Paul, I think you have hit the nail on the head."

He saw no need to tell her anything about her dad. That would only upset her more than ever. She had enough to contend with as it was. He knew he was going to have to tell her about some of the things he had discovered about her dad sooner or later. It was a task he dreaded and would continue to put it off as long as he could. But for now he would say nothing.

They reached the House of Hope and as soon as they got parked, two staff members came hurrying out with a stretcher and carried Adra inside. She still hadn't sobered up enough to realize exactly where she was or what they were doing to her. She was put in a room where they could watch her more closely. They were still mystified as to how she got out of there without anyone seeing her. She was the first one to have managed to escape without getting caught.

On the drive back, Paul mentioned to Vivian about his raise. "Did I tell you that I'm getting a raise in salary?"

"You may have, but not that I recall. Anyway, that's wonderful news."

"Besides that, we can get married any time now. I know how much you want to be a June Bride, but do we have to wait that long before we're married?"

"Not necessarily. We can get married on Valentine's Day for that matter. But, why such a rush. You have waited this long surely you can wait a little longer. This is April, it's only two months away."

"Who are we going to get to marry us? I don't think your dad should do it with the way things presently stand. Besides, he will probably be in the hospital around that time."

"What are we going to do? He will certainly expect to perform the ceremony for his only daughter's wedding. Oh, Paul, I have always dreamed of having a beautiful church wedding ever since I was a little girl. But, with the way things are at the present time it just doesn't seem to be possible. It looks like the only thing for us to do is to forget about a church wedding and have a simple ceremony elsewhere. Say, I just got an idea. Why don't we fly to Las Vegas and get married at one of those cute little chapels they have there?"

"Are you sure you wouldn't mind; can you be satisfied with that? It really doesn't make any difference to me. I just want to get married."

"Then it's settled. That's what we'll do. I'll purchase the airline tickets and we will fly there, get married, have a day or two for our honeymoon, then fly back without telling anyone of our plans," she said, excitedly. "When is the best time for you to slip away?"

"It would have to be right after the Wednesday night service. We would arrive in Las Vegas later that same night, get married on Thursday, have two days for our honeymoon, and fly back late Saturday night. Are you sure you won't regret this later? I want you to completely satisfied and happy with your decision."

"Not only will I be happy, but I'll be happily married too. And if we can pull this off that will be the icing on the cake."

"Then let's do it as soon as you can take care of all the preparations and bring it all together."

Looking back, Paul was pleased with how well the Christmas play had gone over. It had been a huge success. The children had a great time and were already looking forward to next year. The huge Christmas tree went over well also and everybody enjoyed the gifts that were given out. It was nearing one o'clock in the morning by the time they got things straightened out and had gotten home.

Vivian was presently staying with her mother, who had now successfully completed her treatment. She was so happy to be well and at home. She had regained her strength and felt better now than she had in years.

"Why don't you give up your apartment and move in with me, now that your Dad is staying at the club," Adra suggested to Vivian. "He won't be back here and you can save the money you're paying on your apartment."

Adra had finally broken her silence and told Vivian why she ran away. "Your Dad came by and asked me for a divorce. It upset me so much that I become terribly depressed. Seeing no need to continue, I gave up my treatment and ran away."

It had been just what Vivian had suspected.

"Mom, now that you're well again you will do just fine without me. We're planning to get married sometime in the near future and it would be a waste of time for me to move back in with you." She didn't mention what their wedding plans were.

Paul called Vivian to tell her he was going to look for Nora, and when he got back they would slip away and be married. He had gone to the Stellar club sometime back and happened to see George walking arm in arm with the judge and the mayor. He knew he was friends with the mayor, but didn't know he was in cahoots with the judge, too. Seeing them together made him understand how George had been able to get the Tilden boy off so easily.

It was shortly before that incident that Harry Stoddard called him to tell him that George had carried out his threat against him. Two unsavory characters accosted him an warned him that he could get into serious trouble if he wasn't careful what he said about George. They accused him of tipping off the journalist at the Morning Star newspaper. He convinced them that it wasn't him who had done the tipping, nor did he have any idea who it could have been.

Paul knew that George had no intention whatsoever of marrying Nora. He had to find her and try to convince her of that fact so she could get on with her life. He didn't know exactly where she was, all he had to go on was an address on the bill he found from Covington, Kentucky. He drove there and went to the Chamber of Commerce to get the list of homes that were for unwed mothers. Luck was with him. They had two, one on the east side and the other one on the south. He chose the one on the east side, figuring that George would go to that one because it was closest one. Following the directions the Chamber had given him, he had no trouble finding the place.

He knocked at the door of the main entrance and waited. When the door opened, he saw standing before him a little woman about five feet tall, wearing an apron. "I'm Mama Blaume, may I help you?"

"I'm Reverend Paul Langley, and I'm looking for Nora Letty. Would she be in residence here? I'm a friend."

"Yes, she resides here. She's at work now and won't get here until a little after five."

"Thank you, ma'am. I'll call back later then."

He went to get a bite to eat while waiting for Nora to get home.

CHAPTER 15

When George persuaded Nora to move into a home for unwed mothers he took her to Covington, Kentucky, where she would be most unlikely to run into anyone they knew. After she had gotten settled he promised to see her often. He was consistent with his visits at first, as he had said he would be, but, as time went on, his visits became less frequent, coming only once or twice a month. It was hard for her to believe she had been in this place as long as she had. She was now in her seventh month and it seemed to have been a lifetime. With her body being so heavy with child, it would be impossible for her to continue working very much longer. Somehow, she got the ominous feeling that George was slowly but surely deserting her, leaving her to have the baby on her own and to get by as best she could. Even the monthly stipend he was sending was now arriving irregularly. In time, she expected it would stop coming altogether. It was that thought which prompted her to get a job just in case. But, in spite of it all, she just couldn't face the possibility that George would totally desert her.

She made her way home slowly, getting there a little after five. She had one more week to go before quitting her job to wait for her baby's arrival. As soon as she arrived home she found Mama Blaume waiting for her.

"There was a Reverend Langley here to see you, he left, saying he would be back later."

"Thank you. When he returns tell him I don't want to see him." She went to her room to get ready for supper.

Meanwhile, Paul returned to the home and, once again, spoke with Mama Blaume.

"Has Nora gotten home yet?"

"Yes, she's home. But she has asked me to tell you she doesn't want to talk to you."

"Would you mind showing me to her room. I believe I can persuade her to do otherwise."

"I guess it won't hurt to try," said Mama Blaume. She took him to Nora's room and left him standing by the door.

While sitting in her room, Nora got to thinking about George again. Lately, when she thought of him it brought tears to her eyes. She was finding him to be so unpredictable. She wiped the tears away and began to whisper a prayer, something she had been doing more often these past few weeks. She had repented anew of her wrongdoing, asking for and seeking God's guidance. She raised her head, lifted her chin, determined to make the best of it. After all, she wouldn't allow herself to wallow in self-pity.

"I have played the fool," she said aloud to herself, "and I certainly should have known bet..." A knock at the door interrupted her thoughts. She opened he door just wide enough to see who was there. On seeing it was Paul, she said, "Go away! Oh, please go away! I don't want to talk to you."

Paul knew she would refuse to see him, being ashamed for him to see her in the last stages of her pregnancy. He spoke to her through the door. "Please, Nora, open the door. I've got to talk to you. It's very important."

She looked down at her disfigured self and tears began anew. She couldn't face him in this condition. "No, I can't see you now! Go away!"

"Nora, listen to me! It's a matter of grave importance that I talk with you. I know how you feel, but you are in need of a friend in the worst way and I would like to be that friend. After all, I wouldn't have come all this way to find you if it hadn't been of the utmost importance."

She hesitated, torn with the decision whether to talk to him or not. She didn't know what to do. She was so ashamed and humiliated. Yet, she wanted very much to talk to him. Like he said, she certainly was in need of a friend. Reluctantly, she slowly opened the door, stepped back to let him enter.

He glanced over the room and was pleased to see it was comfortably furnished. She had him sit in the only chair and went over to sit on the side of the bed. He came right to the point, explaining the reason for his visit.

"I know what I'm going to tell you will be hard for you to believe but it is the truth. Before I tell you about George, is he still coming to visit you very often? Is he standing by you as he promised to do?"

Nora sat nervously picking at her nails. "Well, he still comes by, but he doesn't come as often as he once did."

"Did you know you're registered here under an assumed name?"

"Not until I received a telegram from him with the name Nora Thompson on it. How did you manage to find me?"

"Only by sheer luck, I suppose— and the providence of God. What matters is that I found you."

"What is it you came here to tell me?"

"Please believe me, I only want to help you in any way that I can. Whether you believe me or not, and whether you realize it or not, George is a disturbed man. He's badly in need of medical attention and possible surgery."

"What makes you think he's mentally ill? Is that just your personal opinion?"

"I'm being as truthful with you as I can, so I have to say yes, more or less. Obviously, there is something wrong with his way of thinking. No man professing to be a minister could do the things he has done, and is still doing, and be in their right mind. Right now, my real concern is the church. If something isn't done soon he is going to destroy everything he has worked for. I know this is difficult for you to comprehend just now, but whatever feelings you may have for George, and I don't mean to be hard or unfeeling, or to hurt your feelings in any way, but you must face reality. Regardless of what he has told you, he has no intention of marrying you. Once the baby is born he will forget you and leave you to fend for yourself."

"No, that's not true! You're wrong!" she cried emphatically. "He will never forsake me and the baby, I know he won't!" She burst into tears again. "As for him being mentally ill, I have to wait and see for myself." She rose to he feet. "Now, will you please go!"

He could see there was no use in trying to persuade her to look at things realistically. As she said, she would have to discover the truth for herself. He rose to go.

"I'll go, but we must talk about this at another time, when you come to see the truth in what I have told you. I'll come back later when you have come to see things as they are.

She nodded here head as if she agreed and opened the door, stepping aside to let him out, then quickly locked the door. He's wrong; he's got to be!, she thought to herself. George loves me, I know he does. She went over and lay down on the bed. She would forego supper. She didn't want anything to eat. She was tired and weary and soon asleep.

Paul arrived home and went about catching up on things while he was away. He was sorry he had been unable to convince Nora of the seriousness of her relationship with George. It was hard to say what he might do next. Especially, once he has been accused of his misdeeds and misconduct as becoming a minister. Paul was in an awkward position. He was planning to be married any day now and, at the same time, preparing to have George charged with the evidence he had gathered against him. He dreaded when the time came, he expected it to be a very traumatic confrontation.

Amidst all of this, for some reason his thoughts turned to Colby. He had been so busy he hadn't got around to visiting him. He had heard that Jesse Latimer had apologized profusely to him and begged him to come back and work for him. Colby, after giving it careful consideration, consented to do so. And they were getting along fine with no problem whatsoever. Colby reaoned that he had to work some-where. Paul didn't want to lose touch with him and his family and, if his dream ever materialized, he would have the church he had longed to have some day, where he planned to welcome them into the church. Hopefully, that would heal the breach George had perpetrated toward them, especially with Perry.

True to his word, as soon as he returned from seeing Nora, he called Vivian, who had now moved back to her apartment. He had let her know the day they would be leaving to get married so she could arrange for someone to fill in for her at work

"Hello," she said, on picking up the phone.

"Hello, sweetheart. I'm back. How are you?"

"As well as can be expected, considering the circumstances. I'm glad you're back."

"So am I. But I have to go back again when Nora comes to her senses. She refuses to face reality and is in complete denial about the whole thing. What she expects is never going to happen." He paused, since this subject concerned her dad, and he wasn't sure if she knew he was the father of Nora's baby. "Are you ready to leave for Las Vegas?"

"No. But I can get ready awfully fast."

"Do you think you can get our plane tickets, arrange to be off from work, and be ready to leave by the weekend?"

"No problem. I've already made the arrangement at work, and all I have to do now is get our tickets."

"That's great! Let's plan on catching the midnight flight right after Wednesday night's service. Is that all right with you?"

"Not only is it okay, we're practically on the plane"

That's what he liked about her, she was so versatile. It didn't take her forever to get ready to go anywhere. "Swell. Let me know the exact time for the departure of our plane and I'll come by your apartment for you."

The flight went smoothly, with neither one of them getting air sick. The flight only took a little over two hours. They rented a car at the airport and drove to one of the hotels there. Since they weren't familiar with any of them they chose the one nearest to the chapel they planned to be married in. They showered then dressed for the ceremony, which would be at three o'clock in the morning when they were married. Paul wore a dark gray suit with a light gray tie, and Vivian wore a silk dress of lavender, with matching earrings and necklace that Paul had given to her for her birthday. Paul couldn't believe he was finally getting married. They were married by a middle age lady minister, while the song "Because" played softly during the ceremony, and in less than ten minutes they were pronounced man and wife.

"You may kiss the bride," the minister said, and then they left the chapel to get something to eat in a nice restaurant. In Las Vegas most places stayed open round the clock. Vivian was bubbling over with happiness as they walked hand in hand from the restaurant to take in one of the live stage shows to be seen there.

After the show they returned to their hotel room. They spent most of the time in their room, only going out to take a bus tour to see the sights and the lights. The time passed quickly and before they knew it, it was time to return home. This was the first time Paul had taken any time off, with the exception of his dad's illness, since becoming an assistant pastor. He had really enjoyed himself and it felt wonderful being a married man. It was what he had been looking forward to for a long time.

Vivian promptly gave up her apartment and moved in with Paul. She would keep her job, as long as circumstances permitted, for they would need the extra money. She would save what she could toward a house they intended to buy when they got to where they could afford one. They were sitting at home the next evening when Paul mentioned to Vivian the pending confrontation he was soon to have with her dad.

"Honey, there's something I have to tell you," he said in all seriousness. "I don't know exactly how to go about telling you this other than coming straight out with it."

"It's all right, sweetheart. So much has happened that I wouldn't be surprised at anything these days. It concerns my Dad, doesn't it?"

"Yes, it does. I hate to have to tell you this, but I've uncovered some things he has done in the past and it is left to me to do something about it."

"I'm so ashamed for what he has done and the way he has acted. I'm surprised you married me knowing all you do about my family."

"You aren't responsible for your parents' actions or for the things they have done. I'm so happy that <u>you</u> married me."

"There has to be something seriously wrong with Dad. What are you planning to do? It could be dangerous for you to approach him alone."

"I have no alternative; there's no one whom I can trust—unless it would be Harry Stoddard—and he wouldn't be the most suitable person at that. Besides, I don't want to embarrass your dad any more than I have to. Maybe something will happen and I won't have to" Little did he know, but his words would turn out to be partly prophetic. His God was on the job looking out for him.

"As I've said before, that's what I love about you. You are so concerned and compassionate toward people."

"I love you too, very much, for being so sweet and understanding, so level headed . And now I think it's time I revealed something else about your dad that I have dreaded telling you for a long time."

"After all the things he has done, what's one more thing?"

"Are you sure that you want to hear this?"

"Yes, I'm sure. I can handle it."

"I hate to put it to you so bluntly, but George is the father of Nora's baby."

"You can't be serious—my Father!"

He was greatly relieved now that she had been told. Then an idea occurred to him, "What do you think about going with me to visit Nora again? She will refuse to see me, but with you along I believe she will relent and talk to us."

"I'll go with you. It may be just what this needs—a woman's touch." They slipped away, saying nothing to anyone about going to Covington, arriving there on Saturday morning around ten o'clock. Paul knocked on the main entrance door and was greeted once more by Mama Blaume. Paul thought it best to talk with Mama Blaume first before going to see Nora.

"So you're back to see Nora Thompson," cracked Mama Blaume. "Right?"

"Right you are," said Paul. "I'd like you to meet my wife Vivian Langley. Vivian, this is, as the girls here call her, Mama Blaume."

"So nice meeting you," Vivian said.

"Pleased to meet you, too," Mama Blaume responded.

"May my wife and I go and knock on her door and see if we can get her to talk to us?"

"Yes, but I don't think she will. I'm sorry, but she doesn't want to see you or anyone else. She asked me to tell you she had nothing more to say to you, that she wanted to be left alone. For whatever it's worth to you, we had a gruff looking man here a day or two ago looking for her. Fortunately, she was at work and he was unable to find her. It turns out he was a hired thug sent here to beat her up and cause her to lose her baby. She is sure that George had him sent here. Anyway, she now refused to see anyone."

"Then she has more reason than ever to see me. That's a little of what I've been trying to convince her of. How did you come to learn what his purpose was for coming here?"

"When he failed to find her, he came back, if you can believe this, to warn us that he would be back; that they didn't give up so easily. She's terrified."

"I'm only trying to help her, trying to get her to understand the danger she is in."

"I believe you. Maybe this time she will listen to reason."

The three of them went to Nora's room and Mama Blaume tapped on the door. "Nora, it's Mama Blaume. Would you please open the door?"

Nora opened the door and all three of them rushed in. "Nora, dear, I had to disregard your wishes. I have come to believe that you are in more danger than you realize. You will forgive me when this is all over and you see we were only thinking of your safety. Now, listen to what Reverend Langley and his wife Vivian have to tell you." Saying that, she turned and left the room.

"Nora, after what has just happened, which is what I've been trying to get you to understand, you must realize how perilous your life has become. You're in grave danger! You know Vivian, she is my wife now."

"Yes, of course, I remember her."

"Nora, please don't be embarrassed that I'm here. You have to trust someone so it might as well be us. This is no joke. We are truly trying to help and protect you from harm. My Dad is ill in mind and body and has done a lot of things too numerous to mention here. You've got to realize that you and your baby are in grave danger!"

"After that goon searched for me the other day, I beginning to realize that now. I'm so scared I don't know what to do!"

"That's the reason we're here," Paul cut in. "Vivian knows her dad is your baby's father. I just told her that. We are of the opinion that George is on the verge of having a nervous breakdown or is losing his mind."

"How awful! I'm so sorry to hear that."

"My Dad has such a winning way about him. I'm sure you know that now. You made a mistake but you don't have to let it destroy you. You need to forget what you thought could have been and get on with your life without him."

"She's right you know. The church has given me enough money for you to fly where they will be unable to find you. Do you know of such a place where you can go?"

"It so happens I have an Aunt Millie that lives in Fresno, California. I could go and stay with her. She would love looking after my baby until I could find a job to support us."

"That's the spirit. Keep hold of that attitude," Vivian said.

"Then it's settled," Paul said. "We all make mistakes. We want to help you correct yours."

Paul took an envelope containing the money from his inside coat pocket, and handed it to Nora. "Take this with our prayers and blessing. You must leave as quickly as you can possibly get away. The sooner the better."

"How much longer do you have before you birth the baby?" asked Vivian.

"I have three more weeks to go yet."

"That's plenty of time for you to get to your Aunt's place. We could drop you off at the airport on our way back home."

"That would be fantastic! I'll pack some things and have Mama Blaume take care of the rest of my things for me."

"Is there anything we can help you with?" Vivian wanted to know.

"No, I can take care of it. There are no words to adequately express my gratitude for what you have done for me. May God richly bless both of you for your kindness and compassion."

They reached the airport and Paul helped her inside with her luggage. He bade her a fond goodbye and wished her well and hurried back to the car and headed for home. He was glad that Nora finally came to see the danger she was in. He thanked God for his blessings and answer to prayer.

**

Nora arrived at her Aunt Millie's and was welcomed with open arms. Her Aunt Millie was excited that they would soon have a little one to love and cherish. Nora's time arrived and she was delivered of a baby girl—the girl she had prayed for and wanted so badly. The baby weighed six pounds, seven ounces and perfectly formed in every way. She was gloriously happy and named her Bretta Kay. But, Nora's happiness would be brief, cut short by a tragedy that would leave her with a broken heart.

When Bretta Kay was only three months old, Nora went to give her a bottle and found her lying dead in her crib. She had died from Sudden Infant Death Syndrome. Her scream brought Aunt Millie running to see what had happened. When she saw the baby was dead she immediately called emergency. The emergency team arrived and, taking the baby from Nora's arms, and saw at once that the baby was gone. A death certificate was filled out and the baby taken to the nearest funeral home.

Nora was completely shattered and went into shock. Aunt Millie had her taken to the hospital where she was kept for almost three days. They brought her out of shock and depression, but Nora was never the same after that. It would be a long while before her heart completely healed, while her arms ached to hold Bretta Kay once again. Each time she saw a mother holding her baby her eyes would follow them longingly. She had been unable to work, and had taken a short leave until she recovered from her loss. She then returned to her job working with orphan children, where the love she would have given to her child was denied her, was now lavished on these children that had no one to love them. She would later write to Paul and Vivian and tell them of her loss of the baby and how she was coping with life. She felt they would want to know since Bretta Kay was Vivian's half sister.

Paul and Vivian were happy with their marriage and had adjusted to it quite well. Winter was almost a thing of the past as they headed into March. Things were coming together where George would be giving an account for his past and present misdeeds. With the evidence he had gathered against George, he was certain he had enough to convict him and prove all that he had been guilty of. However, unknown to any of them, of course, fate was to intervene and bring about a solution none of them would have imagined.

Each day that passed increased Vivian's expertise at cooking. She had never taken the time to learn, always on the go, busy running here and there and having fun. She found that being a wife came naturally to her.

Paul was looking forward to when he would be more financially secure and Vivian could quit her job at the Boutique and stay home. He was anxious to begin a family and hear the patter of little feet around the house. It was almost time for her to come home. This being Friday, he would take her out to eat. They went to a fast food place and had a salad, a roast beef sandwich and a drink. When they returned home Vivian busied herself with some sewing she had been procrastinating with. Paul sat down at his desk to write a letter to his mother he had long been intending to write:

Dearest Mother and Dad,

Looking back, it's hard to believe that the time has gone by so quickly.

So much has happened since I last wrote to you. I hope you both are doing as well as can be expected and that Dad is recovering from his stroke satisfactorily.

Let me know how you all are doing. As for me, I'm doing fine and have never been happier in my life. It seems each day is a new beginning.

I have some good news for you. Vivian and I were married at a quaint little chapel in Las Vegas. We didn't want a big church wedding due to circumstances I will get around to explaining to you later. Vivian has a very pleasant personality and is gorgeous; you will love her as I do. I can't wait to bring her for a visit so you can meet her, which I hope to do in the very near future. I'll let you know when that can be.

Another year has flown by and here we are in March again already. The weather here is not unlike the weather there, cold and blustery, and, of course, the snow. I'm looking forward to spring and warmer weather.

With all our love,

Paul and Vivian

He folded the letter, placed it in an envelope and laid it aside to be mailed in the morning. He asked Vivian if she would like to go to McDonalds' for a salad and a sandwich. She laid aside her sewing, it could wait until later, and went with him. When they had finished eating and returned to the car, Paul noticed the darkening clouds forming overhead and commented to Vivian, "It looks like we're in for a real bad storm. This is March, you never can tell what the weather is going to be next."

"It does look like it's going to be a real downpour doesn't it?" she replied.

By the time they reached home it had just begun to rain while lightening split the sky. They ran into the house and closed the door, shutting out the world and the storm.

CHAPTER 16

It rained steadily throughout the night and had slackened somewhat by the time Paul went to the office. He prepared a program he hoped would hold the youth's attention. He devised a trivia game using the scriptures and leaving out certain words. They were required to fill in the blank spaces with the correct words and the team that got the most of them right would be the winners and win a prize. After the service was over several of them commented how they enjoyed the program.

Vivian was still working and would be up until the time she became pregnant. They both loved children and were looking forward to having a brood of their own.

March went out like a lion, and April came bringing with it intermittent showers. This brought new life to the dormant earth, the trees and to grassy knolls. Although the earth was being reborn, it wasn't the case where the church was concerned. Word had finally gotten out and reached the congregation that George had impregnated his secretary. Even though none of them knew where she was, this revelation concerning the pastor split the church, causing the attendance to drop off dramatically. Paul, seeing what he feared would happen once George's indiscretion was discovered, knew the time had come for him to make his move before the church collapsed completely due to the lack of financial support. He had delayed confronting George as long as he possibly could.

Without letting Vivian know what his intentions were, he made his way to the Skyroom to confront George with the evidence he had compiled against him. This time he didn't bother to knock but opened the door and brazenly barged in. He had hoped to find George alone, but there was someone with him. There huddled behind the desk sat Hiram Jones, the church clerk with George. When they saw Paul walking toward them, Hiram quickly closed the ledger they were using and sat holding it in his lap to keep Paul from seeing its content.

George detected a change in Paul's behavior and knew something was coming up. "Since when have you stopped knocking on the door before entering here?" he inquired a bit testily, resenting Paul's intrusion. "We are having a serious discussion here and would appreciate it if you would come back later for whatever reason you have barged in here for."

"The reason I'm here is far more important than anything you could be discussing here and cannot be delayed any longer." Paul shot back defiantly. "I had hoped to find you alone, George," he was getting a kick out of addressing him as George, knowing how he felt about it, "but, be that as it may, it's obvious that Mr. Jones is in cahoots with your unscrupulous activities."

"I would be careful, Mr. Langley, of accusing someone of something you have no tangible proof with which to back it up." Hiram challenged him.

Paul couldn't resist the taunt. "You'd be surprised what I've dug up on the lot of you!"

"What is this nonsense about anyway, Paul," queried the master of deception, "have you lost your senses?"

"No, George, I haven't. I know perfectly well what I'm doing. I'm openly confronting you with your past and present nefarious activities concerning the misappropriation of church funds and any number of other things you have been illegally involved in. I also know of your fathering Nora Letty's child. The time has come for you to make amends to the people of the church and to make a public confession for your every wrongdoing."

"Why, you ungrateful Judas!" George exploded. "I go out of my way to befriend you, a nobody, give you second stewardship of my church—yes, my church!—and this is the thanks I get for it!"

"It's no use, George. And, it isn't your church. I know everything I need to know about you converting church funds into your own personal account, and of your transactions with the Bank of Switzerland. I know a ledger exists and is hidden somewhere, because I saw it with my own eyes. I also know of your secreting Nora Letty away to keep her pregnancy hidden from the church. You see, I have been conducting a personal investigation on you for several months."

"So, you have been snooping around into my personal affairs. Obviously, you wasn't being honest with me when you concocted that tale about using the flashlight instead of the overhead lights. You're nothing but a big hypocrite yourself!"

"That is merely a moot point at this time and has no bearing on what we have been discussing here. The crux of the matter is this: I'm going to give you ample time to correct your mistakes and make restitution to the church and to those you have wronged. I'm leaving for a long deserved vacation to visit with my parents in West Virginia. If, by the end of the month when I plan to return, you haven't met this demand, then I will be left with no alternative but to expose you to the church officials and let them deal with you as they see fit."

"I will say this, I'm as angry with you as anyone could possibly get! My answer to you is this: whatever the outcome of your accusations turn out to be, you can consider yourself no longer a part of this organization."

Ignoring what George said to him, he turned and walked out of the room and never looked back until he reached the outside. There he breathed a sigh of relief. He had done it! He had taken a big gamble in facing George alone and had done it more out of anger than courage.

He's right, Paul mused to himself, someone would no longer be associated with this place but it wouldn't be him.

"Do you think he was serious?" asked Hiram. "What are we going to do if he carries out his threat?"

"Don't worry about it or give it another thought," George said with confidence. "With my connections we've got nothing whatsoever to worry about. We'll breeze through this without any trouble at all."

When Paul walked into the house the first thing he did was ask Vivian to request her vacation. "I'm going to visit my parents and I want you to go with me. I'm anxious for them to meet you." Then he told her what he had just done. "Well, it's done. I just confronted George with the evidence I had against him. He got awfully angry but didn't become violent. I gave him a month to clear this situation up, and if he hadn't done so by then I would report him to the authorities."

When he finished telling her what he had done she was afraid for him. Knowing her dad, she was sure he would retaliate in some way and Paul wouldn't be safe until all this had been resolved.

They managed to get away the next day. The doors of the church were now locked by the authority of the International Church Board. There were no services being held there due to the fact that the attendance had dwindled down next to nothing. Paul would take steps to remedy that when he returned from his trip.

George, on the other hand, had no intentions of meeting any of Paul's demands he had set before him. After all, he reasoned, who was he to tell me what I should or shouldn't do. If it was taken to court, he knew nothing would come of it. the officials were on his side. What George failed to take into consideration was the International Church Board. Anyway, he hoped it didn't end up in court, he didn't want his time taken up by that. He would solve this by making a few promises, reimburse one here and there and, of course, shed a few crocodile tears, then all would be forgiven and forgotten. That would be the end of it.

He went immediately to inform the mayor and the judge of the predicament they were in. He couldn't remember if Paul mentioned anything about the club. Maybe he hadn't discovered it as yet. They knew what lay ahead of them could be destroy them completely, so they set about trying to figure out what they should do. They decided what this needed was a meeting of the three of them in the Skyroom, George's office, on Friday evening at six o'clock to plan their strategy for a counter attack. With that agreed on they went their separate ways until the time came for the meeting. Meanwhile, George started gathering the money together he would use to bribe the most influential members of the now disbanded church.

Another storm was brewing as dark threatening clouds swirled in the sky, the wind growing stronger, whipping up a frenzy when George pulled into the garage and sat waiting for his partners in crime to arrive. The judge and the mayor got there about the same time.

"It looks like we are in for another bad storm," said the judge looking at the ominously looking clouds.

"It sure looks that way and it doesn't look all that good," rejoined the mayor.

"Let's go on up before the worst of the storm hits," George suggested.

"That's sure is one mean looking sky if I ever saw one." This from the judge.

"I don't think we have anything to worry about. These storms blow in and are usually gone as quickly as they came," George said, in order to calm their fears.

With that bit of advice, they made their way up to the elevator and on up to the Skyroom. George unlocked the door and they went inside. Each man took a chair, one on each side of George. Strange as it seemed, this was the first time either one of them had ever been inside of George's office. They wasted no time getting down to the business at hand, going over every angle they could come up with. They had become so engrossed with their scheming to out fox Paul, they forgot all about the approaching storm. George had a small battery radio but had given no thought about turning it on, therefore, they were unaware of the tornado warning that had just went out over the airwaves. As it turned out, a tornado, making a half-mile wide swath, was bearing down on the city of Blakeville, destroying everything in its path. In essence, it was headed directly toward the church.

Wrapped up in their scheming and conniving, unaware of the raging storm outside, the three men, gathered together there in the Skyroom, were completely taken by surprise when they heard the roar of the tornado, like a mighty steam engine, as it struck the church, totally unprepared for the destruction that swirled and crashed around them. In only a matter of minutes it was all over and the aftermath the tornado left behind was almost total destruction. The church was damaged beyond repair but not completely annihilated.

When the rescue squad came through they found two men dead in the church and one very seriously injured. How one could have survived the onslaught of the tornado was beyond the rescuer's belief. George, for reason known only to God, was miraculously still alive. He had been thrown against a steel girder that had protected him from the roof when it collapsed. He was removed from the shattered church and rushed to the nearest hospital which the tornado had missed.

After the doctor finished with examining him, it was found that he had a broken leg, a broken arm, a broken collarbone, and a severe concussion An operation was scheduled at once. During the operation, it was discovered that he had a brain tumor the size of a walnut pressing on the part of the brain that causes a complete change in one's behavior. He was put into the intensive care unit and listed in critical condition. He would be watched around the clock.

Paul was watching the ABC evening news on television with his dad, while Vivian and his mother were in the kitchen preparing dinner, when the news came on about a tornado hitting Blakeville, Tennessee. Paul watched the scenes of destruction with shock and disbelief. He then made a call to Adra to see if she was safe and made it through the storm. Unable to get through to her, he tried calling the local radio station and fortunately got through to them. He was told of the extensive damage to the eastern section of the city where the tornado made a swath of destruction a half-mile wide where it touched down. Almost everything in its path had been destroyed. He hung up the phone, numb from what he had seen and been told, unable to comprehend the extent of it.

He went to the kitchen to tell Vivian the awful news. "Blakeville has been hit by a devastating tornado. As soon as we've eaten we must leave at once for home. I called your mother, but was unable to get through to her."

As soon as they finished eating, Vivian went to pack their things.

"I'm sorry you have to rush back. We've enjoyed your visit and it was a pleasure to meet Vivian; she is sweet and lovely," his mother said to him.

"Thank you for those kind words. We have to get back so we can help the ones in need. The people of the church will be wondering where I'm at." Paul said. He never mentioned anything about the church being disbanded or the trouble he was having there.

"They bade his mom and dad goodbye and headed for a scene of devastation they could never have imagined. The first thing they did when they got back was to look in on Adra. They were relieved to find

Adra had weathered the storm but her house had been slightly damaged. George was another matter. Told that he was in the hospital not expected to live, they rushed there to see him. They inquired of the nurse how he was doing and she told them he was resting comfortably but was still in critical, but stable, condition, that he had regained consciousness and was asking for Paul.

They stood quietly by his bed and, while whispering a silent prayer for him, he opened his eyes. He recognized them and gave them a faint smile, haltingly reaching out his hand for Vivian to take hold of it. It was then that tears began to trickle down his cheeks. "Can you find it in your heart to forgive me for what I have done, and the pain I have caused you and your mother?" he said, slowly and just above a whisper. "God has forgiven me and I hope all of you can forgive me too. Would you ask your mother to come by and see me?"

"Of course I forgive you, as I'm sure Mother will too. I'm just so thankful to have my "once upon a time" Dad back," she said, crying softly as she dabbed at he tears.

He then turned his attention to Paul. "Brother Paul, I especially beg your forgiveness for the things I said to you. Will you forgive me?"

"Yes, brother George, I forgive you, and I, in turn, ask for your forgiveness, not for the things I said, for they were true, but for my attitude in which I said it. Am I forgiven?"

"Of course I forgive you."

"I thank you for your forgiveness. But, you shouldn't be talking so much, you need to conserve your strength."

"I know, but it's important that I ask as many as I can for forgiveness. The next time you stand behind the sacred desk, please ask the people, on my behalf, to forgive me." He closed his eyes to rest for a few minutes.

Vivian told her mother what her dad had said and she agreed to go see him. When she walked into the room he looked up at her and gave a faint smile, reaching for her hand as he had to Vivian.

"Adra, my love, I must ask you to forgive me for all the pain I have caused you. I'm deeply sorry for what I have done and, had I been in my right mind, I never would have asked you for a divorce." He paused to catch his breath. "I love you and always have and always will. You are the love of my life. Please forgive me—if you can."

"Of course I forgive you, and I love you too. Always have," Adra answered, tears filling her eyes. "Once again, you have made me gloriously happy by reaffirming your love for me."

They had a healing time of reconciliation. Not only was everything forgiven but their relationship was restored to what it was at the beginning. Holding his right hand, Adra said to him, "When you are released from here we will go on our second honeymoon and have a marvelous time together. I'm overjoyed to have you back!"

Paul and Vivian came in for a return visit with George. Vivian didn't know why but something kept drawing her back for another visit with her dad. The first thing they noticed was that George seemed to be recovering nicely and gaining strength daily. It was during this visit that Paul related to George some of the things he had done and he was appalled.

"Did I really do such things as that?"

"Yes, and then some," Paul assured him.

"I have no memory of any of that," George said with remorse. "How shall I ever be able to face anyone, especially the members of the church."

Paul was gratified that he said "the" church instead of "my" church. "We're so thankful that you are all right now and we're praying for you full recovery."

"If I'm ever permitted to be on my feet again," George said, "I'll try, to the best of my ability, to make restitution to as many as possible." His voice was stronger now but not up to his natural volume yet.

"That's all that's required of you. You can't do anymore than that," was Paul's reply. "It will make a big difference and will gain back for you the confidence of the people as well."

Adra was still holding his hand and said, "We've got to be going so you can get some rest. Just remember what I was telling you. I loved you the first time I saw you..." She stopped speaking when she saw his head drop to the side and instinctively knew he was gone. She began to cry as grief overtook her, heart wrenching sobs, as Vivian put her arms around her shoulders and led her from the room.

Due to having no church in which to worship, his funeral service was held at a neighboring church that had escaped the tornado. Paul conducted the service, telling the crowd of mourners how repentant brother George had been and had been looking forward to making restitution to as many people that he could. But, that God, seeing his repentant heart, saw no need of that and took him home. Paul told the crowd that brother George would have been pleased to see so many of his former members had come to his funeral. He then turned the service over to those in charge of internment. He was buried in the nearby cemetery, making it convenient for Adra and Vivian to visit his grave whenever they wished.

***

Paul now had the privilege of building his dream church—a church he had long dreamed of shepherding. It would be a church where people of every race, creed, and color could come together in unity and love to worship God in spirit and in truth. He had run a campaign to raise money to begin the building of this particular church and his plan was to build it on the same spot where the original church had been built. His effort had been successful, he now had the funds to begin to build. He would manage to pay the balance off on he church from the incoming tithes and offerings. He stood watching the men cleaning up the debris from the old church when one of the men came over to him and handed him a ledger they had found among the rubble. Ironically, it was the ledger he had searched so diligently for but could never find. He would see if Adra could retrieve the money and contribute the greater portion of it to the building.

It took one full year to complete the building of the new church. Now it stood proudly in all its splendor for all to see. A huge crowd had gathered for the dedication of the building to God and to His glory. He then held his first service in the new church was named: "The Church of Universal Unity." At the end of the sermon an invitation was given for those who desired to be saved and several people came forward for God's saving grace. The church was a great success and grew by leaps and bounds.

One of those converts was Colby's wife Armeda, and their son Perry. Paul, true to his word, welcomed them into the church and, among others that were baptized, he had both the privilege and the pleasure of baptizing the three of them.

After the service was over he whispered to Colby, "Come to my office and see me after the service. I have an offer I'd like for you to consider."

Colby was there waiting for Paul when he got to the office. He was curious to know what Paul's offer could be.

"There's a lot of people here who could adequately fill the position of Church Clerk, but I wanted you to have it. It pays a small salary and would be a few dollars of extra income for you."

"After all you have done for me, how could I possibly refuse. Of course I'll take the position."

"Thank you, my friend and my brother. But I'd rather you didn't feel obligated to me. What I did for you was nothing more than my Christian duty. You may work at being the clerk at your own convenience. All I ask is that you keep the books current."

"No problem," Colby said, and they shook hand on it.

Harry Stoddard was one of the first to take fellowship with the church, and brought along his wife and son. Paul looked for the others to come drifting in. His only prerequisite was that they repent anew before becoming members of the church.

As he expected, the more the church grew, the more prosperous it became. Along with the success came Satan, bearing temptations of power, money, and worldly pleasures. But Paul steadfastly refused to be enticed; to surrender his morals; his salvation; or his integrity. He was bound and determined to do God's will and always to stay in the center of it. He realized it was not going to be easy.

Before he knew it, June had come round again and each time it came, came the thought of Vivian wanting to be a June bride. He planned for them to repeat their vows on their tenth wedding anniversary so she could feel that she, at least, had a small part of a church wedding.

They were into their second year of marriage before she ever became pregnant. They were about to think they weren't going to be privileged to have any children Then suddenly it happened. She discovered she was pregnant and, to Paul's delight, she gave him a son whom they named Mark. She next had a girl they named Susan. They were a happy and close knit family, and Vivian decided to wait awhile before having any more children.

Paul was under a lot of pressure looking after such a large congregation, and felt the need to get away at least once or twice a year. He always sought out a place far from the hustle and bustle of the city, a place where it was peaceful and quiet and he could commune with God. and commit himself wholly to His will. It was on each sabbatical leave that he and Vivian recommitted themselves to their marriage vows. That felt it kept their marriage strong and true.

Vivian put the children to bed a little early so she and Paul could be alone. They were standing on the balcony where they were staying, looking out over the lake watching a spectacular sunset. Paul impulsively took Vivian in his arms and kissed her—a long, enduring kiss.

"Oh, Paul, I love you so much! You are all I could ever desire in a husband. I love and enjoy our time together away from the noisy crowd, and it's so peaceful here."

"I love you, too! More than you'll ever know." He said, with sincerity. "I shall always remember the first time I saw you on the train and you were with that young man. I was so jealous of him, of him being your friend, never for a moment believing that one day you would be mine."

He held her close and tenderly in his arms and she lay her head on his shoulder. "I'm so happy! I feel so undeserving of your love and this happiness, that I keep expecting it to snatched away from me at any moment."

"You need never fear ever losing my love or this happiness of yours. We shall always have each other's love and we will never allow anything to interfere with our love for each other. Absolutely nothing!"

As they watched the sun setting beyond the lake, they felt so privileged to see one so strikingly beautiful. The sun seemed to float on the water, casting a glimmering trail of light across the surface, turning the sky into a variegated canopy of breathtaking splendor. God was on His throne and they were safe and secure in His love and care.

Printed in the United States
64055LVS00003BA/124-198